Rue
For Repentance

This book is fictitious. The herb properties and herbal remedies detailed in this book are based on ancient folk practice and should not under any circumstances be considered an actual remedy for any ailment or condition.

Random House Australia Pty Ltd
20 Alfred Street, Milsons Point NSW 2061
http://www.randomhouse.com.au

Sydney   New York   Toronto
London   Auckland   Johannesburg

First published by Random House Australia in 2006

National Library of Australia
Cataloguing-in-Publication Entry

Pulman, Felicity, 1945–.
Rue for repentance.

For children aged 12+.
ISBN 1 74166 113 7.

I. Title. (Series: Pulman, Felicity, 1945– Janna Mysteries; 2.)

A823.3

Cover and internal illustration and design by Pigs Might Fly Productions
Typeset by Midland Typesetters, Australia
Printed and bound by Griffin Press, Netley, South Australia

10 9 8 7 6 5 4 3 2 1

the JANNA MYSTERIES

Rue for Repentance

FELICITY PULMAN

RANDOM HOUSE AUSTRALIA

PROLOGUE

THE SCRAWNY, MUD-stained youth froze in his tracks. Someone was coming! He quickly snatched up the snare he'd been about to set, and slipped it down the front of his tunic. Should he be seen, he must seem innocent – but he would do all in his power to avoid being seen for it could mean the difference between his life or death.

Nervous, needing a hiding place, he scanned the forest. A sheltering screen of holly bushes nearby was his best, his only option. He raced towards them and, wincing, eased himself between the prickly leaves, trying not to shake or disturb them in any way, or make any sound that might betray his presence. Once safely inside his thorny cover, he peeped out to see who was on his trail.

Sometimes a guide came through the forest, leading a band of pilgrims, or perhaps a cleric or a nobleman, to safety. When that happened, laughter and chatter usually accompanied their passage, for the travellers would have permission to be in the forest and would be passing through on legitimate business. But this traveller moved silently, and therefore must be alone.

If it was the forester who pursued him, he was in deadly danger. Gravelinges was a royal forest and the king's forester patrolled it regularly to protect it from poachers, to make sure that there were always deer and wild boar for the king and his barons to hunt, as well as hares, rabbits and even fat doves. Anyone caught red-handed would be hauled to the forest court, where justice was summary and swift: if your life was not forfeit, at the very least your hands could be cut off, so Edwin had heard.

Edwin looked down at his hands. They were dirty but not blood-stained, at least not so far as he could see. To make sure, he wiped them across a patch of damp grass, then turned them over and wiped them again. He inspected them carefully. Cleaner now, but it was perfectly possible that there might still be blood under his fingernails, for he had killed and eaten while hiding out in the forest. Rabbits, hares and squirrels, voles, mice and birds – anything to fill his empty, aching belly and keep him alive just a little longer. He felt about him for a small twig and quickly began to scrape it under his cracked and broken nails in a vain effort to lift out the ingrained dirt. All the while he listened as the traveller came closer.

If not the forester, then who? The servants of his liege lord? Edwin's heart sank further as he pondered the possibility that he might have been traced here to the forest. Even now, he might be walking into a trap. He cowered lower in the prickly holly, trying to make himself invisible.

The walker was a youth, and he was alone. Even better, he seemed unarmed. Edwin cautiously eased some leaves aside so he could see the boy more clearly. His eyes narrowed in calculation as he weighed up the choice of staying hidden and taking his chances, or jumping the youth and catching him by surprise. Whether he was here on legitimate business or was an outlaw, the boy might have something worth stealing. He might even have brought food and ale along for the journey. Edwin's mouth watered at the thought.

A fallen tree lay close behind him. Edwin reached out and quietly raised a branch that had broken away, testing its strength and weight. It would do. He had the advantage of surprise. A well-placed blow . . .

Edwin smiled to himself. His muscles tensed. Poised, ready to spring, something yet made him hesitate. He watched as the unsuspecting youth passed close to the holly bushes. The boy looked about him, his face open to scrutiny. 'Who's there?' he cried.

Edwin's eyes widened in surprise. His fingers relaxed their firm grip on the dead branch and his smile broadened. He settled deeper into his prickly hiding place to wait, to watch, and to make quite sure.

ONE

THE FIRST THING she needed, Janna decided, as she followed the faint trail that snaked through the forest, was to find a pool or stream to wash out her filthy clothes. Her lip curled in disgust as she looked down at the peasant's smock and breeches she wore. Men's garments, stolen from a barn at Babestoche Manor. Not only were they far too big for her, they were stained with sweat and dirt. In fact, they stank. She raised her arm to take a surreptitious sniff under her armpit, and nearly fainted from the powerful odour released by her action. Even worse than the smell was the fact that she was itchy all over. Something, or lots of little somethings, was living in her clothes. Janna felt her skin crawl. She longed to scratch her arms, her legs, her body, but she knew scratching would make the itches much worse. Better by far to find somewhere she could strip off and wash herself as well as the garments she wore. Even her eyebrows itched, while her scalp tickled with crawling creatures, real or imaginary.

If the dashing lord Hugh could only see her now! Janna shook her head as she tried to imagine his reaction. There had been admiration in his eyes when he'd looked at her in the past. Admiration, and perhaps something even more than that. But now . . .

Forget it! Forget him, she told herself sternly. Hugh thought she'd died in the fire that had consumed her cottage. Almost everyone thought she had died. Only two people knew she was still alive, but Janna trusted them not to betray her. It was better for her to be gone from sight. Safer. Meanwhile these clothes, these filthy garments, were part of her disguise, and she would have to endure them.

She quickened her pace. She knew not her destination, knew only that she was heading north in a desperate attempt to flee from those who had burned her home and who wanted to harm her. She had heard that this trail went north through the forest of Gravelinges to Wicheford on the other side. Her journey would not end there, but it would put the barrier of the forest between her and all those whom she had once thought of as friends. The thought of their treachery cast a dark shadow across Janna's heart.

The great canopy of branches high above turned the forest into a cool, green dimness. Only a few rays from the setting sun pierced the leafy shield, pebbling the path with coins of gold. Bright spongy moss coated tree roots, while sticky-footed ivy clung to dead and living trees alike, encasing them in ruffled coats of green. The soft groans and murmurs of wood pigeons gave way to an alarmed rattle of wings as they flew from Janna's approach. She felt as if she was walking through an enchanted wonderland, yet loneliness and sorrow walked beside her, step by step.

She scanned the silent forest for signs of water, and licked dry lips. She'd been walking for a long time. How much

6

further did she have to go? Everyone knew that Gravelinges was enormous, but how big was enormous? Could she walk through the forest before nightfall, or was she already running out of time? She had no way of knowing where she was. Huge beech and oak trees towered above her, silent watchers in the dark forest, interspersed with birch, ash and hazel too, their summer green brighter than the dark patch of holly ahead. Janna shivered. The forest was a dangerous place to be, especially at night, when it became the demesne of wolves and other fierce creatures.

Her footsteps quickened, but then slowed again almost immediately. The trail was barely discernible in the dim light. She was further through the forest than she'd ever gone before, and could not rely on familiar landmarks to guide her. Janna was afraid that, in her hurry, she might misread her way, might become truly lost.

A faint rustle ahead froze her to a sudden stillness. Her heart thumped with fright. Slowly, her gaze sifted the landscape. There was a tall thicket of weeds in an open space ahead, which might give shelter to anything from a rabbit or deer to an outlaw. She watched for shaking leaves, for any signs of movement, but all was still now. Her gaze moved to the clump of holly bushes and then on and over the flat leafy cover spread beneath several huge oak trees.

Nothing moved. Janna turned slowly in a full circle, watching and listening. Then she took a few steps forward, pressing her feet carefully on grass and weeds so as not to make a noise, for she sensed now that she was not alone.

A silvery trilling set her heart leaping with fear. A pale yellow-grey wood warbler, flushed from cover, flew upwards.

She felt the stir of air from its flight on her cheek. Sweat prickled her shoulder blades. 'Who's there?' she cried, her voice high and wavering with fright. Too late, she recalled that she was wearing a man's clothes. 'Is anyone there?' she tried again, striving for a deeper tone.

Silence. Janna's ears stretched to hear a noise that wasn't her own. She could feel eyes watching her every move. She whirled abruptly, hoping to catch – what? Something animal – or human?

Janna swallowed hard, feeling again the sweat of fear as she recalled the last time she'd been lost in Gravelinges in the dark. She'd stumbled across the path of a wild boar. In her panic to escape she'd run in a circle around it, enraging it to such a degree that it had charged and charged again. If Godric hadn't been out poaching that night . . .

Godric. Janna's mind skittered hastily away from the image of the sturdy villein. She didn't want to think of Godric right now. He lay too heavily on her conscience for comfort.

No noise, no movement, save for the frightened thudding of her heart. Janna forced her legs to move once more, taking one reluctant step after another while she assessed her predicament. Wild animals didn't only come out at night, she reasoned, but if it was a wild animal stalking her now it would not trouble to conceal the noise of its passage. Which meant that the watcher must be human.

Perhaps it was the king's forester? Her mouth twisted in a grimace. She had only her feminine wiles to talk her way around the fact that she was trespassing in the royal forest, and she doubted they would be enough to save her – especially dressed as she was now! But if the forester was following her, surely he would have shown himself, would have challenged her just as soon as he noticed her?

Not the forester then. Could it even be Godric, who sometimes came through the forest on legitimate business, guiding people through to safety? Briefly, desperately, Janna wished that it might be Godric. In spite of feeling deeply ashamed, she longed to see him, longed for the comfort of his familiar presence. But she dared not call out again, for it was more likely that the silent watcher was an outlaw. Janna had heard frightening stories of those who fled the king's justice. They hid in forests and preyed on travellers, seizing whatever they might find and showing no mercy to any who would prevent them.

Icy fear pricked up her spine. God rot it, she thought, wishing she was safely home in her cottage with her mother and Alfred, her cat. She drew in a deep breath to steady herself. Her home, and those she loved, were gone, all gone. She was alone out here, with no kith or kin to comfort her and only her knife for protection. She drew it out of its sheath and, feeling slightly braver with a weapon in her hand, she began to walk on.

Her way became more open, the tree cover now quite sparse. Janna realised she was no longer climbing. She seemed to have reached the high point of the forest, for the open weedy growth ahead lay downhill before being swallowed into darkness under the trees. She walked towards it and looked about. It must be very late for the sun, always slow to disappear in the summer months, was now gone and the light was fading fast from the sky. Even if she hurried, Janna knew she could not get through the forest before nightfall.

Nor could she keep on walking for she would stray off the path. Already it was so faint as to be almost indiscernible. She'd heard tales of travellers who'd been lost in Gravelinges for days, weeks even. If they survived, they were half-mad with fear by the time they were rescued. Whatever else she did, she must not lose her way.

Should she then remain here through the night, and continue in the morning? She looked about her, feeling a shiver of unease. She shouldn't light a fire. Although the flames would bring warmth and a measure of protection from any wild animals that might be lurking nearby, they might also attract the attention of the king's forester. She couldn't risk that. Nor could she risk making a nest of grass out here in the open. If she slept on the ground she would be in danger from any wild creature, animal or human, large or small, that crossed her path. Better, perhaps, to wedge herself up in a tree for the night, she decided. It would be uncomfortable, but she would be in a position to protect herself; she would be safe.

With her knife, Janna drew a large and careful circle around her feet to mark the faint trail she was following, then cut a long staff of hazel and staked it in the centre so that she could see it from a distance. After a moment's thought, she pulled out her old kirtle, which she'd hidden under her smock, and tied it to the top of the stake. She stepped back and surveyed her handiwork. Her kirtle had been burnt to tatters in the fire. It was useless to her, but it made a good beacon. Besides, she no longer needed the disguise of a fat stomach, for anyone who met her from now on would be a stranger to her. Even if, by unlucky chance, she were to come across someone from her past, they shouldn't recognise her either. She was no longer Janna, daughter of the *wortwyf*, the herb wife who had died in mysterious circumstances. She was now a youth called John.

Janna nodded to herself, satisfied. With frequent glances at her home-made marker to prevent herself from roaming too far, she began a careful inspection. She was looking for a tree with a lot of branches to cradle her and keep her fast should she fall asleep and forget to hold on. She also kept a lookout for any sign of water, or even some juicy berries. Her stomach growled with hunger; her throat scratched with thirst. A few pale discs caught her eye. She pounced on the small puffball mushrooms, and inspected them carefully before peeling them and stuffing them into her mouth. They were still white and tender enough to eat raw. Although they'd be better stewed, they brought saliva into her mouth and helped to fill her hollow belly.

Janna tried to ignore her discomfort, ignore too the itches that plagued her, and the tickling, biting midges that swarmed around her face. But she could not ignore the uneasy sense that she was not alone. If the watcher was human, it seemed he was in no hurry to accost her. Perhaps he intended to wait until she fell asleep?

Janna's heart thumped hard and heavy in her chest. She found it difficult to catch her breath. I'll stay awake all night, she promised herself, and gripped her knife more tightly as she searched for a tree with branches reaching down low enough for her to haul herself up. There was a thicket of yew ahead, a dark, dense tangle of knitted branches and spindle leaves. Her mother's voice came into her mind: 'Yews are

ancient and sacred trees. The druids built their temples nearby, believing them to be sites of burial and resurrection.'
Janna took a step towards them, then stopped as she remembered her mother's warning.

'The fruits and seeds are highly poisonous, so you must be careful, Janna. Stay away from them, if you can. They're otherworld, and they're dangerous.'

The trees rose before her like a solid wall; she could not penetrate their depths. They would make a perfect hiding place. Could she risk it? It wasn't as if she was planning to eat any part of them! Then Janna remembered what else she'd been told: that faeries believed that yews had the power to make them invisible, and used yew to conjure up a darkness in which they might disappear. Janna, too, sought to disappear; she hurried over to them and eased herself into their sheltering arms.

Climbing was so much easier wearing breeches, she realised, as she pulled herself upwards from branch to branch. In fact, just about everything was so much easier for a man than a woman!

When she could no longer see the ground below, she judged she was high enough to be unobserved, and secure enough to defend herself should anyone climb up and attack her. She wedged her body into the interlacing branches, and hooked her arms around them for safety. It was almost completely dark now. She couldn't see anything other than her immediate cover, but she knew her home-made beacon was close enough for her to find in the morning.

With a sigh, she closed her eyes, then quickly snapped them open. She must not go to sleep. She touched the purse at her waist, heard a faint crumple of parchment and the clink of coins. Everything she owned that was of value to her was in her purse, including her journey's purpose: the clues that might lead her to her father.

With the last of the light gone, the night became cold. A light rain began to fall. Janna pulled the hood of the gorget over her head, and huddled deeper into her prickly shelter in a vain effort to stay dry. The rain kept on, soaking through the gorget as well as her smock and breeches. It was too gentle to cleanse the filthy garments or drown the creatures that tormented her with their biting, but it was persistent enough to chill her to the bone. Janna shivered, and debated climbing down from her tree. She was cramped from crouching among the branches. If she walked about, her blood would flow freely once more and she might get warm.

If she wandered about in the dark, she might also get attacked! She would certainly get lost. Janna stayed where she was, and continued to shiver as she listened to the sounds of the forest at night: the haunting call of an owl overhead; the scuffle of a scavenging badger below and, in the distance, the anguished howl of a wolf. Secretive rustles betrayed the hunters; squeaks of distress marked their prey.

The night wore on, black and dismal, all trace of moon and stars hidden behind dense cloud. In spite of her best efforts, Janna's eyes closed. She slept, jerked awake, and slept again.

When she next awoke, the sky was beginning to lighten with dawn, and the birds of the forest were celebrating the birth of a new day with chirps and cheeps, trills of interrogation, whistles, and snatches of songs. Janna rested quietly for a moment, listening to their conversations. But her body felt numb with cold; she was desperate to get down from her tree. Her limbs were cramped and stiff and, as she clambered downwards, she slipped off a rain-slicked branch and crashed through prickly foliage to land with a thump on the ground. She groaned with the pain of it. A brief vision of her home flashed into her mind: the fire warming and lighting the small cottage, the fragrance of dried herbs, hot griddle cakes and rich vegetable pottage, her mother's busy efficiency, and Alfred's welcoming purr . . .

Tears came into Janna's eyes. She felt once more the wrenching grief of her mother's death, an aching sense of loss. There was also the added frustration of knowing that her mother had been on the brink of divulging the secret of her father's identity, a secret Janna could never know now unless she could find out what was in the letter she carried. But for that, she would need to be able to read, and that was something Eadgyth hadn't taught her. Janna thought about the parchment, with its undecipherable marks. Only the name at the end meant anything to her. John. It was her father's name, she was sure of it. She burned with curiosity to know what he had written to her mother. Eadgyth had loved him, she knew that now, yet his words had been enough to make her mother pack up and run, and keep his identity for ever a secret.

Janna came back to the present, becoming aware of her surroundings once more. She choked back a sob. She was lonely and frightened. Yet she knew that somehow she must find the strength to carry on, for she'd made a vow to herself: to seek her unknown father and, with his help, bring the man guilty of the murder of her mother to justice. So she scrubbed the tears from her cheeks with a grubby hand, then eased herself up into a sitting position and carefully massaged the base of her sore spine. She stretched out her legs, rotating first one foot and then another. Satisfied that nothing was broken after her fall, she stood up then, and walked over to the stake she had left as a marker. She pulled it from the ground, removed her bundled kirtle and threw it into the shelter of a clump of bushes. The stake she kept, for it gave her an extra weapon to protect herself, should she need it.

Remembering her sense that she was being watched, she glanced about, searching for signs. A sudden crackle of twigs set her heart leaping into her throat. She backed behind a tree, then realised the noise came from a grazing deer. Fascinated, Janna stood still, watching it. Its belly was swollen, reminding her that the fence month might already have begun, the time when the forest was forbidden to everyone so that the does might drop their fawns and nurture them in safety. She had to get out of the forest as soon as she could.

The doe stepped on delicate feet towards Janna, head bent as it nibbled grass, lulled into a sense of safety by Janna's stillness. She extended a cautious hand towards it. 'Tck, tck, tck,' she called softly. Startled, it jerked its head up and surveyed her with liquid brown eyes. Then it bent its head once more, and resumed feeding. She smiled at it, feeling a sense of peace as she contemplated the creature's innocence and trust.

She tiptoed past it, fighting her reluctance to leave the safety of this open space for the dense forest that lay ahead of her. She must get through the forest today. Not for anything would she spend another night like the one she'd just passed.

She walked on and under the sheltering trees, then stopped, unsure now if she was on a path at all, for the way ahead seemed unmarked and undisturbed. She looked upwards, hoping to determine her direction by the position of the sun, but the forest had closed over her head and the sky was barely visible. Hastily she retraced her steps, and felt relief as she reached the clearing once more. She tilted back her head to find the sun, but dark clouds banked thick across the sky; there was no trace of golden radiance. Even as Janna glanced about, rain began to fall once more, soaking through her already wet clothes. 'Hell's breath,' she muttered miserably, knowing that she would give up almost anything if it would buy her food and shelter. She longed to be free of the forest. Its silence oppressed her.

To stand still was to give in to despair. Janna began to prowl around the open space, trying to bring life to her chilled feet and limbs. She looked down at her leaking boots, wishing she had wooden pattens to protect them. While she paced about, she pondered what to do. Finally, she shrugged. She couldn't follow the path home, for she had no home any more nor was there anyone in the village willing to give her shelter. It seemed she had no choice but to try to find her way through the forest. She walked back to where she'd left the trail, but there was no sign of it now. Fear almost paralysed her. It took all her strength not to open her mouth and scream for help in the hope that someone, anyone, be he forester or outlaw, would come to her aid.

She curled her hands into fists, feeling her nails dig into her palm. The pain helped to calm her. Breathe, she thought, remembering Eadgyth's instructions to a panicky patient.

She took a slow, deep breath, feeling time pass as the cold air sucked through her nostrils and down into her chest. Slowly, she expelled her breath through her mouth, blowing it out in a thin stream. It looked like smoke from a fire in the chill morning.

After several more breaths, and feeling slightly calmer, she looked about her, seeking signs. But there were none. 'Just keep going along the edge of the clearing,' she told herself. 'The path must be here somewhere. Have patience, and you'll find it.'

Step by cautious step, she began to circle the open space. A new thought alarmed her now. How would she be able to tell the difference between the track she'd come from and the track that would lead her to where she wanted to go?

Without warning, her foot slipped from under her and she slid down through layers of leaves, down into icy cold water. It sucked up around her, filling her boots and making her gasp for breath. Speechless with shock, Janna flailed about until she found her footing. She realised then that in fact the water came only to her thighs.

She looked about her at the great, leaf-filled depression in which she stood, and decided that she must have fallen into a large and ancient dewpond. She tried to step out, but slimy mud, formed from the detritus of the centuries, held her boots fast. Janna stood on one foot and leaned on her staff to help her balance while she wriggled her other foot until she'd managed to work her boot free. She took off the boot and threw it to safety, then cautiously lowered her bare foot to the bottom of the pond. She shuddered as it sank deep through the icy slime. She wriggled her booted foot, tugging hard until the sucking mud released it. A second boot joined its companion on the leafy bank. With a gasp of fear, Janna suddenly snatched up her purse and opened it, belatedly understanding the danger if the precious parchment inside had got wet.

The outside of the purse was damp, but its contents were dry. Janna released her breath, uttering a quiet 'thank you' to whoever might be listening. She flung the staff onto dry ground, and untied her girdle. Purse and girdle followed the staff and boots to safety. Time now to attend to her greatest need: water! She scooped twigs and leaves out of her way, bent her head and began to drink, relishing the icy wetness in her dry mouth and parched throat. She drank until she could drink no more, but now another idea had come into her mind. She was already wet and uncomfortable. She had nothing to lose save the family of biting creatures that inhabited the garments she wore. With a quick glance around her to make sure that she was alone, she gingerly lowered her body deeper into the water. Anchoring herself in the freezing mud, she stripped off the stolen gorget and smock, untied her breeches, and gave them all a good scrub before dressing herself once more. The gorget came last, but the hood clung cold and wet around her head and water dripped into her eyes. She took it off and cast it out onto the grass.

Remembering the itches, she ducked her head under and massaged her fingers through her hair, giving it a thorough rinse in the freezing water. She could feel the strangeness of its short stubble, all that was left after the ravages of the fire and her efforts to trim it short with her knife. At last, when she was satisfied that every little creature must be drowned, she felt her way towards the rim of earth that circled the large leafy basin. A memory teased her mind. Godric had told her about the ancient road built through the forest by the Romans. Could this dewpond have been fashioned to provide water for the soldiers and merchants who had once traversed this land?

Something sharp pierced Janna's foot, and she cried aloud, forgetting for the moment her need for secrecy. She raised her foot above the water, and frowned as she inspected it. The tender skin of her instep was cut and bleeding. What could have been so sharp that it had pierced her skin like that? Not a flint, surely, but a sword perhaps, or a dagger? Janna knew that such things were sometimes found in water. She'd heard that it was once a custom for the ancients to throw their weapons into rivers and pools in order to propitiate the gods and seek good fortune. Coming across a pool in a huge forest such as this must in itself have seemed like good fortune to the old ones. They might well have shown their gratitude with costly gifts.

She took a deep breath and ducked down, carefully feeling through the icy mud for something sharp. Her own knife was quite small, no match for a wild animal or an outlaw. The staff she'd found was better than nothing, but with a real weapon in her hand she would feel much, much safer.

Janna's lungs were bursting. She shot upwards and gasped for air, greedily sucking it in. Her teeth chattering, she was tempted, so tempted, to get out of the pool. Instead, she forced herself to take another deep breath and duck down into the darkness. She groped about in the slimy mud. Nothing. She surfaced once more, her whole body shaking with cold. One last time, she promised herself, and filled her lungs with air.

This time her search was rewarded. Janna felt the blade's sharpness bite into her hand. She snatched it back, then cautiously stretched out her fingers, feeling inch by careful inch until at last she touched the blade again. Her chest was on fire. She was desperate to take a breath but she stayed down, carefully patting along the flat of the blade until she came to the solid shape of its hilt. She closed both hands around it and tugged, feeling the sword slide free. She shot up, breaking the surface with a triumphant whoosh of escaping air. She breathed deeply, savouring the air's freshness, and looked down at the muddy object in her hands.

It was longer than a dagger, but shorter than the swords worn by noblemen such as the lord Hugh. Part of the hilt was broken off, but there was enough left for her small hand to grasp the weapon. She swished it around in the water, carefully breaking off lumps of caked mud and grit and rinsing it clean. The blade was rusty, its sheen dulled from its long immersion in the water. But it was sharp enough to inflict a grievous wound, Janna realised, as she gingerly put her foot to the ground and limped out of the dew pond.

Wiping her injured foot clean, she eased it into her boot. She put on her other boot, picked up the gorget and looked about for her purse and girdle. There was no sign of them. Janna frowned and looked more carefully, unable to understand the significance of their disappearance. Where could they be?

Panic constricted her chest. She began to search frantically, thinking she must have misread the direction in which she'd thrown them. Perhaps they'd slid beneath a bush or got buried somewhere in long grass and bracken? She scoured the clearing, widening the area of her search to poke into banks of tall nettles and patches of flowering weeds, although she knew in her heart that she'd not mistaken the direction. They had gone. Someone must have been there all along, watching her, waiting for just this opportunity to steal from her the only clues she had that might lead her to her father.

TWO

JANNA BOWED HER head as a wave of grief and loss swept over her. She had so little, yet even this had been taken from her. A few silver pennies – yes, they might be of use to a desperate vagabond, as might the ring and brooch if he could trade them. But, for Janna, the real value of the contents of her purse lay in the parchment she'd carried, the letter she'd found from her unknown father. She was sure the letter was the key to everything, if only she could read it. Would an outlaw be able to read? Janna doubted it. He'd surely keep the other things, but would he perhaps throw away the letter, thinking it worthless?

A faint glimmer of hope lifted Janna's spirits. If she could only follow in the thief's footsteps, perhaps she might find the parchment discarded along the track. She looked about her once more, this time seeking the shelter nearest to where she'd cast her boots from the pond. The thief must have hidden somewhere while he watched her and waited to pounce. He might well have left some signs of his passage.

A dense thicket of hazel stood close by. Gripping the sword tight in her hand, she headed towards it. She examined the trees carefully, as well as the ground surrounding them, in case there were any signs to be seen: a thread snagged on a withy perhaps, or bruised and broken herbage. Her search was rewarded by the sight of a footprint indented in a patch of soft earth. Another print followed, leading away from the thicket. Janna stepped forward in the same direction, alert for any further clues to point her way.

Several times she thought she'd come to a dead end, but she trusted her instincts and kept on, following the most obvious route through the trees. Although she constantly checked the ground around her, there was no sign of her father's letter. But scuffed moss, a broken twig, some flattened grass or herbs, a sliver of snagged bark all helped to point the way. She placed her feet lightly, carefully, while words repeated in her mind like a prayer: 'Please let him throw away the parchment. Please let me find my father's letter.'

She found herself now in a dense patch of the forest, hazel and holly hedged by a wall of prickly brambles. There seemed no way through. Baffled, Janna stopped and looked around her. Then she stepped forward for a more careful inspection. Every instinct told her she was close to her quarry, but the brambles barred her way. Or did they? Here they were bent one way, there another, cunningly plaited to disguise a thin and twisting passage through. Quiet as a hunting owl, Janna eased herself to the left then to the right, pushing deeper into the prickly heart of the brambles, until suddenly a small clearing opened before her. She walked into it, then hastily slid sideways behind the trunk of a large beech for concealment. She could see the thief clearly. She gripped the sword tighter and watched him.

He was sitting with his back to her. Janna saw a faint glimmer of light as he held the gold ring up high to inspect it. Her other treasures lay on the ground in front of him. Clearly, he was gloating over his day's work.

A wave of rage coursed through her, as fierce, as white hot as the blazing sun. Without thought, she launched herself towards him, arm raised and sword at the ready to strike him flat with the blade and, if necessary, run him through. How dare he take her treasures, how dare he!

Swift and silent as she was, still the young man heard her and jerked upright to face her. His upraised arm deflected the sword's blow. The blade missed the side of his head and hit him flat against the wrist instead. He grunted with pain but was still able to grab her wrist and wrench the sword from her grasp, flinging it safely out of range. Enraged, Janna swung back her foot and kicked out, aiming for his groin, hoping to cripple him with pain. But she was too slow and he read her mind. Just as her foot came forward, he released her and jumped nimbly out of her way after giving her a shove so that she lost her balance and fell. Before he had time to flee, she launched herself at his ankles and tugged, pulling him down on top of her. She rolled free and raked his face with her nails. 'Devil's spawn!' she gritted through her teeth. She began to pummel him with her fists. 'Dog's droppings! Pond slime!'

She kept up the attack, feeling proud of the fact that she was getting the better of the rogue, until she realised he was making no effort to defend himself. Instead, he'd curled into a ball to present the smallest target to her flailing arms and fists.

'You can stop hitting me, mistress. I won't harm you,' he muttered. As she understood the import of his words, shock stopped Janna mid-blow. Wide-eyed, she jumped to her feet and snatched up the sword, ready now to grab her treasures and run.

'H-how did you know I was a girl?' she stammered.

His face reddened slightly. He grinned at her, but did not answer. Janna felt her own face redden as she worked out how he'd managed to fathom her secret. 'You watched me bathe, you . . . you bastard, damn you to hell!' She closed her eyes as she remembered how she'd stripped off and washed both herself and her clothes. Mortified, she lashed out once more.

He took a hasty step out of her reach. 'I turned my back to you as soon as I realised what you were. Who you are!' he protested.

Janna wondered whether she could believe him. It was certain that he'd seen enough to know the truth! She comforted herself with the thought that mostly she'd crouched down in the water to wash, and that she'd both undressed and dressed in the pond. She remembered then the rustles she'd heard the night before, her sense that she was being watched. She eyed the youth warily. He hadn't harmed her – not yet. But that didn't mean he might not try in the future.

'Why are you wearing men's clothes anyway?' he asked, his grin returning as he commented, 'Certes they don't become you, nor do they fit you very well!'

'They do well enough.' To prove her words, Janna tugged on the cord holding her breeches in place to tighten it, then hitched the breeches higher so she no longer trampled the fabric underfoot. 'And don't change the subject either!' she flashed, recalling the reason she had followed him. She bent and snatched up the ring which the young man had let fall in the surprise of the attack, and hastily shoved it into the purse that lay on the ground nearby, hearing the comforting crump of parchment as she did so. The brooch and silver coins had also been dumped on the grass. They swiftly followed the ring to safety. Janna straightened then, and subjected the thief to a defiant glare, ready to spring at him once more to protect what was rightfully hers.

He held up his hands in a gesture of peace. 'I'm sorry,' he muttered. 'I . . . I have nothing save the clothes I am wearing. I was going to use what I stole from you to travel somewhere safe, to find shelter and buy food. But I won't try again, I promise.'

'Why are you here in the forest?' Janna demanded, not in the least mollified by his explanation. 'What are you hiding from?'

'Why are *you* here?' He turned the question back on her. 'What are *you* hiding from?'

Janna was silenced, but only for a moment. 'I asked first,' she muttered.

A grin stole over his face once more. 'I'll make a bargain with you. I'll tell you my story if you'll tell me yours,' he said. He waited for her grudging nod before continuing. 'I am on the run from my lord. He's a cruel man, cruel as the devil. He beat me.' The youth touched his dirty face. Janna saw a jagged scar on his chin, and winced in sympathy.

'I ran away 'cos I decided I'd rather live as an outlaw than stay at the mercy of that swine,' the youth continued. 'I've been hiding here in the forest ever since, catching whatever I may to eat, and drinking water from that pool you fell into.'

'How long have you been here?' Janna strove to keep any hint of warmth from her voice, lest he believe she might take pity on him and share with him her treasures.

'I don't know the time in days exactly, but I reached the forest as the trees were just coming into bud from their winter sleep. I think it must be mid-summer now?'

Janna nodded. 'Close enough. The fence-month may well have started already. You must certainly leave the forest as soon as possible, as must I.'

'Why?'

''Tis the time when the does give birth to their fawns. The forest is forbidden to all at that time so that mothers and their babies are not disturbed. 'Tis a dangerous time to hide here, for the forester will be on constant watch to protect the king's deer for the hunting season to come.'

The young man nodded thoughtfully. 'I'll have to take my chances. I can't leave until the seasons turn full circle.'

'Why?' Now it was Janna's turn to ask the question.

'If I can stay hidden for a year and a day, I shall have earned my freedom from my lord.' He grinned ruefully. 'That's if I can stay alive for that long.'

In spite of her best efforts, Janna felt some sympathy for the ruffian. His story touched her. So, too, did the realisation that, although he'd stolen her purse, he'd made no effort to harm her, or keep her goods once she'd tracked him down. She, too, had stolen something: the clothes she wore, and from a poor peasant who could ill-afford to lose them. She was in no position to judge what anyone might do when pushed to the limit of need. 'What will you do after a year and a day?' she asked.

The young man shrugged. 'I would like to become an apprentice, to learn a trade, but I have not the money for that. So I will do anything at all that might help me earn my bread and keep.'

'No-one will give you work and shelter once they know you're a runaway serf,' Janna pointed out.

'They will if they think I've come from Wales. That's what I'll tell them. They won't care who my lord was, so long as I show willing and work hard.' The youth flexed his muscles. 'I am strong,' he boasted, 'and I can turn my hand to anything I'm asked to do. I'll have no trouble finding someone to take me in, I promise you.'

Janna nodded thoughtfully, while her mind ticked over in a tumble of ideas. If she helped him, so too might he help her. She held out her hand. 'My name is Johanna, but I'm known as Janna,' she said. 'I, too, am in hiding. That's why I'm dressed like this. I call myself "John", for he was my father – a man of wealth and importance,' she added proudly.

The youth nodded. He relaxed his wary stance, sprawling back against the grass. 'My name is Edwin.'

'If you come from Wales, shouldn't you should call yourself by a Welsh name? Hoel or Gwyn, something like that?'

'Edwin, Hoel, it makes no matter so long as they believe I'm a free man from across the border.' He shrugged, and patted the grass beside him. 'Sit down,' he invited. 'I won't hurt you.'

Not taking any chances, Janna hooked the purse onto her girdle, and tied the girdle firmly around her waist. Then she sat down as she was bid, sword close at hand, keeping a careful distance from Edwin.

'So where are you bound? And why are you hiding?' he prompted.

Janna took a deep breath, hardly knowing where her story should start. With the fact that her cottage was burnt to the ground and she was homeless? Or a few days before then, when the nightmare first began?

'I am Janna, daughter of Eadgyth the *wortwyf*,' she said. 'My mother used her knowledge of herbs to heal the sick. Just a few days ago, she was called on to physic the lady of Babestoche Manor, Dame Alice, and her newborn babe.' She paused, debating whether or not she should tell Edwin how her mother had also looked after Cecily, one of Dame Alice's tiring women, and how Eadgyth had drunk the poisoned wine that was meant for Cecily.

'My mother taught me all she knew, but she is dead,' Janna continued, choosing her words carefully. 'She died in mysterious circumstances, and I have sworn to avenge her death and bring the culprit to justice. But I need my father's help for this. Although I know who caused my mother's death, I cannot accuse the man for he is all-powerful whereas I am but a humble outcast. So now I'm going in search of my father.' She patted the purse at her waist. 'My mother never told me who he was, but I hope that this letter and these pieces of jewellery will help me find him.'

'No wonder you took after me in such a fury!' Edwin gave her a rueful smile. 'I'm sorry,' he said again, adding, 'But why do you dress like a youth and travel in such secrecy?'

Janna sighed. 'The man responsible for my mother's death turned the villagers against me. They burned my cottage to the ground, thinking I was in it. It is safer for me if everyone

thinks I died in the blaze, but just in case anyone sees me . . .'
She swept a hand down her body, indicating the clothes she
wore.

Edwin's lips pursed in a silent whistle. He regarded Janna
thoughtfully for a moment. 'It seems to me that, if we can't
stay here in the forest, we should journey together. We might
be able to help each other,' he ventured.

Janna nodded in agreement. 'Your lord searches for a lone
runaway, while you understood what I was quickly enough.'
She slid a sideways glance at him, and he reddened once
more.

'Yea, well I was in a . . . a position to see more of you than
most,' he said, shame-faced.

'Than any man has ever seen before,' Janna said tartly.
'Had you not seen what you saw, would you say I could pass
for a youth?'

He looked her fully in the face now. He was taller than
her, and Janna noticed that he was also a little older than her
own sixteen years. His face was comely rather than handsome, and he had an attractive smile. She noticed the scratches
on his dirty brown cheek, freshly made and dappled with
beads of blood. She, too, had left her mark on Edwin. 'You
should wash those scratches,' she said. 'I'll find some herbs
that will help them heal.' She felt sympathy for the mis-
treated youth, but she would not say sorry; she wasn't quite
ready to forgive him yet.

He nodded his thanks. 'You dress like a man,' he said
then, 'but you walk and talk like a girl.' He jumped to his
feet, put a hand on his hip and took a few mincing steps.

Janna was surprised into laughter. 'I do not!' she protested.

'You laugh like one, too.'

Janna gurgled into silence. 'I can't dress like a girl,' she pointed out, making her voice purposely deep. 'These clothes I'm wearing are all that I own.'

'That's better,' he approved. 'And if you walk like so . . .' He began to stride about, his arms loose and swinging freely by his side. Janna scrambled up and began to copy him, walking first beside him and then in front, so that he could watch her.

'Like this?' she asked.

He grinned at her. 'You fight like a girl, too.' He gently touched his scratched face with his dirty hand.

Janna kept silent, refusing to feel guilty for protecting what was rightfully her own.

'If you're going to live as a boy, you'll need to learn how to defend yourself in a fight. You haven't the strength to fight fair, but your instinct was right.' Edwin patted his groin. 'A hard kick here will cripple your attacker and give you time to run like the devil himself. But you were too slow. I knew exactly what you had in mind.' He forked two fingers and, before Janna had a chance to react, he stabbed them towards her eyes. 'You could also try to blind your opponent like this, or . . .' Edwin's fingers closed together. 'You can use your hand to break his nose, or his neck.' His hand became a blade as he chopped up towards Janna's nostrils and then sideways at her throat. She felt the side of his fingers slam hard against her skin, and swallowed involuntarily.

'Hit hard, hard as you can. And be quick, you have to take your enemy by surprise,' Edwin continued. 'But what will you do if he comes from behind you?' Giving Janna no time to reply, he ducked behind her and grabbed her, pinning her arms to her side and holding her close to his chest. With a startled cry, she tried to fight him off. 'What will you do then?' he whispered. His breath blew warm against her ear. She felt a deadly fear as she realised she was powerless in his grasp.

Still he held her, while she struggled uselessly in his grip. He gave a small huff of amusement and continued to hold her tight. The sound enraged Janna and she increased her efforts, but to the same end. She could not get away from him.

'You stamp down on my foot. Hard,' he told her. As Janna's knee came up he released her suddenly, and skipped away out of danger. 'Don't signal your actions,' he warned. 'And don't give your enemy any chance to escape.'

Janna nodded slowly. Suddenly, she sprang towards him. Her fingers stopped a hair's breadth from his eyes.

'Yea, that's it. Now go practise on someone else!'

Janna scowled at him. Her heart was still racing after the fright he'd given her. Unrepentant, he grinned back. 'You'll do, John – so long as you remember who and what you are!'

'I'll remember.' She squeezed her fingers together and tried a few practice chops at the air, pretending that she was aiming at an opponent's neck. And his nose. Her fingers formed into a V to stab at unseen eyes. For good measure, she stamped down hard on an imaginary foot.

Edwin craned his head back to look up through the green veil of leaves. 'There's not enough sunlight to tell which direction we should walk in,' he said. 'Do you know the way through the forest?'

'No.' Janna's face fell. 'I lost the path at that clearing by the pool.' She looked about her. 'I have no idea where we are now.'

'We're at the place I've made my home.' He jerked a thumb behind him. Looking past him, Janna noticed a small shelter fashioned from branches and stuffed with mud and leaves. Longer branches were laid on top of the primitive walls to form a rough roof; they were covered with a layer of reeds for extra protection. She had to look hard to see the shelter, for it was almost indistinguishable from the surrounding forest. It would give Edwin some cover from rain, but was too small for anyone to live in any comfort. Nearby was a small circle of blackened flints, with three branches meeting at a point above the space in the middle. Janna realised she was looking at Edwin's fireplace.

'What do you do for food? Do you have any?' she asked, suddenly ravenous.

Edwin shuffled his feet, looking shifty. 'I trap small creatures with this,' he admitted, pulling a snare of plaited fibres from the front of his tunic. 'I cook them and eat them.'

Janna felt juices seep into her mouth. 'I'm so hungry,' she said. 'Do you have anything we can eat now?'

'No.' He smiled slightly. 'I could offer you some water, but I saw you drink your fill in the pool.'

'You have water? And something to cook in?' Janna's gaze flicked around the forest floor, settling on several plants of interest to her.

Edwin nodded.

'Then light the fire,' Janna instructed. 'Before we go anywhere, I'll make us a pottage of herbs to fill our bellies for the journey.'

'We can't, not in daylight! The smoke will betray us.' Edwin cast a nervous glance about him.

Janna hesitated. Her stomach growled with hunger. She was famished. 'Let's risk it,' she said. 'The forester is probably miles away, and even if he does see the smoke we'll be gone before he can track its source.' Not giving Edwin a chance to protest, she drew out her knife and hurried towards a clump of nettles. She kept an eye on Edwin's movements as she plucked the nettles by the stem and carefully cut away the stinging leaves. A patch of chickweed drew her on, and she harvested a handful of green shoots before moving over to gather some dandelions and a snippet of wild garlic to add flavour. Although her treasures were safe in her purse, she still wasn't sure how far she could trust the young outlaw. It was true that they might be able to help each other; nevertheless, Janna reminded herself to be wary, to stay on guard just in case she'd misread his intentions. So she watched him.

His boast had not been an idle one, she thought, as she recalled how powerless she'd been in his grip. In a fair fight between them, he would be the winner. He was taller, and he had a wiry strength that became evident as he wrestled with a dead branch to break it up for kindling. The fire laid and the tinder struck to light it, he poured some water from a crudely fashioned jug into a small iron pot and hooked it over the flames to boil.

Reassured that they had a common purpose, Janna ventured further, looking for mushrooms to add bulk to the brew. She couldn't find any more puffballs, but a few oyster mushrooms fanned out from a rotting tree stump and she gathered those, along with some late white mushrooms that nestled in an open grassy patch. She inspected them carefully for insects and to make sure they were truly an edible variety and not any poisonous look-alike. Satisfied that they were sound, and that she'd gathered enough to satisfy their hunger, she searched now for a bird's nest. Some eggs, or even some berries, would make a welcome addition to this most basic of broths. The nests were empty and berries still unripe, but she espied something even better. Janna smiled with antici-pated pleasure as she hurried towards the big white splats of lacy elderflowers peeping through the green cover. She held up the front of her smock like an apron, and dropped in what she'd already gathered, then cut several elderflowers to add to her collection, finally circling back towards the fire-place. The pot hung over the fire, steam rising in the cold air, but there was no sign of Edwin. He had vanished.

With a sinking feeling, she looked about for him. 'Edwin?' she called softly, remembering to keep her voice pitched low. 'Where are you?'

There was no response. 'All the more for me, then,' Janna muttered, trying to keep up her spirits. Carefully laying aside the elderflowers, she threw the mushrooms and plants into the pot and, shivering, stepped closer to the fire to warm herself and dry her clothes. All sympathy for the outlaw had gone along with his disappearance. Beaten by his lord indeed, she thought, as she recalled the scar on his chin. Got that in a free fight more like, probably while he was trying to steal from someone else!

A slight rustle set her fumbling for her knife. She whirled around, frantically trying to recall the moves Edwin had taught her. The eyes. The nose. The neck. The foot.

As she saw who it was, she relaxed. Wearing a proud grin, Edwin strode forward and dangled a limp furry form in front of her nose.

'Erk! What's that?' Janna jumped backwards.

'A leveret.' He set down the hare and pulled out his knife.

'But it's only a baby!' Janna protested.

'That's right. I found it lying in a clump of grass.' Edwin looked down at his prize. 'It must have been ailing or I wouldn't have caught it.' He began to strip the fur from the small body.

Janna shuddered, but she didn't stop him when he threw the leveret into the broth. He peered in after it, and sniffed suspiciously. 'That's poisonous.' He pointed at one of the mushrooms.

'No, it's not.'

'I don't eat fungus. It can kill you.'

'I know. You have to be careful. But that's a white mushroom, and there are also some oyster mushrooms. They're quite safe.'

Edwin looked at Janna. 'How do I know you're not trying to poison me?' he muttered.

'You don't,' Janna said cheerfully, 'but you don't have to eat them if you don't want. I'm hungry enough for both of us.' She offered him an elderflower. 'Have one.' She stuffed the sweet lacy flower into her mouth and chewed it with relish.

Edwin took a cautious bite, looking dubious. Then he licked his lips in appreciation, and quickly scoffed up the rest. It seemed he'd decided to trust her after all. Janna smiled to herself, and picked up another flower.

They ate the pottage with their fingers, taking pleasure from the hot food. It went some way to settling the ache of hunger in their stomachs. Even the hare was shared between them, although Janna tried to close her mind against what she was eating as she picked the flesh from the small bones.

'A feast fit for King Stephen himself,' Edwin commented, and licked his fingers. Janna pulled a face at him. If Edwin really believed that, he must be truly deluded. But his ready grin showed her that, even if he'd never attended a banquet, his imagination was every bit as vivid as her own.

'Are you ready to leave now?' he asked, when every last morsel was finally eaten. He stood up, and looked about for the jug and the pot that had held their meal.

'You should first break up your shelter,' Janna suggested, 'just in case the forester comes this way.'

'He won't. I've never seen him anywhere near here.' But Edwin began to dismantle the branches that had made up his home. Eager to be gone, Janna lent a helping hand by throwing away the flints that marked the fireplace, and scuffing the scorched earth inside the circle to disguise it.

She picked up a last lump of flint and clay, but it flaked and began to crumble in her hand. It slipped from her grasp so Janna gave it a kick instead. The clod fell apart under the impact of her boot. She was about to walk away when she realised that there was something twisted and misshapen in its centre. With quickening interest, she crouched down to examine the remains more carefully.

It was a small figurine, fashioned from pale clay and baked hard as iron. Janna jumped up and fetched the jug that Edwin had put by. There was still some water in the bottom, and she poured it carefully over the figurine, wiping away the last clods of earth that disfigured it. A mother holding a child came to life in her hands. Janna caught her breath as their features washed clearer. Was this Jesus with the Virgin Mary? Or was this something much, much older? She looked at the little statue, tracing the lines of the mother's face, the tenderness of her expression as she looked down at her child. A lump came into Janna's throat as she thought of her own mother. She stole a quick glance at Edwin. He was still busy pulling his shelter apart and hadn't noticed. Janna opened her purse and placed the figurine carefully inside. It was ancient and precious but, even more important to Janna, holding it had brought some comfort, some ease to her own aching, lonely heart.

'Now are you ready?' Edwin demanded as he walked over to her and picked up the sword. He handed Janna the staff she had carried, and raised an enquiring eyebrow.

'That's my sword. I found it,' Janna said indignantly.

'Do you know how to use a sword?' He made no effort to hand it over.

'Do you?' she challenged, and snatched it from him.

'Some of us villeins used to practise our fighting skills against each other. We'd talk of cracking our lord over the head to pay him back for all the beatings he gave us. But we had no swords to practise with, only stout sticks.'

'Then here's a stout stick for you.' Janna handed over her staff, then stepped aside and waited for him to pick up the pot and jug. 'Where did you get those?' She pointed at them.

He looked away and didn't reply, instead setting off towards the clearing. Janna didn't need to be told that he'd probably stolen them. But who was she to judge, when they might well have made the difference to his survival, she thought, as she began to walk after him, consciously imitating the easy swing of his stride.

'We need to make up some story to tell, once we come to a village or town.' She addressed her remark to his back. 'If we're going to be Welsh, perhaps we should call ourselves something other than Edwin and John.'

'It's too hard. Complicated. What if we forget and don't answer when people talk to us?' Edwin threw the question over his shoulder without checking his stride.

Janna thought for a moment. 'Could our mother have been Saxon, wed to a Welshman?'

'Good idea. It might also explain why we don't speak as the Welsh do.' Edwin turned, flashing his easy smile at her. Janna found herself smiling back at him. She began to relax, rolling her shoulders to ease tight muscles. The past few days had taken their toll.

'And where are we bound?' Edwin asked.

Janna shook her head. 'I don't know,' she confessed. 'I can't read my father's letter, so I don't know where to start looking for him.'

'What about Winchestre?'

'Why there? What about London?'

'Winchestre is the royal city where the Treasury is kept. If the king isn't in Winchestre, people will know where he's gone.' He looked back to make sure she understood him. Seeing her look of incomprehension, he continued impatiently, 'You said your father was wealthy and important. If you don't know where your father's manor is, surely your best hope is to find him through the king?'

Excitement blazed across Janna's face. 'I didn't think of that!' She touched the purse hanging from her girdle, feeling the shape of the folded parchment through the rough woven fabric. Winchestre! It was worth a try. It was an added comfort that Edwin seemed to be trying to help her. But she couldn't afford to lower her guard, she reminded herself. He'd been living wild in the forest, putting his own interests before anything else. She must take care never to come between him and his freedom when they came to a town or village, for she might well pay too high a price if she was careless.

ThReE

'Do you know the road to royal Winchestre?' Janna asked, as they came once more to the forest clearing where she'd spent the night.

'No. Do you?'

Janna shook her head. 'But once we reach a village we'll look for someone who knows the way.'

'First we have to get through to the other side of the forest. Which way should we go?' Edwin asked, coming back to a more basic question.

Janna shook her head once more. 'I was hoping you knew how to find the path,' she said. 'I don't even know which direction I've come from.'

Edwin laughed. 'You came from over there,' he said, and pointed.

'Then we must keep walking this way.' Janna pointed in the opposite direction.

As they skirted the shallow dew pond, a smile twitched Janna's mouth. Reaching out, she gave Edwin a hard push.

'Hey!' he yelled as he slid down into the icy water.

'You saw me having a wash, so now it's my turn!' Janna retorted, and began to laugh as she noticed Edwin's horrified expression. 'Go on,' she encouraged. 'If you clean up the scratches on your cheek, I'll find some herbs to help them heal.'

'But I don't want to be clean!' Edwin protested. 'I put the mud on my face and clothes so I can blend into the shadows when the forester comes along.'

'Oh.' That made sense to Janna. 'But we're walking out of the forest now, so you won't need to hide for too much longer,' she pointed out. 'If you're really dirty, people will notice you, and they'll talk about us. You'd better clean yourself up, Edwin.' She flashed a wicked grin. 'I'll wash your back, if you like?'

'You'll turn around, and not look again until I say so,' he contradicted firmly.

Smiling, Janna complied.

'So what will you do when we get to Winchestre?' Edwin asked. Soft splashings told Janna that he was profitably occupied.

'I'll ask around, see if anyone can help me find my father.' Ready to fulfil her promise to Edwin, Janna began to wander about, keeping a lookout for pink flowering betony, mallow, strong-smelling yarrow, or the creamy flowers of wood sanicle.

'You need to find someone who can read,' Edwin pointed out.

The thought of a stranger reading her father's letter made Janna uneasy. Her mother had gone to such lengths to protect the secret of her birth. She risked setting her father against her for all time if private, maybe even dangerous, information about his liaison with Janna's mother became known to others.

'I just thought of something else,' Edwin continued. 'Does your father support the king or his cousin Matilda in their battle over the crown?'

'I know not,' Janna admitted. She spied the bright yellow flowers of ragwort and stopped to pluck some sprigs, wrinkling her nose at the strong smell from the bruised leaves. But it made for a good cleanser and healer, as did the hairy Herb Robert growing nearby.

'If he is of fighting age, your father may not be in Winchestre at all,' Edwin warned. 'Not only does King Stephen wage war against his cousin and her half-brother, Robert of Gloucester, but he's also having to fight his barons, to keep them under control. They're using this time of unrest to grab more land, they're becoming too powerful. Maybe your father is one of them, Ja . . . John?'

Janna straightened slowly, feeling discouraged as the difficulties of her search became apparent to her. 'I have to start looking somewhere. Winchestre seems as good a place as any.' She stayed silent for a few moments, lost in thought. Coming back to the present with a start, she asked, 'How do you know all this if you've been hiding here in Gravelinges?'

'I follow the travellers, I listen to them talking.'

'Just like you followed me?'

Edwin suddenly stopped splashing. 'Yes,' he admitted after a pause. 'I was desperate, you see. I planned to surprise you, to fell you with a blow and rob you of whatever you carried. Then I suspected you might actually be a girl. I was curious, and so I stayed hidden to see who you were and what you did.'

'And last night?'

'I kept watch over you.' The splashing started up again.

Janna gave a snort of disbelief. She raised her voice so as to be heard over the noise of the youth's ablutions. 'You were hoping I'd fall out of that tree and break my neck, so you could rob me without blame!'

'No!' he protested. 'I wondered why you were in the forest by yourself. That's all.'

Janna wondered how far she could trust him. 'Hurry up,' she said gruffly. 'I certainly don't want to spend another night out here.' With you. The words remained unsaid, but she didn't care if Edwin understood her true meaning.

Yet in spite of everything, her lips curved into a smile as he said cheerfully, 'You've only had one night in the forest. I've had days, weeks, *months* out here! I was even beginning to talk to the trees and the birds and the animals. Imagine!'

Janna could. After all, she used to talk to the hens and goats she and her mother kept on their small plot of land. Even the bees in their hives used to get a daily update on what was happening in their lives. She could quite under-stand how a lonely youth might find comfort in pouring out his troubles to something that would neither judge him nor give him a harsh reply. In fact, she fancied Edwin might have had little in the way of warmth and companionship even before he came into the forest.

'You've heard all about me, but you haven't told me much about yourself,' Janna commented, as he emerged from the pool. His skin was clean now, and the marks from her nails showed clearly. Janna pulled a regretful face over the damage she'd done.

'Phwoar!' Edwin's nose wrinkled in disgust as he smelled

the ragwort. But he stood quietly until Janna had finished spreading the astringent juice over the scratches on his cheek. He was shivering in his wet clothes.

'Why don't you take off your tunic and squeeze out the water?' she suggested.

He nodded, and did as he was bid. Janna drew breath in a shocked gasp. His back was marked and criss-crossed with scars from old beatings. Some were still not quite healed and looked red and painful. 'Come here,' she said. She made Edwin bend over so she could examine the wounds more closely. With a gentle touch, she used the remains of the ragwort to cleanse the worst of them. 'I'm not surprised you ran away,' she said, as he pulled on his tunic once more.

'Like I said, he was a vicious old devil.' Edwin began to step around the clearing, examining it carefully for signs of the path they should follow.

'So where does this vicious old devil live? Where have you come from?' Janna prompted, curious to know more.

'He has a manor near Tantone in Somer Shire. I walked for many miles, for it was in my mind to seek work in Winchestre, or even in London. Then I became lost in this forest. I decided to hide here until my time was up for by then I'd realised that my lord had sent his servants in pursuit of me.'

'Why did he do that? Why did he bother?' Janna didn't mean to disparage Edwin, but she was genuinely curious to know the answer. Certain it was that a lord would pursue a missing serf, but the chase would not last long, especially if the serf was as poor and as lowly as Edwin appeared to be.

'He is miserly as well as vicious. He guards what is his and holds on to it far beyond reason. Everyone on his manor has cause to hate and fear him, for everyone has been called to account for some act of carelessness, some slight or misdeed, some imagined oversight. We have all been punished, even when we were not guilty. Walter of Crice will not listen to any explanation or any excuse but takes the whip to all, even to his own wife and children, so it is said. In truth, I think he goes out of his way to find reason for punishment, for he seems happy only when he's causing misery for someone else.'

Janna was silenced by the bleak picture he painted. Yet her imagination couldn't leave it alone; she was sure he hadn't told her the full story. 'Were you accused of something? Is that what made you run away?' she persisted.

Edwin looked up abruptly, abandoning his search for the path. A wash of colour swept over his face. 'My lord's favourite steed went missing, and I was held to blame for it.' His voice was harsh, bitter with hatred as he made the confession.

Was that guilt or indignation that stained his countenance? 'And did you steal his horse?' Although Janna kept her voice carefully neutral, both of them knew that Edwin was guilty of one theft at least.

'Of course I did not!' he flashed. 'Do you see it here? I would have kept it if I'd stolen it! And I would have ridden to the far end of the kingdom to escape that devil.' He cast his eyes downward, his face set in sullen lines as he began to search once more for any faint signs of a way out of the forest.

Janna berated herself for asking such a stupid question. Yet the thought still troubled her: what if the horse had gone lame? Edwin might well have had to abandon it somewhere. 'If you didn't take it, then who did?' she asked, anxious to understand.

Edwin shrugged. 'I don't know. It was a fine beast, any man might covet it. All I know is that my lord will not rest until he reclaims it – which means he will not rest until he finds me. There it is!'

Bewildered by his unexpected admission, Janna cast about for signs of the horse, then realised that Edwin was pointing at a faint mark in the grass. Ready to forgive him, and forgive herself for her lack of trust, Janna flashed him a grateful grin. 'Well done!' she said, and gave him a whack across the back, instantly regretting the action as she recalled the deep cuts she'd just treated.

'Ow!' he protested loudly.

'Isn't that the sort of thing men do to each other?'

'Who goes there in the king's royal forest?' A loud shout startled Janna into silence. They stared at each other, momentarily numb with fear. Then, putting a warning finger to his mouth to caution silence, Edwin grabbed Janna's hand and began to run, pulling her with him along the trail he'd found. Janna sprinted beside him, hoping she could trust Edwin to find the way. Even in her fear of being overtaken by the forester, she revelled in the freedom of movement the breeches gave her as her legs pumped up and down, pounding down-hill through the trees.

'Stop! In the name of the king, I bid you stand and give me your names and your reason for trespass in the king's royal forest.' The voice was uneven, somewhat breathless. The forester was chasing them. Edwin tugged harder on

Janna's hand, and she kept on running. Both of them knew that there'd be no mercy shown if they were to stop and meekly surrender.

They ran on, stumbling into hollows and tripping over rough flints hidden among the tangled, weedy undergrowth. They let go, needing their hands to protect themselves from the brambles that snagged their clothes, whipped their faces and tore at their skin. A long strand of sticky goosegrass wrapped around Janna's ankle; she yanked her foot free and, panicking now, put on a burst of speed to catch up with Edwin. The sounds of pursuit were louder but she was tiring. A pain cut into her side, sharp as the sword she carried. *Aelfshot*. The Saxons believed this sudden stab was caused by darts shot by elves, but Janna knew she felt it only when she'd run too far and for too long without rest. 'You go on,' she panted hoarsely as Edwin turned to check her progress. 'I'll find a tree to climb.'

'No!' He stopped and grabbed hold of her. 'My safety lies with you, just as yours lies with me. We're in this together. Quick!' Instead of heading deeper into the trees he hauled her towards an opening in the forest. Janna had no choice but to follow him, and saw the sense of his action when he dived headfirst into a patch of tall weeds. At once he was hidden from sight, and Janna wasted no time going in after him, although she felt exposed and vulnerable away from the shelter of the trees. Bracken and tall herbs formed part of their shield, but so too did stinging nettles and prickling thistles, and Janna had to fold her lips hard together to stop herself crying out. She lay still, listening to the pounding of her heart and the heavy rasp of her own panting breaths.

She pressed her lips tighter to stifle the sound, while the thudding footsteps of their pursuer came closer.

'Come back!' he shouted as he passed close beside them. 'I know you can hear me. Come back here at once!'

They stayed silent, even when a blackbird alighted nearby to forage for a juicy worm. It took one startled glance at them and squawked loudly before taking off to find a less menacing hunting ground. All sound from the forester ceased. Janna couldn't see him, but she could sense him waiting, and watching. She prayed that they, too, were invisible, and that Edwin would keep still until all danger had passed. For herself, she was too frightened even to blink. Any movement, the slightest sound, might give the forester the clue he needed to find them.

Time passed. Janna felt as if she'd been lying hidden for an eternity. She desperately wanted to poke her head up, to see where the forester was and what he was doing, but she lay silent beside Edwin instead and waited for the danger to pass. Her heartbeats had begun to quieten, her breathing had returned to normal by the time the forester eventually set off. They could hear the diminishing sounds of his voice calling out in the hope that he would be heeded and obeyed.

More time passed. The pressure of Edwin's hand on her arm confirmed the need for stillness and silence, lest the forester be waiting down the track to trap them when they showed themselves. She became aware of Edwin trembling beside her. She thought at first that he was fearful, until the shudders grew stronger and she realised he was shivering with cold in his wet clothes. 'We should go on now, before you freeze to death,' she breathed softly into his ear.

He nodded and cautiously raised his head above the cover of the weeds. Once he'd made sure the forester was really gone, he stood up and began to run on the spot, rubbing his arms to get the blood flowing through his body. Janna nodded in approval but, seeing the warning finger come to his mouth once more, she didn't say anything. Instead, she extracted her sword from the weedy growth, then jabbed a thumb towards where they'd left the path. On receiving his nod she set off, trying to place her feet quietly upon grass so that no crackling leaves or twigs might betray them, ready at an instant to melt into concealing undergrowth. Suddenly, she became aware that she couldn't hear Edwin. Had he run off and left her? Alarmed, she spun around, and was reassured to see him pacing silently behind her. He grinned at her. She flashed a smile in reply, feeling a little guilty that she'd doubted him.

The trail was wider now, and more distinct. It was becoming well-trodden, just like the beginning of the trail on the other side of Gravelinges. It, too, must be used by farmers in autumn, some of whom, for a fee, were allowed to bring their pigs into the forest to eat the beechmast. With a sudden lift of her spirits, Janna assumed they must be coming close to Wicheford, and safety.

'Stay where you are!' A triumphant cry punctured her confidence and set her pulse leaping with fright. Her first thought was to hide, but even as she searched desperately for cover, the forester sprang out onto the path to confront them. She stepped backwards, cannoning into Edwin. He shouldered her aside and, with one almighty shove, sent the forester staggering to the ground.

'Run!' he shouted.

At least we've had a chance to rest, Janna thought, as she sprinted beside him. She felt proud that she could keep pace with Edwin even though she was a girl, but she knew she would also tire more quickly. Still she ran valiantly, following the trail down through the trees, through gloomy shadows under leafy canopies where every bush and thicket seemed to conceal a threat to their safety, and through open weedy clearings where she felt even more vulnerable to the hunt.

'Stop!' The cry sounded behind them. The forester was in pursuit once more. Janna forced her aching limbs to pump harder, sucked breath deep into her burning lungs. To be caught by the forester was bad enough. To be caught after striking him to the ground and running away would invite a punishment too dreadful to contemplate. Flight was the only answer, their only hope of salvation. Fear added a burst of speed to Janna's feet.

They ran on. Janna felt now as though she'd passed into a new dimension, a place where her body no longer seemed part of her consciousness. Her chest rose and fell with her breaths; her feet flashed briefly in front of her, left, right, left, right as they sped onwards, but she felt nothing past the desperate need to escape. She sensed Edwin check slightly and matched her stride to his, looking past him to see for herself what had given him pause. Only a narrow fringe of forest separated them now from water meadows and a river lying ahead. Behind them, the forester kept shouting, but in front of them danger also lay, in the form of a mounted man. By the stillness of his stance, and the direction of his gaze, Janna understood that he'd already spied them and that trying to hide from him was futile. Nor could they turn back. And so they kept on running, while he spurred his horse to meet them. They came together at the edge of the forest.

'What frightens you? What do you run from?' In spite of his handsome mount and the elegance of his tunic, the man spoke in the Saxon language. The realisation gave Janna the courage to answer truthfully.

'We're running from the king's forester.' She kept the sword hidden behind her back, knowing that the man would suspect the worst if he saw it. His expression hardened. Janna wondered if she'd misjudged him. The king's forest laws were popular with no-one save those of his favourites who'd been granted hunting rights in the royal forests. The Saxons especially had reason to hate and resent the edict set in place by William the Bastard, who had conquered their country and killed their king. Forced off their own lands, forced to work for their hated enemies, thegns and villeins alike were also prevented by forest law from cutting wood to build their homes, or trapping wild creatures to fill their empty bellies. Was this man on their side, or was he only speaking their language?

'Take shelter in there. Hurry!' The man pointed at a long, timbered shed nearby. It was so close to the forest edge Janna hadn't noticed it before.

'Thank you,' she breathed, even as Edwin pushed her towards it.

The door had hardly closed behind them when they heard a cheerful shout. 'Master Roger! What brings you through the forest in such a hurry?' This time, the man spoke the language of the Normans, but Janna had been taught to speak it by her mother and she understood his words. Edwin, however, tensed.

'He's trapped us here like rats, and now he's going to hand us over to the forester,' he hissed into Janna's ear.

'No, he's not. Sssh. Let me listen.' Janna bent and put her ear close to a space in the wooden palings. She heard the jingle of the bridle as their rescuer dismounted to talk to the forester.

'Where are they, Serlo? Two youths? You must have seen them.' The forester also spoke in Norman French now. His voice was rough with fatigue; he struggled to catch his breath. The chase had taken its toll.

'I've seen no youths. Are you sure they came this way?'

A short silence confirmed that the man's shrewd question had hit home. Just as Janna eased a sigh of relief, the forester said petulantly, 'They were following the trail through the forest. They must have run past you.'

'Do you doubt my word?' Their rescuer sounded angry now.

'No, no. I'm just surprised you haven't seen them.'

'If they realised you were after them, they might still be hiding in the forest. Did you have them in your sights all the while?'

'I did not!' The forester's voice was sharp, accusing, as he continued, 'One of the ruffians struck me such a blow that I fell to the ground. By the time I got after them, they had disappeared from my view. I was sure they were coming this way and so I made haste to follow them even though I can scarce move from the pain of the attack.'

Janna stiffened, sure that the forester's lie would make their rescuer think twice about his chivalrous action. While Serlo might be prepared to save villeins fleeing from a harsh and unjust law, he wouldn't harbour anyone who'd resort to violence to escape from a king's man. She peered through the crack, in time to see the forester rubbing his head, an aggrieved expression on his face. Hardly daring to breathe, she waited through a long silence as their rescuer weighed the pros and cons of confessing his lie or continuing to shelter a pair of dangerous villains.

'What are they saying? Do you understand any of it?' Edwin whispered nervously.

'Yes. Sssh.' Janna clamped a hand over his mouth and leaned closer to the gap between the wooden stakes, straining to hear whatever might be said.

'. . . but if I see them, I'll be sure to keep hold of them and send word to you.' Janna felt slightly cheered as she understood what Serlo was saying. He had hold of them already, but hadn't spoken of them to the forester. That must mean he was prepared to let them go free, once the danger had passed. She released Edwin, and put her eye to the crack, trying to see what the forester would do next. Fear slammed into her with the force of a body blow as she found herself staring directly into his eyes. Had he seen her? Did he know someone was hiding inside the shed? She dare not blink lest she betray their presence.

'What are you . . .?' Edwin subsided into silence as Janna gave him a hard jab in the ribs. Her eyes stayed fixed on the forester, who continued to stare at her. Moments passed. Hours. Months. Years. And then the forester turned to Serlo and asked, 'What's in the shed over there?'

'Nothing now, Master Roger.' Their rescuer gave a shrug. 'It's a winter shelter for my sheep, to keep them out of snow and flood, but the time for that has passed now. See how well my flock is doing. We shall have a goodly stock of wool to sell at the fair this year, and a bountiful harvest too if the weather stays kind.' There was pride in Serlo's voice as with one hand he grasped the forester and drew him around, while with his other hand he indicated a flock of white-faced sheep, grazing peacefully under the watchful eye of their shepherd. The generous sweep of his hand encompassed all the fields beyond the river: dark, ploughed earth lying fallow, golden barley and ripening wheat. Janna felt a great warmth towards him as she understood how successfully he'd managed to deflect the forester's attention from the sheepfold and their suspected whereabouts. Serlo kept a grip on the forester's arm and, still talking, led him away, following the green wall of trees at the edge of the forest.

Once she judged they were safely out of earshot, Janna whispered an explanation of what had transpired to Edwin, including the forester's version of how he was attacked.

'I gave him a shove and he fell over,' Edwin protested. 'I didn't mean to hurt him, I just wanted to buy us some time.'

'I'm sure you didn't hurt him. There was no sign of any mark on him, but that didn't stop him trying to make a greater cause against us. Lucky for us, his ruse didn't work.'

'So what do we do now?' Edwin asked, restless and anxious to be gone.

'Nothing, for the moment. I don't know where Serlo's taken the forester. They may still be close enough to see us if we leave. And where would we go? We can't cross the river in daylight, and we can't really go back to the forest either, not if the forester is still about. I suggest we stay here until nightfall, and make our escape then.'

Edwin grunted uneasily. 'Serlo? Is that his name? He thinks I hit the forester. He thinks we're dangerous. He may want to hand us over to the sheriff instead, and claim a reward for his trouble.' He shook his head. 'I think we should leave now.'

'It's not safe. At least, not yet. Let's wait a while,' Janna insisted.

Edwin huffed a sigh. 'It's all very well for you to say "wait". You're not the one on the run. You didn't thump the forester. You're not suspected of stealing a horse either.'

'You can go if you want to, but I'm staying here.' Janna sat down. To underscore her words, she shifted around so that her back rested against the timbered frame of the shed. She stretched her legs out in front of her, and closed her eyes. Just for safety, she casually folded her hands over her purse. If Edwin decided to make a move, it would not be with any of her belongings – at least, not without a fight.

'You still don't trust me, do you?' His voice was amused. Janna felt embarrassed that he'd read her mind so easily. Or was it shame for doubting him? Uncertain now, she recalled how he'd taken her hand, matching his speed to hers as he pulled her along. He hadn't run away to save himself. Instead, he'd helped her hide from the forester.

'No, I don't trust you,' she said truthfully, pushing aside her uneasy conscience.

'I've already apologised for stealing your purse. It's safer for both of us if we stay together, but we have to trust and even like each other if we want people to believe that we're brothers.'

'Stay together? I thought you were leaving right now?' Janna opened her eyes to study him.

'No. Not yet. You're right. It's not safe. We'll go as soon as it gets dark.' He stretched out beside her.

'Go where? We still don't know the way to Winchestre.'

'Sssh. I hear voices. I think they're coming back.'

The voices grew louder. Janna tensed, waiting for betrayal, but the voices passed, becoming softer until there was silence once more. Just as they started to relax, the door of the shed flung open with a sudden crash. A tall figure blocked the light, and blocked all chance of their escape. It was the horseman, Serlo. They scrambled to their feet to face him.

Serlo was in his mid-years, his freckled face burnished red by the sun and topped with a shock of red hair. From his commanding air and confident speech, Janna guessed he must be the lord of this manor. A quick inspection confirmed her guess: his tunic was made of good linen and decorated with a border of embroidery. His boots, although mud-spattered, were made of fine leather. 'Now,' he said threateningly, 'you'd better tell me what really happened in the forest.' He planted his hands on his hips and puffed out his chest. 'Tell me the truth, for you can be sure I'll beat it out of you if I suspect either one of you is lying.'

Janna was thankful then that she'd understood his conversation with the forester, and that she'd repeated it to Edwin. They might otherwise have tried to bluff their way out of trouble, and would have earned themselves a beating for it. But how much of the truth should they tell? She stole a quick glance at Edwin, then looked away. One of them had to say something. It had better be her, for Edwin had far too much to lose. She would speak for both of them – and in as low a voice as possible!

'We thank you kindly, sire, for hiding us from the forester,' Janna began, thinking it wise to flatter their rescuer as well as show themselves humble and well-mannered, so that he might think twice before believing all that the forester had said of them. As an added precaution, she addressed him in the Saxon tongue, not wanting him to know that she'd heard, and understood, his conversation with the forester.

Serlo grunted acknowledgement, all the while looking them over as if to assess their worth. He frowned as he took in Edwin's damp and tattered appearance, his half-starved, wild air. His attention moved then to Janna. She quickly looked away, not wanting to show her full face to him lest she betray her real identity. Instead, she studied the earthen floor intently as she launched into explanation. 'We are two brothers from beyond the Welsh marches, sire, come to seek employment wherever we may find it.'

'Has your lord given you permission to leave his manor?' Their rescuer eyed them suspiciously.

'We . . . we are not tied to anyone, sire.' Janna's thoughts raced as she tried to come up with something to satisfy the man's curiosity. 'Our father was Welsh, a craftsman, but he died when we were just babes. Our mother found a living . . .' Janna flushed as the man's eyes narrowed in calcu-lation, '. . . working in an alehouse.' If the man believed her mother was a whore, he might well think her daughter one too! Except she wasn't a daughter, she reminded herself.

'My name is John,' she said hastily, 'and my brother is called Edwin.'

'You do not speak like a Welshman, John.'

Janna felt a flash of triumph that he'd not seen through her disguise. 'Our mother was of Saxon stock, sire, and sick with wanting her home and her kin around her.' She was rewarded by the brief flash of sympathy in his eyes. But he was not yet done with them.

'One of you struck the forester. Which of you was it?'

Janna glanced at Edwin. As she opened her mouth to defend him, he said, 'It was me, my lord. I gave the forester a hard push, to give us time to get away from him. He fell to his knees, but I didn't hurt him. I didn't strike him either.'

'I should put you in to the sheriff for such an act.' Yet a faint smile curled the man's lips upwards.

Emboldened, Janna asked, 'Will you allow us to leave now, sire? If the forester is gone and it is safe?'

'No.' The smile grew broader as the man shook his head.

'No?' Janna's voice skidded dangerously high. Her heart beat fast with fright. Did he mean, after all, to give them over to the sheriff?

'There is much to be done on the manor, and I am short of labour, especially as half the villeins are struck down with some poxy disease. You may stay a while, and repay your debt to me by doing their work for them.' He was no longer smiling. Janna knew that even though his words were couched as an offer, he expected to be obeyed. She glanced at Edwin, uncertain what to say or do. To her surprise, he nodded acceptance.

'Good,' the man said briskly. 'My name is Serlo, and I am

the reeve of this manor.' Janna felt a moment's surprise that she'd so misjudged his position here. But Serlo was still speaking. 'You will follow my commands and work in return for your bread and lodging until I no longer have need of you. Do not cross me for I will raise the hue and cry should you try to leave.'

Janna's heart sank. She fingered the shape of the small statue in her purse, the mother hunched so protectively over her child. It gave her the courage to ask the question. 'How long will you keep us here, Master Serlo?'

'What does it matter? You said you were in search of work. I am offering it.'

Janna wondered how to convey to him the urgency of her quest to find her father, without giving too much away. As she struggled to find the words, Edwin forestalled her.

'We are grateful for your kindness, Master Serlo. Be sure that we will pay our debt to you in full.'

'Come with me.' Mounting his horse, Serlo beckoned them to follow behind. Janna cast a glance at the sword she'd salvaged from the pond, now lying half hidden behind a rough wooden feed trough. Edwin caught her glance and shook his head. He started off after Serlo and, after a moment's thought, Janna stowed the sword out of sight, along with Edwin's jug and pot, then scurried after the pair. Serlo had said that the shed stood empty through the summer. The sword should be safe enough for the moment, but she would come back for it once they were given permission to leave.

It was a long walk over the marshy ground of the water meadows. Mud and dung stuck to Janna's boots and she again wished she had a pair of wooden pattens to protect them from all the muck. Serlo led them across the river and up to the manor house. He bade them wait while he entered the yard and dismounted to fetch some implements. To Janna he handed a heavy wooden mallet; to Edwin a pair of long-handled sticks, with a Y-fork on one and a small sickle blade on the other. Once more he mounted, and walked them on and up into the fields beyond. Some of the ploughed fallow land was studded with fat horned sheep and their long-tailed lambs. They nibbled at new shoots of weeds and grass, and dropped the dung that would be spread to make the soil more fertile for the next cycle of planting. The earth was dark, marked with patches of white chalk and studded with flints that glinted in the watery sunlight. Scarlet poppies turned their faces to the sky, bright splashes of colour among the green wheat growing nearby. Looking more closely, Janna could also see an abundance of prickly purple thistles, red deadnettles, charlock, dock and hairy pink corncockle. The flowers made a pretty picture, but Janna knew they would spread and choke the wheat if left unchecked.

Weeding fields and spreading dung was back-breaking work. It was normally done by the villeins of the manor in return for a small plot of land and shelter for their families, yet these fields seemed almost deserted. She wondered how Serlo could be so careless of his lord's property, and why his lord let him get away with it. Then she remembered the poxy disease, and understood why the reeve was forcing their service to his cause. She became aware that he was talking to them, throwing words carelessly over his shoulder as he rode along. She hurried to catch up with him and Edwin. To her dismay, the reeve's words confirmed her fears.

'I'm behind with everything here because of this cursed pox. The sheep are still to be washed and shorn and the hay to be cut, just as soon as we get some sunshine. There are new ditches to dig, and hedges to repair around the growing corn. But you can begin by weeding the corn, and breaking up clods and picking large flints from the fallow fields, anything that might get in the way of the plough. You can also spread the sheep's mundungus to make next season's crops grow better. While you are here, you will sleep with the servants in the hall and break your fast with them. Mistress Tova, the cook, will give you food and ale to take out into the fields for your dinner and supper. I don't want to see you back at the manor until it's dark. I am out around the manor farm every day in my lord's absence, so make sure I'll be keeping an eye on you and how hard you are working.'

Janna groaned inwardly. With the sun rising early, and the summer light fading late from the sky, it made for a long day's labour. She cheered herself with the thought that at least they'd be meeting new people, any of whom might know the way to Winchestre. Their service here could not last for ever; sooner or later they would be given permission to leave.

Edwin gave her a hard nudge. 'What?' she asked, startled out of her reverie. He began to walk with exaggerated strides, swinging his arms manfully by his side. Puzzled, Janna stared at him, then became aware that Serlo was watching them both and frowning with suspicion. Suddenly catching on, she squared her shoulders and lengthened her stride. 'He's only young,' Edwin called, as he drew nearer to Serlo, 'but he's strong.' He jerked a thumb towards Janna. 'He's a good worker, you'll see.'

Another grunt met this observation, but Serlo turned then and set his horse for home. Edwin flashed a grin at Janna and she pulled a rueful face at him. It was so easy to forget her new disguise. So easy, and so dangerous.

FOUR

AFTER A FEW days out in the fields, Janna ached all over. Her fingers were torn and bruised from picking up sharp flints and hacking into thistles, while her back felt bent out of shape from bending over to beat out hard clods of earth with the heavy mallet. In her nose was the stink of sheep dung. Although she'd washed her hands and feet in the river before coming in for the night, she could still smell it.

She stretched out on her straw pallet, trying to find ease for her tired body and her unquiet mind. To stop herself from the misery of recalling her past life with her mother in their small cot at the edge of Gravelinges forest, which always brought with it the slow burn of anger at the injustice of what had happened to her, Janna thought instead about Urk and what had happened that day while she was out culling weeds.

Urk was by far the oldest of the group of children who had been sent into the fields to scare away the crows, rooks and other scavengers that swooped down to eat the ripening corn. The youngest, aged three or four, banged drums and shouted. The older children carried slingshots, and it was a matter of competition and pride between them who could fell the most birds. Behind the children came Urk's mother, cutting weeds and keeping an eye on the youngsters to remind them of their purpose should their natural high spirits lead them astray.

Urk was tall and heavyset, and slow by nature. He reminded Janna of a scruffy hen she'd owned, which she'd called 'Laet' because it was always last to get to the feed. The hen would not have survived if Janna had not fed it separately. Janna suspected that Urk's mother might also give her oldest son special treatment. Yet he was a merry lad, with a sweet smile and a willing nature. He was also the most accurate of them all when it came to using the slingshot. This day he'd had the misfortune to bring down a dove in front of Serlo, and had his ears severely boxed as a result. Janna cringed as she remembered how Mistress Wulfrun had pleaded on her son's behalf.

'He doesn't understand what he's done wrong, Master Serlo. Please don't punish him so.'

'It was eating the wheat, Master Serlo,' Urk chimed in. 'You told us to kill all the birds who ate the grain.'

Serlo glowered at the unfortunate boy, then gave him another clip across the ear. 'Doves are for my lord's sport, not yours,' he shouted, as if the boy was deaf rather than slow. 'Don't you dare kill another – don't ever touch the doves again, or I'll take your slingshot from you and you'll never get it back!'

Urk's lip quivered; he looked on the verge of tears. 'And no more playing with fire either!' Serlo turned on his heel and marched off.

Mistress Wulfrun placed her arm around her son and gave

him a hug. 'Don't take it to heart,' she comforted him. 'Master Serlo doesn't mean it.'

Feeling sorry for the boy, Janna bent once more to her task. Suddenly, she found Mistress Wulfrun beside her, with Urk a pace behind. 'Master Serlo is usually more patient with him,' the woman confided, as she stooped to cut weeds. She glanced at Urk. 'And you don't play with fire, do you, son?'

'No.' Urk stood still, watching them. Janna wondered if he was too afraid now to use his slingshot.

'He woke up one night when he was small,' Mistress Wulfrun explained further. 'We were all asleep but he wanted to go outside. I think he was just curious to have a look around the manor in the moonlight. He had the good sense to take a rush light so he could see his way, but when he walked into the byre a cow mooed and frightened him. He dropped the light into a pile of hay, and the byre caught on fire. He didn't do it on purpose – and there was no harm to the animals,' she added quickly, forestalling Janna's question. 'But my son got such a fright he started screaming. Everyone came running. The animals were led to safety, but the byre burned to the ground.' She looked at Urk, concern scoring deep lines across her pleasant, homely face. 'Of course, he shouldn't have gone near the manor, and my lord was very good about it, very understanding. But Serlo was angry, I think because he feels responsible for everything that takes place here. He is usually fair in his dealings with us, but it seems he has neither forgotten the fire nor forgiven my boy.' She looked at Janna. 'I can't be with him all the time. Will you also keep watch over him out in the fields, John, when I'm not here?' she pleaded.

'Of course I will, mistress.' Janna didn't know what else to say to comfort the woman or her son, but she wished now that she'd thought of something, anything, to ease the situation, to make Urk feel better about himself, and his mother less worried about him. She yawned, and shifted about on the straw pallet, trying to compose herself for sleep, but her bed was prickly and her whole body ached. Contributing to her unease was the company she kept. All Janna's life there had been only her mother and, later, the cat Alfred in their cottage. Now she was expected to sleep in the hall with all the servants of the manor, most of them men and boys. Edwin had set their pallets into a corner, away from the crowd around the fireplace. He'd put Janna next to the wall, keeping himself between her and the others. She was grateful for his protection, but even so she lay awake, unaccustomed to the night noises, the sighs and murmurs, the cries of nightmares, and the odours of farts and sweaty clothes and dirty feet.

When at last she fell asleep, her dreams were full of endless fields spread before her. She stooped over them, with the smell of animal excrement in her nose and the knowledge that her tasks would never be done. And so it seemed still when she woke to yet another grey dawn and the realisation that a new day lay before her, and one after that, and then another and another. She groaned softly. Hot tears stung her eyes.

'What's wrong?' Edwin stirred beside her.

'Nothing.' Janna was conscious of the servants nearby, any one of whom might be wide enough awake to carry the tale to Serlo if she confessed to Edwin how sad and desperate she felt. She wiped her eyes on the back of her sleeve, and tried not to sniffle.

Edwin seemed to understand. 'My body is one big ache, and my arms feel like they're on fire,' he muttered, as he stood up and squared his shoulders to face the day.

'At least our bellies will soon be full!' Janna felt a little more cheerful as she stored her straw pallet in an alcove off the hall. She looked about, but there was no sign of the bread and ale with which they normally broke their fast. The table stood bare, and Janna's stomach rumbled with hunger. Beckoning Edwin to follow her, she hurried down the stairs and on towards a stone building nearby. There might be other pickings waiting for them in the kitchen, a scrap of bacon perhaps, or even a pasty. Saliva flooded Janna's mouth at the thought, and her steps quickened.

She loved going into the kitchen. It was a source of wonder to her that anywhere could hold such an abundance of food. She took a deep sniff, anticipating the delicious smells of meat roasting on a spit over the fire, newly baked bread, the rich aromas of a bubbling pottage, the spicy fragrance of herbs. Instead, she smelt a sharp and acrid stink. A young maid stood at the large table in the centre of the room, chopping onions and weeping over her task.

Janna sniffed again and realised that it wasn't onions she could smell, but smoke and burnt offerings. Bewildered, she looked around for the cook, but there was no sign of Mistress Tova, only Serlo and the kitchen servants. Hands on hips and face red with anger, Serlo was berating one of the skivvies. Feeling sorry for the boy, yet reluctant to attract the reeve's attention, Janna stopped abruptly. Edwin crashed into her. 'What are you . . .?' His words died on his lips as he took in the situation. But it was too late. Serlo had seen them. Tilting her chin in assumed bravado, Janna waited for him to address them.

'The cook has gone and got the pox now. She's all over spots,' he said, by way of explanation. 'And no-one seems to know anything about baking bread.' He flung out a hand towards some flat, blackened rounds which must once have been small loaves.

'I can bake griddle cakes, Master Serlo,' Janna said quickly, keen to lend a helping hand and, if possible, get the young boy out of trouble. She noticed the flare of surprise in his eyes as he turned to face her and realised, with a sinking heart, that she'd have done much better to hold her tongue. 'My . . . our mother taught me how,' she added, sneaking an anxious glance at Edwin as she did so.

'Hmph,' Serlo grunted. He cast a glance around the kitchen, at the silent kitchen hands and lowly skivvies huddled near the door, waiting only a chance to disappear from view. His glance settled on a young woman, and he reddened slightly. 'Hasn't your mother taught you how to cook, Gytha?' he demanded, in a softer tone than he'd used with the boy.

'No, Master Serlo, she has not.' The girl tossed her long dark ringlets. Janna waited for an explanation or an excuse for her lack of skill, but none came.

Curious, and rather impressed by Gytha's impertinence, for Janna judged the girl a little younger than herself, she leaned slightly to one side for a better view. Gytha was beautiful, she decided, with a pang of envy and of pain as she mourned her own lost locks, and her rough disguise. Evidently Gytha was the cook's daughter, yet she wasn't often in the kitchen for Janna hadn't seen her there before. Now, she faced Serlo with pride, secure in her own beauty and a position that seemed equal to Serlo's own.

He's smitten with her. Janna's lips curved upwards into a smile as she understood his sudden fluster. But he was well in command of his emotions when he turned his hard gaze back on Janna. 'Make some griddle cakes then, John, quick as you can. There's much work to be done.' With a last suspicious glance at Janna, he hurried out.

'I'll help you.' The beauty moved towards Janna with a friendly smile. 'I wouldn't admit it to him,' she jerked her head in the direction of the disappearing reeve, 'but my father taught my mother the arts of the kitchen while he was alive, so she was able to keep his position here after he died. In turn, she has taught me all she knows. I can cook, and cook well, but I will not be a skivvy to the likes of Serlo. I have set my sights much higher than the reeve.' A dreamy smile tugged at the corners of her mouth.

'You will cook for the lord of the manor when he returns?'

'No, indeed. I shall do more, much more for my lord than cook for him.'

Could Gytha really mean what she was saying? Even as she scolded herself for her nosiness, Janna's insatiable curiosity prompted her to probe further. 'You are my lord's mistress?'

'Certainly not!'

'I beg your pardon,' Janna apologised hastily. 'What I meant to ask is: are you betrothed to him?'

'Not yet.' A calculating expression briefly marred the young girl's beauty. 'But it's only a matter of time before he recognises that our destiny lies together.' Head tilted to one side, she studied Janna. 'You're new here, aren't you, John?'

'Yes.' Janna answered without thinking. 'Yes,' she said again on a deeper note, hoping the girl hadn't seen through her disguise.

'My name's Gytha,' she said, and took Janna's hand. 'Come on, I'll show you where everything is kept. It'll be a blessing if you can do the cooking while my mother is ill. Not for anything would I have Serlo tramping around after me, breathing down my neck and telling me what to do.'

Yet you have no hesitation in shifting the burden onto my shoulders, Janna thought. With a wry smile, she acknowledged that she would far rather slave in the kitchen all day than break her back out in the fields.

She rinsed her hands, and began to rub fat into the flour, noticing how fine and white it was compared to the gritty brown flour which was all she and her mother had been able to afford. She poured some goat's milk into the mixture, hiding a smile as Edwin sidled over. He edged closer to Gytha, looking hopeful. Gytha fluttered her eyelashes and gave him a demure smile.

'This is my older brother, Edwin,' Janna said, amused. Gytha might have designs on the lord of the manor, but it seemed she couldn't help flirting with any marriageable prospect around. 'What ails your mother and the villeins, mistress?' she asked. It was possible she might know of a preparation that could help them.

'They burn with fever and they're covered in itchy spots. They are too sick to leave their beds.' Gytha looked genuinely concerned now, and Janna could understand why. She'd seen the ravages of this disease before, how it could scar skin and destroy hearing and sight, and even kill if taken badly enough. No wonder Gytha looked frightened. She obviously had ambition for her future, an ambition dependent on her youthful beauty.

'You should stay away from your mother. I hope it's not too late,' Janna advised. 'Once one gets the disease, most everyone else around and about will get it too.' She hung a flat tray over the kitchen fire and waited for it to heat.

'Put some eggs with that.' Gytha whisked into a larder and came out with several eggs cupped in her hand. Trying not to look too impressed by such riches, Janna cracked them open and spilled the contents into the bowl. Once the eggs were beaten into the milk and flour, she ladled the mixture in small dollops onto the tray. Her stomach growled with hunger. She fought to restrain herself from peeling off the cakes and stuffing them straight into her mouth.

'My mother looks so ill. The spots plague her so she can't stop scratching.' Gytha seemed genuinely wretched now. 'I wish I could do something to help her.'

Janna thought of the potions she and her mother had made when a similar disease had struck down a number of villeins in a hamlet near their own. 'If you wish, I can brew a decoction for the fever and make up a lotion to soothe the itchy spots,' she promised, adding quickly, 'but you must help me first. These cakes are almost ready. Perhaps you could fetch the ale and take it up to the hall?'

'And what would a youth like you know about fevers and lotions?' Serlo's voice made Janna jump. She hadn't heard him return. She cast a nervous glance behind her. 'Our mother was a . . . a healer,' she stammered, thinking it safest to keep as close as possible to the truth. 'But she also worked in an alehouse,' she added hurriedly, as she recalled what she'd first told Serlo.

'She was a very skilful healer, Master Serlo,' Edwin cut in swiftly, anxious to take the reeve's attention off Janna. 'People came from all over to see her when they had a pain or a disease.' He couldn't possibly know that for a fact, Janna thought, but even if he was making it up, he was actually speaking the truth.

'Then let your brother do the cooking, and you can see about making my villeins well again,' Serlo told him. 'The sooner they can go about their tasks, the sooner you can both leave the manor farm.'

'I . . . I have not my brother's talent for healing,' Edwin stuttered. 'I can't cook neither.' He brightened as he thought how to embroider the tale. 'In fact, our mother always said that young John here was by far the more skilled when it came to indoor work such as this. I am more use out in the fields.' He raised an arm and flexed the muscle to make his point.

'Then you can work alone in the fields today. Your brother will stay here and brew his concoctions to make my people well again.' Serlo gave them a curt nod, and stepped back to watch their final preparations. Even though most of his attention was reserved for Gytha, Janna could understand how the proud beauty sought to avoid him. Such close proximity to Serlo was making her nervous, and that in turn made her clumsy. Janna stifled a cry as her wet, greasy fingers slid off a bowl and it crashed into pieces on the floor. Scarlet with shame, she kept her head bent as Serlo berated her for her carelessness. Her gratitude towards the reeve was waning; she was beginning to wonder if they might have been wiser to take their chances with the forester.

Once they'd all broken their fast, the men left to go about their work while Gytha returned to the kitchen to supervise the servants over preparations for their dinner at midday. Janna made her excuses, and escaped out to the kitchen garden to seek the herbs she needed to bring relief to the cook and the manor's villeins. She was pleased to recognise several plants her mother had grown in their own garden. She plucked some feverfew, intending to add it to a syrup with mint and valerian to help dull the pain and cool the fever. She continued to browse among the herbs, searching for marigold, septfoil, elecampane or mallow. Roots, flowers or leaves could be useful in a potion to expel the poison or a lotion to cool and soothe the itchy spots.

Harvesting the herbs, smelling their fragrance, reminded Janna of the last time she'd collected herbs for healing. She'd been in the manor's kitchen garden at Babestoche, and there was a child's life at stake. She sighed. The past was behind her, she reminded herself. Her own mother was dead, and so was Dame Alice's baby. He had been ailing from the start. She would wager that not even King Stephen's own physician could have kept him alive. Still, for the sake of Dame Alice, she wished she could have saved the child. If her mother had only acknowledged that Janna was growing to adulthood, and had trained her to administer to the sick instead of merely letting her prepare and make up the potions for them, it would have helped Janna so much in the dark days following Eadgyth's death. It would have helped Janna now. Miserably she acknowledged that because of Eadgyth's lack of trust, she had not the knowledge or experience to properly diagnose the true causes of illness, nor her mother's skill when it came to binding wounds, setting broken bones, or even administering a healing massage. But she had watched her mother on many an occasion, and for now that would have to do.

Clutching her handful of herbs, she hurried back into the kitchen. A quick glance told her that Serlo had left off interfering, and that Gytha was now supervising the plucking of fowls, the gutting of herrings and the dicing of vegetables that they – or someone – would be eating for dinner. Janna resolved that if any of it came her way, she'd keep half for Edwin. She'd seen his hunger as he ate the griddle cakes she'd prepared, how every last crumb had been wolfed down. In spite of his strength he was too thin, but regular food would soon restore him to full health and vigour. Perhaps, then, he might have a chance with the lovely Gytha?

Ignoring the activity going on around her, Janna carefully washed her hands and the herbs she had collected, just as her mother had always done. Then, with Eadgyth's instructions whispering through her mind, she set about preparing what was needed to help the sick. She had only Gytha and Serlo's description of the disease to go on, but even so she was almost certain that she had seen its like before. She knew how to make the preparations that would give ease, even if she wasn't sure she could cure the pox. Of course, prayers and holy relics might also help – for certes the priests would think so – but so far as Janna was concerned, she had little knowledge of such things and the patients must look to that sort of cure for themselves.

She hung a pot of water to boil over the fire, moving to one side a dish of savoury pottage to make room for it. 'This won't take long,' she told Gytha, when the young woman protested. She added leaves and roots to the steaming water. Leaving the decoction to simmer, she began a survey of the kitchen, bemused at the array of spices she had not encountered before, and the abundance of corn, fruits and vegetables stored in huge barrels and baskets in the larder. A hock of ham hung beside the fireplace, being cured in the smoke from the fire. She took a deep breath, inhaling the rich and potent mix. Bread and vegetable pottage had been their staple diet, but she and her mother had often known great hunger at this time of the year, after what little grain that remained had grown mouldy and the new wheat was still too green to harvest.

She prowled around the kitchen while she waited, testing and sniffing the spices. Some she remembered from her encounter with the spice merchant at the market at Wiltune. She wished now that she'd asked their purpose. At the time they had seemed so far out of her reach, she'd been reluctant to bother him with too many questions. Still, she could taste and sample to satisfy her curiosity now, and this Janna proceeded to do, enjoying the unexpected heat of some, the elusive fragrance and piquancy of others. She could see how they might add flavour to meat, vegetables and puddings. She itched to try them out.

'Pray, take me to see your mother, Mistress Gytha,' she said, once her medicaments were ready. 'I shall try to ease her discomfort.'

The cook and her daughter did not share the servants' sleeping quarters upstairs in the hall of the manor house, but had a separate cot of their own, set close behind the kitchen. Janna had come to know the cook in the mornings when she and Edwin broke their fast and waited to collect their dinner. She was a disapproving, thin-faced woman whose tongue had been sharpened on the misfortunes of others. But she was a sorry sight now, Janna thought, as Gytha pushed open the door and led the way into their cottage.

Mistress Tova lay on a straw pallet. She looked flushed and uncomfortable. Her hair lay in lank strands on her forehead, and her restless fingers scratched first at her face and then at her arm.

'Don't scratch!' Janna said quickly. 'The sores will become full of pus and take much longer to heal.'

The cook's gaze moved from her daughter to Janna, who came forward then so that she might see her patient more clearly. With a conscious effort, she made her voice deeper. 'I beg your pardon for speaking sharply, mistress.' She was about to curtsy but remembered in time to catch herself and bobbed awkwardly instead. 'I am here to help you. My mother was a healer, and she taught me something of her craft. I've made up an infusion for you to drink. It will dull the pain and cool your fever. There's also a lotion to bathe your skin. It will soothe those itches and help the spots to heal. You must not scratch them or you will be left with scars afterwards.' She held up a phial and a jar of lotion, so that the cook could see what she carried.

The woman nodded, even managing a faint smile. 'I would be glad of some comfort, John, for in truth I think my head is about to burst. And my skin feels as if it's been branded by the devil's own fire.'

Janna was somewhat relieved to hear the cook's words. Her mother's patients had described their symptoms in similar fashion. As she set about ministering to Mistress Tova, the woman gave her daughter a sharp glance. 'Get back to the kitchen, Gytha, and make sure you prepare a goodly feast, just in case my lord returns today. John can minister to my needs.'

Gytha ducked her head in obedience and vanished outside, leaving Janna alone with the cook. Janna kept her head bent, for Mistress Tova's sharp eyes and avid tongue seemed to miss nothing.

'You are very young,' she said now. 'You have not even a hint of a beard.'

Janna cleared her throat. 'I may be young, but I am strong, mistress,' she said, fending off any implied criticism.

'And skilled too, it seems.' The cook sniffed the draught that Janna handed to her. 'Pray tell me what is in this? I'd like to know how you have prepared it, for it is usually my task to minister to any who might fall ill here on my lord's demesne.'

As Janna detailed what she had used and her method of preparation, the cook nodded approvingly. Her eyes were alight with interest. After a first suspicious sip, she drank the mixture down. 'And how did you prepare this?' she asked, when Janna unstoppered the cooling salve she had made.

'Septfoil?' she queried, interrupting Janna's recitation.

'It's sometimes called tormentil.' Using a small piece of cloth to keep her fingers free of contact with the sores, Janna began to dab the lotion onto the cook's skin.

The cook was silent for a few moments. 'You have a wide knowledge,' she commented.

'My mother was very skilled at healing. She wanted me to learn her craft and so she taught me what she knew.' It was the truth.

'And your brother? Does he have the knowledge too?'

'He has no aptitude for healing. He . . . he likes working outdoors, tilling the earth and caring for the animals.' Janna hoped that was true of Edwin.

The cook grunted. 'Master Serlo will keep him up to the mark. He is a hard taskmaster, but a fair one, you'll find. Do as he tells you and he's kindly enough. Go against him, and you'll live to regret it. He tends the manor farm as if it was his own and he expects the same from all of us. Indeed this is his life, for he has no family to think about. My lord is fortunate he has Serlo to look after everything in his absence.'

'Master Serlo has indeed been kind to us,' Janna acknowledged. She continued to dab the cooling lotion onto the cook's face and arms.

The cook gave a quiet moan as the liquid touched several spots she'd scratched raw. 'Am I hurting you, mistress?' Janna asked.

'No, indeed.' Mistress Tova gave Janna a watery smile. 'I am grateful for your aid and comfort.'

'If you will remove your kirtle . . .' Janna remembered her new identity just in time. 'You could also use this lotion on your stomach and back. I will leave it here with you.'

'Thank you.' The cook nodded gratefully.

'And I will mix up some more medicaments, and visit you again tomorrow.' Janna moved towards the door.

'I am sure Master Serlo would be very grateful if you could also attend those villeins who are too sick to work, John. There is so much to be done, and too few hands now to do it. I know the reeve is anxious, for my lord is expected home soon. He will want to give a good accounting of his steward-ship during my lord's absence.'

'I will do what I can to make them all well,' Janna promised. Curiosity prompted her to probe further. 'You have a very beautiful daughter, mistress. I pray that she will not contract your disease.'

'As do I,' the cook said promptly. 'My daughter is of an age to wed, and I have great hopes of a good match for her. In fact, Master Serlo has already spoken to me. He would be a good catch for Gytha. I have urged her to consider his offer, but . . .' She hesitated. Pride overcame prudence. 'I believe my lord is also attracted to Gytha and I know she cares for him. If he was to suggest that they wed . . .' The cook smiled at the thought.

'Then I hope they'll find happiness together,' Janna murmured. 'God keep you, mistress. I'll call in tomorrow.' Smiling to herself over the high hopes of the cook and her daughter even while wondering if they were deluding them-selves, she opened the door and let herself out of the cottage.

FIVE

THE NEXT FEW weeks were busy for Janna. She physicked her patients and so found her way around the manor farm and the hamlet outside the manor gate where dwelt those villeins who gave service and goods to their lord in exchange for land to tend and somewhere to live. Urk and his mother she'd already met, but Janna now came to know everyone else in that small community, husbands and wives, sons and daughters. At first they were watchful, suspicious of this young stranger, this boy who claimed to possess the power to heal their hurts and lessen their misery. They asked instead for Mistress Tova, and Janna had to explain over and over again that the cook herself was struck with the pox and confined to her bed. But at Serlo's urging, and as they themselves began to feel the benefit of Janna's healing salves and lotions, they came to accept her, and welcomed her into their homes.

For Janna, this was something new. She didn't know much about living in a close community, for she and her mother had always dwelt alone at the edge of the forest. Janna found she enjoyed the villeins' friendship and their appreciation. Tending the sick also gave her new confidence that her years of watching Eadgyth so closely might count for something after all. With practice, she might yet come to possess her mother's skills with healing. It was a source of pride to Janna that Mistress Tova made a good recovery, with only a few scars to show where the spots had been. Gytha escaped unscathed. Others were not so lucky and bore the scars of their misfortune, but it was a consolation that no-one died.

As soon as they were well enough, the villeins returned to work in their own fields, although their time was restricted by Serlo, who insisted they also catch up on tasks on the lord's lands that they'd neglected while they were ill. Rainy days postponed haymaking so, instead, Edwin and Janna continued to cut weeds, dig ditches and repair the hedges that protected the fields of corn from hungry animals. Whenever she could, Janna fled to the kitchen garden to tend the plants and herbs that grew there, but the days were long and the work was always hard.

Janna had reasoned that the sooner the villeins were back on their feet and out working in the fields, the sooner she and Edwin would be free to leave. Yet Serlo continued to find work for them to do and made sure they kept busy. He seemed determined that they would repay their full dues for his silence. He rode around the manor and kept an eye on everyone and everything. He always knew exactly what was going on and what needed to be done. Janna had come to admire and respect the reeve for his good care and husbandry of the manor, even while she grumbled over the toll paid by her body. Yet she was aware too that she was growing stronger and more able as the weeks went by, and she gloried in the fresh air, exercise and freedom that her new life afforded her.

Of the lord of the manor there was still no sign, although Gytha was forever preening herself in case he returned unexpectedly.

'He's much older than me, but not so old as Serlo,' Gytha confided on one occasion, when Janna found her admiring her reflection in the still waters of a small duck pond. 'He has at least twenty-five years.' She puckered her lips to blow a kiss to herself.

'And he has not spoken of marriage?'

'He wishes first to make his way in the world.' Gytha tossed her head. Janna could see that she was out of sympathy with her lord's ambition.

'Why should he wish to do that?' Janna spread out her hands to encompass the fields stretching before them. 'Surely this fine demesne brings him in a good income?'

'It is not his to inherit.' Gytha sounded resentful. 'It's not fair! My lord works so hard, he aims to make this the finest manor farm in the shire, but his cousin will take it all when he comes of age. My lord will be left with nothing!'

Janna nodded in understanding. It was becoming the custom for the first born to inherit everything, which made life very difficult for those sons who came after. They had few options other than to enter the king's service and hope to earn bounty in battle, or else go into the church. A third option, and the best from their point of view, was to marry a woman with a dowry and lands of her own. Looking at Gytha, Janna felt sorry for the young beauty. She might have her hopes pinned on the lord of the manor, but unless he was either blind in love or very stupid, he would be looking to wed someone far more suited to his ambition than the cook's daughter.

'When you grow up you should try to be just like him, young John. He's such a man to admire. He's very brave, and very handsome. He's the handsomest man I've ever seen,' Gytha gushed.

Janna wondered just how many men Gytha knew that she could make the comparison with such confidence. 'When does he return?' she asked, thinking that perhaps even now he might be off scouting marriageable prospects.

'We expected him long before this.' Gytha scowled. 'He went to visit his family, but the country is in such unrest he might have been summoned by the king to his castle in Sarisberie. It's not so far from here. Or he might have gone on to Winchestre.'

Janna's ears pricked up. 'Do you know the road to Winchestre?' she asked quickly.

'No, I do not.' Gytha pouted, her mind fixed on her own problems rather than Janna's question. 'Really, there is no reason for him to be anywhere but here,' she groused. 'While there's fighting between the king and his barons, who keep changing their allegiance in the hope that it might profit them, none of the trouble comes anywhere near here. As for the empress's claim to the crown, my lord told us there was a council of peace between Stephen's queen and Matilda's half-brother, the Earl of Gloucester, at the end of May. It was arranged by Bishop Henry, the king's brother, who hopes to bring about a reconciliation between the king and his cousin.'

This was welcome news to Janna. 'Pray God he succeeds, for all our sakes,' she said.

Gytha nodded absent-mindedly. 'Perhaps my lord is still with his family,' she said, coming back to the topic that most interested her. 'Perhaps even now he is arguing his right to keep this demesne. Oh!' She clasped Janna's hand in sudden hope. 'Pray that he succeeds, John, so that our future here together may be assured.'

Janna wondered whether to sound a note of caution, but decided it was none of her business. 'I hope your wish may come true, mistress,' she said, and gently removed her hand from Gytha's grasp. She did not wish to become involved in the young woman's schemes.

It was not so easy, however, to keep herself detached from the villeins and the servants of the household for, having come to know them all as she ministered to their needs, she was popular and much sought after as a result of her kindness and skill. She stood in the kitchen early one morning, waiting for the cook to pack up their dinner and half-listening to Mistress Tova's gossip. Janna had taken special care to stay on friendly terms with her, for it meant that she and Edwin might gain extra meat, or a piece of fowl, or a stale pastry or some fruit along with their bread and ale for the day. Their hard work out in the fields meant that they were always hungry, so Janna was happy to put in extra time and care in return for extra food.

'Of course, that girl would look at anyone who wore breeches.' The cook's lips tucked down with disapproval as she continued in her petulant whine. 'Only yesterday, I saw her walk past him. She pretended to stumble, and kicked aside her kirtle so that she could show off her bare legs. I've seen the way she looks at him! One of these days, you mark my words, that girl will —'

'Who do you mean?' Janna was already tired of the cook's spiteful gossip; her long nose seemed made for poking into where it wasn't wanted. Besides, Janna was keen to be out in the fields for, in spite of the hard work ahead, she thought the day might bring some sunshine, a change from the spitting rain that had plagued them these past few weeks.

'Bertha, of course. Haven't you been listening to me?'

'Yes indeed, mistress, of course I have,' Janna said hastily, anxious not to get on the wrong side of this woman who seemed to wield almost as much power within the household as Serlo did in his master's demesne.

'You must warn your brother about her.' Mistress Tova clicked her tongue vigorously. 'He's handsome enough, I grant you, but he shouldn't encourage her. No good will come of it, you'll see. She'll break his heart before she's done, for she's a flighty girl and besides, she has her sights set much higher than Edwin.' There was an extra note of sourness in the cook's voice. Janna wondered if she considered Bertha a rival to Gytha's chances with the lord of the manor. Her suspicions were confirmed as the woman continued her gripe. 'Not that she'll get anywhere with my lord. A keen eye for a pretty girl my lord might have, but he's not for the likes of Bertha.'

Janna nodded agreement, even while wondering how the cook could show so little common sense when it came to her own daughter. Yet she had some sympathy for Gytha, and also for Bertha, as she remembered her own dealings with the handsome Hugh, a Norman nobleman, whom she'd met at Babestoche Manor while she was trying to save the life of Dame Alice's newborn son. He'd been so kind to her after her mother had died. She was also quite sure she hadn't misread the admiration in his eyes when he'd looked at her. But Hugh, too, had his way to make in the world. Janna knew that he was not for her, although his kisses had shaken her heart and soul, shaken everything she'd thought and believed in. How easy it would have been to love him, even knowing that it could lead only to disaster! She shook his image out of her mind. Hugh belonged to her past life and besides, she was a youth now, and so would not attract the eye of any man, be he as highborn as Hugh, or as lowly as Godric, who had protected her so bravely.

She turned her face away so that the housekeeper wouldn't notice her sadness. The voice continued, relentless as a midge in summer. 'Young as you are, John, you should also guard yourself against Bertha's wiles. I tell you, that Bertha will set her cap at anyone. Young or old, it matters not.'

Janna wondered if the cook realised she was contradicting herself, but was too weary to question it. Instead, she pondered what the luckless Bertha had done to attract so much spite and ire. Bertha was the carpenter's daughter. She was slightly older than Janna, and while she was no beauty, she had a pleasant countenance and always had a friendly word for everyone. Perhaps it was her popularity that soured the old biddy. It was a popularity that her own daughter did not share because of her airs and graces and her deliberate efforts to keep herself apart. Perhaps others on the manor also resented the favouritism shown to Gytha by Serlo, for servants and villeins alike worked every hour of daylight while it seemed that Gytha could please herself what she did. She was seldom in the kitchen, preferring instead to sit beside the well in the yard, or under a sheltering tree, where all might view her dainty stitching and admire her efforts at embroidery.

'. . . but you'll see him soon enough.'

'Who?' Janna realised her mistake as soon as the question left her mouth.

The housekeeper pursed her lips. 'If you are not bothered to listen to me, you'll have to stay ignorant, John,' she said. 'Besides, I haven't all day to stand here gossiping.' As if it was all Janna's fault.

'I beg your pardon, mistress,' she said meekly, and made her escape before the housekeeper relented enough to regale her with another half-hour of malice.

'You'll see him soon enough.' The cook's words piqued Janna's curiosity as she left the manor and trudged up to the fields beyond.

'Is someone coming to the manor today?' she asked Edwin, in case his intelligence was better than hers.

'Maybe the lord. He's supposed to be here for the hay-making. It's late, but they'll start cutting the grass as soon as this rain stops.' Edwin looked worried. 'I hope he won't ask too many questions about us.'

'Who is he?' Janna was surprised to realise that after all this time, she didn't even know whose manor they were on.

Serlo held such firm control over everything, she'd almost forgotten the manor belonged to someone else.

Edwin shrugged. 'Don't know his name. Don't care, so long as he doesn't find out who we really are.'

'I hear he's quite young and very handsome, although to hear Gytha tell it you'd think he was as ancient as God.'

Edwin laughed. 'He might be as handsome as the devil himself, but it can't matter to you. You're a youth, remember?'

'Oh, he'd be far too busy to look at me, even if I were a girl,' Janna said cheerfully. 'I'm told he has his eye on Gytha, and that Bertha has her eye on him.'

'What?' Edwin swung around to confront Janna. He took a savage swipe at a patch of deadnettles.

'It was just idle gossip. You know what Mistress Tova is like.' Janna felt uncomfortable, remembering now how Edwin had sidled up to Gytha when he first saw her.

'She's a wicked old crone,' Edwin muttered. Turning his back on Janna, he began to hack into thistles as if his life depended on eliminating every single one.

With a sigh, Janna looked about her. No matter how many thistles they cut, there were always more to find; she was beginning to think the harvest would be more bountiful if they reaped thistles rather than corn!

Although they used a pair of long-handled sticks to cull the tall, prickly weeds, Janna's hands were scratched and sore. She could feel the sting of their spikes through her smock and breeches whenever she came too close. She hated them! Now, she turned her back on them and, instead, began to cut into a clump of hairy pink corncockle.

In the new freedom her tunic and breeches provided her, she'd almost forgotten how it felt to be constrained in a long kirtle. Her past life was beginning to seem more and more like a dream, and yet her quest nagged at her conscience: she needed to find her father. She wanted justice for her mother's death. Finally, she gave voice to her thoughts.

'If Master Serlo won't give us permission to leave the manor, we must ask the lord if we may go.'

'Master Serlo needs our help with haymaking. He told me so only yesterday.'

'You work too hard, that's the trouble.' Janna paused a moment to survey Edwin's efforts as, seemingly tirelessly, he slashed through the spiky thistles. 'If we were both of us as useless as Gytha, he'd get rid of us tomorrow. Today, even.' She bit her lip as she remembered the distress she'd already caused Edwin. She wished she'd held her tongue.

'Gytha has other uses so far as Master Serlo is concerned,' Edwin said dryly.

'True enough.' Janna felt slightly reassured that Edwin had come to realise he was wasting his time on Gytha. She decided to jolly him along. 'And what is this I hear about Mistress Bertha showing off her legs to you?'

'Who told you that?'

'Do you need to ask?' Janna continued before Edwin had a chance to respond. 'I'm meant to warn you that she's a flirt, a flighty girl, and that she'll break your heart.'

'Mistress Bertha cares nothing for me, whatever Mistress Tova might think!' Edwin's voice was gruff with embarrassment.

Janna looked at him. Edwin's wild, half-starved look was gone; he was filling out, becoming a man. Janna had seen how some of the young women looked at him when he passed by, although he never stopped long to talk with them, to tease them or flirt with them as they obviously wished he would.

'You might not stand a chance with Gytha, but I reckon you could have your pick of anyone else if you weren't so shy,' she observed.

Edwin flushed. 'Look at me!' he countered angrily. 'I'm a fugitive from my lord's demesne. How can I woo a maid when I have nothing to offer her, nothing at all?'

'That'll change when you've waited out your year and a day,' Janna comforted him.

'Yea, it will. But only if we can get to Winchestre, and if I can find work to earn my keep.'

'Then we might as well get started,' Janna said cheerily. 'You won't mind if I ask the lord's permission to leave?'

'I'd rather stay until we're told to go,' Edwin countered. 'Serlo is a good reeve, far better than my own lord, and we have food and shelter here. Trust me, it's much more comfortable living here than living wild in field and forest, having to scavenge and steal to stay alive. Besides, Serlo saved us from the forester. We owe him for that.'

'We've already worked hard enough to repay him a hundredfold,' Janna grumbled.

'It's safer for me to stay here, tucked out of sight.' Edwin thought a moment. 'It's not as though you have any real plan to find your father. A few weeks more can't make any difference either way.'

Janna gave a grudging nod, accepting the truth of Edwin's words.

'Besides, I hear there's to be a great feast after haymaking is done, with much ale and merrymaking. You wouldn't want to miss that, would you, even if it means you'll have to ask a maiden to dance with you?'

Janna threw back her head and laughed at the thought. As she brought her attention back to the task in hand, her gaze sharpened and she straightened abruptly to look ahead. Her heart skipped a beat. She felt light-headed with shock.

That sleek, black destrier! She could swear she'd seen the horse before. She'd even been on its back, riding in front with Hugh sitting behind her, his arms around her to keep her safe. So close they'd been, she had wished the ride might last for ever. She squinted her eyes against the light, trying to see the rider more clearly.

He was clean shaven, with brown, shoulder-length hair. A green cloak almost covered his long tunic. She looked into his dark eyes.

Yes, it was, it truly was! Her legs folded under her and she collapsed onto the ground, faint and giddy with fear. She bent her head to her knees, knowing that the rush of blood would make her feel better. More than anything, though, she needed to hide her face. Hugh thought she was dead, burned in the fire along with her cottage. It was safest for Janna if everyone thought that.

'What is it? What's the matter?' She heard Edwin's anxious voice through the heavy pounding of her heart.

'Hide me, Edwin! Stand in front of me.' Janna didn't raise her head. 'That's my lord Hugh coming our way. What's he doing here?'

There was silence as Edwin surveyed the figure coming towards them. 'I noticed him before,' he commented then. 'He's come from the forest, and he rides alone. He must know the way, or there'd be a guide with him else.'

'I suspect he knows the way very well.' Through her own fear and confusion, Janna had found the answer to her question. 'I suspect he's done the journey through the forest many times.' She remembered how Gytha had talked about her lord and how he managed the manor on behalf of his family, and wondered why she hadn't made the connection before. How could she have been so stupid! Hugh himself had told her that he was visiting his aunt to report on his custodianship of her property, while Hamo, Hugh's cousin, had boasted that in time, he would inherit everything. 'The lord Hugh has been away visiting his aunt at Babestoche, which is on the other side of this forest,' she said slowly. 'Dame Alice must own this manor farm, for Hugh is her nephew and Gytha has told me he's in charge here until his cousin comes of age. Oh, Edwin!' Her voice shook as she looked up at him. 'This is the worst possible place we could have chosen to come for shelter!'

'Have courage,' he murmured, as he bent and sliced into a patch of nettles. 'You are a youth now, remember, and the lord comes very near to us. You'd better get back to work or he'll certainly stop and give you a piece of his mind.'

Conscious that it was good advice, Janna scrambled to her feet and began to hack into a patch of yellow-flowering charlock, deliberately turning her back on the oncoming horseman. All her senses were strained as she listened to the sound of the horse's hooves and the jingle of its bridle. In spite of herself, a slow blush mounted her cheeks.

'God be with you,' Hugh's cheery voice rang out.

'God be with you, sire,' Janna mumbled in reply. She didn't turn around, but heard Edwin's voice echo her own greeting. To her horror, the sounds had stopped, which meant that the horse had too. She risked a quick glance behind her, not wanting to turn around but wondering if it would be considered rude to ignore Hugh and keep on working.

'You are strangers to my manor, are you not?' Hugh sounded puzzled. Janna waited, her heart thudding, for Edwin to reply.

'We are, my lord. Your reeve, Master Serlo, gave us shelter in return for our labour. He has asked us to stay and help with the haymaking.'

'Which is very late.' Hugh cast his eyes skyward, assessing the chances of the sunshine continuing.

'There has been much illness as well as bad weather, sire,' Edwin hastened to explain.

Watching from under lowered lids, Janna saw Hugh nod silently. 'Who are you? What are your names?' he asked.

'I am Edwin, and this is my brother, John.'

Janna turned to Hugh. She ducked her head in obeisance and kept it bent to avoid his gaze.

'And where are you from? Do you have permission from your liege lord to leave his manor?'

As Edwin launched into an explanation, Janna turned to attack a patch of thistles.

'Your young brother seems determined to earn his keep,' Hugh interrupted, sounding amused. Janna did not dare to look at him.

'He's young, sire, but he's a good worker. Our mother always said that young John here was never at rest until all was done and proper.'

Edwin sounded so convincing! Janna stifled a giggle.

'I can see your mother was right. I'll have a word with Serlo when I find him. Maybe you can stay on to help with the harvest too. There is always a need for good and willing workers.' The jingle of the bridle told Janna that Hugh was on the move once more. Only when the sounds had faded into the distance did she dare to raise her head and look about her.

'There, you heard him! He wants us to stay.' Edwin sounded wistful. 'I'd like that, John, I really would.'

'Don't even think about it!' Janna said furiously. 'Didn't you listen when I told you that the villagers set fire to my cottage, with me in it? It's too dangerous for me to stay here!'

'You didn't tell me he had anything to do with it.' Edwin jerked his head in the direction of the dwindling figure of Hugh.

'No, but . . . but . . .' Janna couldn't tell Edwin that it was Hugh's uncle by marriage, Robert of Babestoche, who had incited the villagers to rise against her. If Hugh found out who she really was, it would only be a matter of time before Dame Alice and Robert found out too. Janna had managed to escape with her life once; she didn't intend to take any further chances.

'But . . . but what?' Edwin raised an enquiring eyebrow.

'He was part of it. Hugh, I mean,' Janna muttered. 'It's not safe for me to stay here.' Even as she said the words, she knew that she wanted to stay, just to be near Hugh. Being so close to him again had utterly unnerved her. In spite of her short hair and villein's garb, she longed to show herself as she really was, and tell him the truth: that she was alive, that she had escaped the fire that was meant to destroy her and her cottage. Then she remembered Gytha, and the light died in her eyes. It seemed that Hugh had a weakness for pretty serving girls and also the glib tongue to convince them that they were special in his eyes. 'We have to leave. We must,' she insisted.

'We can't. Not without Serlo's permission.'

'He can't stop us if he doesn't see us go.' Janna wondered why Edwin was being so obstinate.

'He can raise the hue and cry after us with the forester and with the sheriff. I've done enough running away, Ja . . . John. Please, let's stay here as long as we can.'

Janna was silent, torn between wanting to help Edwin and to protect herself.

'We probably won't see him again,' Edwin urged. 'He'll be far too busy and important to bother with the likes of us. Our dealings are with Master Serlo, not him. Besides, he doesn't suspect a thing. In fact, he thinks well of you for being such a hard worker!'

Janna gave a grudging nod, acknowledging the truth of Edwin's argument. 'Then you must speak for me, protect me from him,' she conceded, adding fiercely, 'but only until our time is up! Then I'm going to Winchestre, whether you come with me or not.' She bent to slash at the hated weeds once more.

SIX

AFTER HER unexpected encounter with Hugh, Janna spent as little time in the hall as possible in case he came in and found her there. She broke her fast at speed and, while Edwin waited about afterwards for Hugh or Serlo to give the villeins on week work their orders for the day, she would hurry to the kitchen and wait for Mistress Tova to pack up dinner and supper in a sack for those who had no land to provide for themselves. Listening to Mistress Tova meant that Janna was well up on the doings of the manor, and the gossip that was attached to them.

Not everything was going smoothly and Mistress Tova had plenty to say about that too. A fox had got into the henhouse one night. The rumpus had woken the servants sleeping in the hall, and they'd rushed down to investigate, but several hens had already been savaged and killed. The maid in charge of feeding them and collecting their eggs had been in a lot of trouble, although she tearfully repeated over and over again that she was sure, positive, absolutely certain that she'd shut the coop tight for the night.

Next, a young lamb had been found dead. The sheep had all been washed prior to shearing. They'd been put back in

97

their fold but the lamb was found some distance away, although the shepherd said he'd counted them and had stayed guard in his little hut all night. The lamb's carcass was cut and bloody. It was certain that no natural illness or weakness had killed it, while the shepherd swore no wolf could have carried it off either. He, too, had felt the sharp edge of Serlo's tongue.

On another occasion, cows managed to escape from their byre and plunged through a hedge into a field of ripening wheat. Before the hayward could sound the alarm, their hooves and their appetites had destroyed a large portion of new grain, which meant there would be less for the harvest and therefore less to tide everyone over through winter and the hungry months before the next harvest.

What intrigued Janna most was her suspicion that the incidents had been planned, and for a purpose. Walking past the henhouse on the day after the hens had been savaged, she'd noticed a small bunch of rue beside the gate of their run. It had seemed odd at the time, so odd that she'd paid close attention when she found another bunch of rue near the sheepfold after the slaughter of the lamb. Was the herb dropped by accident, or had the perpetrator regretted his act of violence after the event? Was this his way of saying he was sorry? No-one seemed to think anything of it, but Janna couldn't believe in happenstance. Perhaps to the others the rue was just a useful herb, but she understood its special significance. 'Rue is for repentance,' Eadgyth had told her. 'Rue stands for regret.' The bunches of rue must surely mean that these things had happened for a reason. But what could that be?

The question had niggled her so that, after the cows went wandering, Janna searched for rue near the byre. It had taken some finding, for by then the animals had been found and herded back. The ground around about was muddy and the herbs had been trampled underfoot, but Janna found enough scraps to know that a bunch of rue had been picked and placed there.

No accident then, but for a purpose. Who was responsible, and why? Janna had a growing suspicion that she knew the answer to the first question, and possibly even the second. She resolved to keep watch, and wait until she had some grounds for accusation. Meantime, she hoped with all her heart that her suspicions were wrong. She became aware that Mistress Tova was still talking.

'There have been too many accidents since my lord Hugh's return. This sort of thing never happens while Master Serlo's in charge.' Mistress Tova gave Janna a long and meaningful glance, before adding hastily, 'Of course, Gytha is delighted to have my lord back at the manor again, but even so . . .'

Janna stopped herself from defending Hugh, not wanting to betray any special interest in him to the gossiping cook. But she couldn't help worrying about it, for although Serlo had questioned everyone after the incident with the cows, no-one seemed to have any knowledge of how they might have escaped the byre, nor any intention of revealing the secret if they had. The cowherd seemed blameless; his family could vouch for his presence in their midst at the time the animals must have gone astray. Someone else was therefore responsible, and Serlo was making every effort to find the culprit. Janna was quite sure that the reeve suspected her and Edwin, being the newest arrivals on the manor farm. He'd certainly questioned them for a long time.

Janna's thoughts went back to that interview, and how uncomfortable she'd felt under Serlo's accusing gaze as he'd made them recount where they'd been and what they'd been doing. He had a nasty rash on his hand, Janna remembered, and she'd sought to divert his attention by offering a healing salve. But he'd brushed her concern aside, clearly determined not to be deflected from his purpose: someone was going to be held responsible for the destruction; someone was going to get the blame. Yet at the end he'd made no accusations, but instead had ordered every villein out into the field to plant peas, beans and vetches, so that there might be something to eat in place of what had been destroyed.

'Of course, you and Edwin are newly come to the manor.' Mistress Tova's voice broke into Janna's thoughts. She didn't have to say anything else for Janna to know what she was thinking.

'Edwin and I aren't responsible for any of these accidents. We know nothing about them!' Janna hoped that her denial would be believed, and also passed on with the rest of the gossip that Mistress Tova shared around so freely.

The cook looked thoughtful. 'No-one wants to think the worst of you, John, not when you were so good about curing us of the pox. No.' She went quiet for a moment, as if wondering how far she could trust Janna with her suspicions. 'No,' she continued, 'it seems that we're just having a run of bad luck.' She tied up the sack of food and thrust it towards Janna. 'I've put in a small meat pie for your dinner,' she said generously, and Janna beamed her thanks.

The sun had finally come out, the long days had settled into sunshine, and haymaking had started at last. Hugh was present for the ceremony that marked its beginning, when at dawn the hayward tied a bunch of flowering grasses to his scythe and crossed himself in prayer before making the first cut. Janna had stayed as far away from Hugh as she could, mingling with the villeins as they followed the hayward in a line through the water meadows, scything the long grass that would keep the animals from starvation during the lean winter months when the meadows were flooded. When she next looked around for Hugh, he had gone. She smiled with relief, her smile returned by the women and children who followed behind them. Their task was to spread the grass out to dry, and turn it so that it bleached to a pale gold in the hot summer sun. The sweetness of cut grass, and the fragrant herbs that were felled with it, scented the air.

All able-bodied villeins, plus their wives and children, were expected to take part in this boon work for their lord, just as they were pressed into service at other busy times on the farming calendar. Their reward, at the end of each day of haymaking, was to take home as much hay as they could carry on their scythes. Only when all the grass was cut, dried, bundled and stored would they be released from their extra days of labour. While this caused some grumbles, they mostly worked with a will so that they could finish the task and get back to tending their own fields.

After the fuss about the straying cows, there'd been no further incidents. Janna had begun to convince herself that the culprit was truly repentant, and that they could all rest easy now. So she was happy and quite unsuspecting as, sack of food under her arm, she walked past the stables on her way down to the water meadows for the day's haymaking. The sound of Hugh's voice stopped her. After a quick look around the yard to check that no-one was watching, she sidled over to the door and peered around it. Hugh was in a stall with his destrier, swearing loudly as he inspected its hoof. Janna knew an instant of alarm, but then calmed her fears with the thought that horses often went lame and that this must just be happenstance. As she watched, Hugh removed a loose shoe and then carefully extracted an iron nail from the horse's hoof, swearing profusely all the while.

To allay her suspicions, Janna inspected both sides of the stable door, looking for any telltale sign. It was bare of everything but the latch. She felt a rush of relief until she realised that what she sought and feared to find was lying on the ground in front of the door: the aromatic silvery green leaves and small yellow flowers of rue, half-hidden under her boot.

Janna snatched them up. This was proof, if proof was needed, that this was no coincidence. All these so-called 'accidents' had been planned deliberately. As she hurried through the water meadows, she cast the sprigs of rue into the long grass to hide them. Who could be responsible? One by one, she went through everyone she knew, trying to find a possible culprit.

It was a puzzle. While many of them might have the opportunity to carry out these acts, there was only one person she could think of who had any reason to do such things. From everything she'd heard and witnessed, Hugh was a good overlord, kind and fair, while Serlo was respected and trusted by everyone. Why should anyone want to harm either man, or his reputation, or the manor farm itself, at least anyone other than a child?

Urk. Everything pointed to him. He was free to come and go. No-one paid much attention to him, or took him seriously. And he, alone of anyone she knew, had a reason to cause trouble and then repent his actions.

Although she'd tried to keep her promise to Mistress Wulfrun, it was impossible to watch Urk all the time. Janna was sure the boy brooded over his punishment at the hands of Serlo and that he might well want to hit back at the reeve. The posies of rue seemed to confirm his regret afterwards for what he had done. Janna wondered whether she should warn Urk's mother, yet she didn't want to cause the woman even more grief and worry. Instead, she resolved to double her watch over Urk, and also to warn him that she knew what he was doing and counsel him over the consequences. She must make him realise that, if he was caught, retribution would be horrible both for himself and for his family.

Pleased to have formulated a plan of action, Janna skipped a few steps and then, after checking that no-one was about, she tried a couple of cartwheels, copying the actions of some children she'd seen larking about. She'd been dying to have a go and, to her satisfaction, she almost succeeded. She had another try and then another. A bit wobbly, she decided, but she was sure she'd improve with practice. She strode on, feeling happy, healthy and almost content. She was used to the labour now, and revelled in the growing strength in her muscles and her freedom to run, to shout, even to turn cart-wheels and do anything else a boy might do. She smiled to herself, and hurried on to join Edwin and the others who were busy forking up the dry grass and stacking it into bundles. Urk was among the group. He was almost as tall as Janna, and far stronger and quicker. He gave her a smile. It was the perfect opportunity, and Janna took it.

'Are you very angry with Master Serlo, Urk?' she asked, moving closer to him so that they could talk without being heard.

'No. I'm scared of him.'

It was true. Janna had seen him cower away and try to hide whenever Serlo came near. 'I wonder, did you hurt that baby lamb we found the other day? The one that was all bloody and lying out in the field?'

'No! I like baby lambs.' Urk's lips set in a straight line, and he forked the hay with renewed vigour.

'Do you know who hurt it?' she pressed.

'No.' Urk shook his head without slackening his pace. 'It's not right to kill baby lambs.'

'No, it isn't,' Janna agreed, feeling rather at a loss. 'What about the cows that got into the field?' she tried. 'Do you know who let them out of the byre?'

The boy shook his head, not bothering to answer.

'Or the hens? Do you know how the fox got into their coop?'

'No.' Urk kept on forking up hay.

'What about my lord's horse? Was it you who hammered the nail into its hoof?' Janna pressed.

'No!' He stopped and turned to her then. 'I'm scared of horses. They're too big.'

'None of those things was an accident,' Janna said. 'Someone did them on purpose. Someone who wants to cause trouble to Master Serlo and the lord Hugh. Do you know who that could be, Urk?'

He lowered his head and began to kick out at the green stubble left from the newly cut grass.

'It's all right to tell me if you know anything about it,' Janna urged. 'I won't tell anyone else what you did, I promise, just so long as you stop.'

'But I didn't do anything!'

'If Gabriel says he didn't do it, then he didn't do it.' Mistress Wulfrun materialised on the other side of Janna. 'I know what you're thinking, John, but he's a truthful boy. I've never known him tell a lie, even when he's got in trouble for it.'

'Gabriel?' Janna asked, confused.

'We call him Gabriel,' Mistress Wulfrun explained. 'He may not be the brightest star in the sky, but he's kind and loving, and he has such a sweet smile we believe he's been touched by God's own hand.'

Urk smiled at Janna, as if in proof of his mother's faith in him. 'I didn't do none of those things,' he said, softly but firmly.

Janna wondered whether she could believe him and his fond mother. 'I hope that's true,' she said, 'because you can be sure that when Master Serlo finds out who was responsible, that person will get such a beating he may be half-killed.' She read the fear on Urk's face and was briefly repentant, yet she'd spoken only the truth. If Urk's conscience was clear, then Serlo couldn't touch him or his family. Meantime she had delivered her warning. It was all she could do.

In spite of Urk having the only reason she could think of to do these things, she found that she believed he'd told her the truth. But if not Urk, then who? Edwin? It hardly seemed likely when he was so keen to stay on at the manor, and was so grateful to Serlo for giving them food and shelter. Yet Janna had formed the impression lately that Edwin was keeping something hidden from her, some sort of secret. She hadn't thought much about it, for although the two of them had become firm friends, she thought of him only as a friend and no more than that. She certainly didn't expect him to confess every little thing to her. But where once he'd been always at her side, now he was sometimes missing, gone about some errand of his own. To kill a lamb? To lame a horse?

No! Janna shook her head, unable to imagine Edwin doing any of those things. Besides, he seemed happy enough. He certainly didn't seem to be harbouring the sort of hatred and spite that must lie behind acts of this sort.

What most worried Janna was the thought of what disaster might happen next. If someone was causing problems for a reason, he'd be unlikely to stop until his purpose was achieved. What could that purpose be? If she could only find that out, she might be able to put a stop to these so-called 'accidents', which, in turn, would help ensure her and Edwin's safety.

Questions continued to bedevil her as the villeins prepared to enjoy medale, the drinking festivity to celebrate the end of haymaking. The grass had been cut and dried, and collected into stacks with thatched covers to protect it through the winter rains, or carted off to be stored in the barn. For the moment, their task was done, although Serlo had already warned that sheep-shearing and harvesting were next and that he expected them to stay on and help. She took comfort from the notion that he couldn't suspect them of causing the problems – unless it was at Hugh's urging that he wanted them to stay.

It was with a sense of anticipation that she followed Edwin up to the manor hall on the night of the celebration. Mistress Tova, Gytha and the rest of the kitchen servants had been busy. Trestle tables were set up to form a large square and were laden ready for the feast. Wooden platters were piled high with food, with brimming pitchers of honey mead and ale set beside them.

'This'll do me,' Edwin said cheerfully, as he surveyed the spread. 'You can have the leftovers.' He patted his stomach and gave Janna a wolfish grin.

Janna laughed, but her mirth vanished as she looked beyond Edwin and saw Hugh standing beside Serlo at a table raised up on a platform. He was surveying the crowd below.

'I have to go,' she muttered, and swung around.

'You can't miss out on medale!' Edwin caught her arm and dragged her back, looking horrified at the thought.

'But he's here! My lord Hugh is here!'

'So what? Why are you so afraid of him? What makes you think he'll even remember you?'

It was a fair question, Janna acknowledged, and one she couldn't answer unless she told Edwin how kind Hugh had been to her after her mother died; how they'd played ball with his cousin, Hamo; and how he'd taken her home on the

back of his destrier afterwards. And then he'd kissed her! She
blushed at the memory.

'Stay,' Edwin urged now. 'He thinks you're my brother. He
doesn't know who you really are. Don't let him spoil the feast
for you.'

Janna risked another glance in Hugh's direction, her heart
jolting painfully as she noticed who else was standing beside
him. Gytha. She wore a new gown for the occasion, home-
spun but with a greenish tinge that became her dark locks
and creamy complexion, and added a bewitching green
tint to her hazel eyes. Hugh sat down at the high table,
accompanied by Serlo and several others. After he'd said
grace, Gytha began to serve him, bending over so that she
could smile into his eyes.

Janna stood still, swept by a tide of pure envy. She wanted
to flee, to hide from the sight, yet a painful curiosity bid her
stay, to watch the interplay between them so she would
know for sure whether the girl's trust in Hugh's intentions
was well-founded or misplaced.

'See?' Edwin nudged Janna, unwittingly adding to her
distress as he said, 'You don't need to worry that he'll notice
you. He has eyes only for Gytha.'

'As she has for him,' Janna said bitterly, wondering how
Edwin could sound so cheerful. 'Don't you mind?'

'About Gytha? No, why should I?'

So Edwin was over his infatuation with the cook's
daughter. Good, Janna thought. She must work on him anew
to get him to leave the manor with her. She might feel sorry
for Gytha if the girl's high hopes for Hugh came to naught,
but she'd feel even sorrier for herself if Hugh defied common

sense and became betrothed to the young girl. It seemed flight was her only choice if she was ever to know peace of mind. She sat down beside Edwin, but she found now that she'd lost all appetite and could only look without interest at the mound of food he'd piled on the trenchers of bread in front of them.

'Do you mind if I sit with you two?' Without waiting for a reply, Bertha took a seat on Edwin's other side, flashing a cheerful smile at Janna as she did so. The two of them set about wolfing down huge portions of fish, fowl and mutton, but Janna felt too sick to eat. Instead, she picked up her cup of ale and drained it, then sneaked a glance at Hugh and Gytha.

It was clear that the girl was doing all in her power to woo him. Janna wondered if it was only wishful thinking that made her question whether Hugh was quite so enamoured with the serving wench as she was with him. She knew Hugh to be courteous, and so he was now, bending his head to listen to something Gytha was saying. Yet his gaze roved the room until he caught sight of Janna. She blinked and looked quickly away, while her face flamed scarlet. His glance had been questioning; he was frowning at her. Had she done something wrong? Worse, did he suspect that she or Edwin might be behind the laming of his horse and the other disasters that had befallen the manor? Janna wanted to leap up, to go to him and protest her innocence. With an effort, she stayed seated and tried to look as if she was enjoying herself. She sneaked another look, to find Hugh still watching her. Her heart thudded painfully, her chest felt too tight to breathe. She cast about for a chance to escape, but knew there was none. She would not be able to leave the hall until after the lord had arisen from the table and retired to his solar. It would be unforgivably rude to do so. In case Hugh was still watching, she poured herself another mug of ale and quaffed it down, trying to look as unconcerned and as boyish as possible.

'You should eat something, John,' Bertha urged, and held out a portion of fat hen in her fingers. 'You'll never grow as tall and strong as your brother, else.' She smiled at Janna.

Distracted from her dark thoughts, Janna felt a flash of amusement as she took the food from Bertha's fingers. 'Thank you,' she said, wondering if the cook's sour gossip had some truth in it. Was Bertha indeed flirting with her as well as with Edwin – and everyone else who wore breeches, if Mistress Tova was to be believed? Janna ate the fowl, her appetite reviving somewhat as she savoured the delicacy, so that she continued then to help herself from the trencher.

'Are your family here tonight, mistress?' she asked Bertha, seeking to distract herself from the scene being played out at the high table.

'Yes, indeed.' Bertha waved an arm towards the tables opposite. 'That's my father and mother, and my two sisters sit next to them. Not for anything would any of us miss this feast.' With an expression of bliss on her face, she began to tear the flesh off a chicken bone with her teeth.

Janna had met one of Bertha's sisters when she'd taken medicaments to cure her of the pox. Now she looked with interest at the rest of Bertha's family.

'Bertha's little sister wants to meet you, John,' Edwin told her, with a sly smile. 'She thinks you're very handsome. Perhaps you might like to dance with her later?'

Janna choked on a piece of fish, and began to cough. Edwin thumped her on the back. Scarlet in the face, she quaffed down some ale. 'Fish bone,' she spluttered, by way of explanation.

Bertha smiled in ready sympathy. 'I had an uncle who choked to death on a fish bone,' she said, and embarked on a long story, giving Janna a chance to recover her equilibrium.

Only when every last morsel was eaten were the tables cleared away and stacked. Now I can leave, Janna thought, but Hugh still stayed seated at the high table, gazing serenely at the scene in front of him. Gytha leaned over him to pour wine into his goblet, her arm against his, her breast almost brushing his cheek. Janna clenched her hands and turned away, knowing she was trapped for the while.

Several villeins stood together at one side of the hall. Janna recognised the shepherd with his pipe, then noticed that the others also carried musical instruments. Occasionally she'd heard someone playing a tune in the marketplace; sometimes people sang words to the music, or even danced around. Janna hadn't paid them much mind. Her mother only ever hummed a tune when she thought she was alone and no-one was listening. Janna thought there must be something shameful about it because Eadgyth had been so angry when Janna had asked if she would teach her the song. Music had never been part of Janna's life, so she could hardly contain a gasp of surprised pleasure now as, with one accord, the villeins turned to the eager crowd gathering around them and began to play.

The shepherd held his pipe to his mouth and blew through the holes in it, dancing his fingers up and down to produce the sounds. One of the villeins struck a small drum, setting up a rhythm for the dancers, who were now swirling around in pairs, stamping their feet in time to the beat, and shrieking with delight. The third member of the party held a wooden bowl with a long neck along which several strings were tied. His fingers plucked and stroked the strings so that his sounds and the sounds from the pipe spoke to each other, sometimes blending together and sometimes taking turns to create different sounds altogether. Janna listened, enchanted, while her feet tapped in time to the rhythm.

'John? I would have a word with you.'

Hugh's voice dragged Janna from her reverie. She gave a start of surprise, and looked anxiously for Edwin and Bertha to save her. But they had joined the throng of dancers and she sat alone.

She leapt to her feet and bobbed her head. 'Sire,' she murmured, remembering to keep her voice deep. She did not dare look at Hugh. Instead, she moved closer to a shadowy recess where the light from the candles scarcely reached.

'I believe I have you to thank for ministering to my workers when they were ill with the pox. I am grateful to you. Serlo tells me we would have been even further behind with everything but for your cures.' Janna felt her hand seized. Something round and cold was pressed into it. Hugh released her hand and she looked to see what he had given her. A·dull glint told her what it was: a silver penny! She thrust it into her purse.

'Thank you, sire,' she stammered, glancing quickly up at him before looking away again.

'I have a horse gone lame — a nail awry in a loose shoe. Will you see if you can do aught to help? Arrow is in pain, and I fear he may become crippled if the wound festers.'

'Yes, sire. Of course I'll do all I can.' Janna's heart lurched at the thought of ministering to Hugh's destrier under his watchful gaze. She kept her head bent.

'Come to the stables tomorrow, after you have broken your fast. I'll wait for you there.'

Janna nodded. 'Sire,' she whispered, wishing that he would go and leave her alone yet wanting him to stay, wanting this moment with him to last for ever.

'You have no need to fear me, John.' Hugh's voice was kindly. But his next action filled Janna with alarm as he reached out and tilted up her chin. She had no choice but to look full at him.

'I thought so,' he murmured, coming closer to peer at her in the shadowy darkness. 'You remind me of a young healer I once knew. Her name was Johanna. Do you know of her, John? Was she perhaps a sister, or a cousin to you?'

'No! No, sire. My brother and I come from Wales.' Janna's voice shook as she told the lie. She longed to confess to Hugh, and to ask if he had kept his promise to her, but she dared not. 'We have no living kin here in England,' she said, in case he still harboured suspicions about her.

'And yet you look so like her,' Hugh mused, adding as if to himself, 'They say Johanna died in a fire.'

And were you sorry to hear that? Janna pressed her lips firmly together so that she could not ask the question, although she longed to know the answer. It was some comfort that Hugh remembered her; she took more comfort from the regret in his voice when he said, 'Johanna had a great gift for healing, and so did her mother. They are much missed at the manor of Babestoche, and in the neighbouring hamlets, for there is no-one now to physic the sick and help the dying.'

'Surely there is a midwife in the village, my lord?' Janna knew he was mistaken about the villagers' regret, but she wondered what had become of Mistress Aldith, one of the few of her mother's acquaintances who had shown her any kindness.

Hugh shrugged. 'Her business is to birth babies, but my aunt has little faith in her, that I know. Whether she can do else, I know not.' His gaze sharpened on Janna's face. 'Where did you learn your healing ways?' he asked.

'From . . . from my mother, sire.' Janna knew she should stick to her story. Others had heard it, and could repeat it to Hugh if he asked. It would increase his suspicion if she told him something different now. 'She was Saxon born, but when she wed my father, she went to live with him in Wales. He died when we were still quite young, but my father had a cot and enough land to keep us so my mother stayed on, for her own family were either dead or gone away.'

'I thought Serlo told me your mother worked in an alehouse?'

'So she did, sire, sometimes, for she had us to help her about our home,' Janna improvised rapidly. 'As soon as he was old enough, my brother tended the fields and planted the corn. He also looked after our sheep and goats, while I helped by growing vegetables for the pot, and herbs for my mother's medicaments. My mother was settled in Wales.

It was her home. And ours, until she died.' Janna knew she was gabbling, but she hoped the wealth of detail might help to convince Hugh. She hated lying to him, hated it, but she knew that her safety depended on it.

'Why, then, did you leave Wales?'

Janna gulped. 'I . . . er . . . my oldest brother has wed. He has taken the land and the cot for his own, so Edwin and I decided to seek a living in Winchestre. We are free born, sire,' she added for good measure.

'This isn't Winchestre,' Hugh commented dryly.

'No. No, sire, it isn't. But we have no money of our own so we are forced to find food and shelter along our way, which we repay with our own labour.'

'Then I wish you both good fortune.' Hugh paused a moment. 'I've watched you and your brother. You are hard workers, and your skill as a healer is also welcome here. You may stay on my manor as long as you wish.'

'Th . . . thank you, sire.' Janna stepped away from Hugh and bowed her head, desperate for him to leave. To be so close and not tell him the truth was a torture to her. When she looked up again, he had returned to his place at the table but he watched her still, his face screwed up into a thoughtful frown. Knowing she must act, and quickly, Janna turned to a young girl standing nearby. She was Bertha's young sister, Janna realised, and she was looking at Janna with a hopeful expression on her face. Without giving herself time to think, Janna grabbed the girl's hand and led her into the throng of laughing, dancing villeins.

Just as she had no notion of music, so Janna didn't know how to dance either. It didn't seem to matter among all the noise and confusion, but still she tried to copy the actions of those around her, clapping her hands and stamping her feet in time to the beat. When the villeins linked arms or whirled their partners around by the waist, so did Janna, and when they formed into a long line and danced around the high table, so did Janna along with Bertha's sister. She hoped Hugh was still watching. She hoped he was satisfied that she was who she claimed to be. But in truth, she thought, as she stole a quick glance at him, it was Gytha who held his attention now, for she held a plate of sweetmeats before him, tempting him both with the delicacies and with her eyes.

Janna looked quickly away and concentrated on following the pattern of the dance. She was just beginning to enjoy herself when a sudden shout sounded above the music. 'Fire!'

At once there was pandemonium. Some began to scream, some froze to the spot with terror, while others pushed past and over them in a desperate effort to get through the door and down the stairs to safety. It took some time for the hall to clear and everyone to realise that the danger lay not in the manor house but outside in the fields.

One of the haystacks was alight. They could see the glow above the palisade of sharpened stakes that fenced the manor house and yard. Cold dread gripped Janna as she listened to new cries of alarm. If the fire moved on and destroyed the other haystacks, the winter fodder would be burned and the animals would starve. Yet everyone milled around, waiting to be told what to do until Hugh shouted out above the hubbub: 'Follow me to the stream!' He raced ahead through the gate, and everyone fell into line behind him.

Janna saw that Hugh had already left instructions with Serlo for he, along with a group of his own, ran towards the shed where all the farming implements were housed. Undecided how best to help, Janna followed the crowd through the gate and up into the field, then stopped to watch. In the light from the flames, she saw that Hugh was now dividing the villeins into two groups, sending some towards the small stream that ran down into the river, and beckoning others to follow him to the flaming haystack. As Serlo and his helpers raced to the stream with leather buckets from the shed, the villeins began to form into a long line, making a chain that led from stream to haystack. At once they began to fill the buckets and pass them from hand to hand up the line. Serlo stayed by the stream to keep the buckets moving, while Hugh took up station beside the haystack to direct the flow of water onto where the flames were fiercest.

Once the contents were thrown, the buckets were thrust at a knot of children waiting nearby. They took turns to race back with the empty buckets to the stream to be refilled. Janna noticed Urk among them, carrying two buckets at a time and racing faster than anyone. Had he been in the hall with everyone else before the haystack caught alight? She couldn't be sure. All her attention had been on Hugh, and then on her dancing partner as she tried to convince Hugh that she was a youth. It was certain that Urk was on the spot now, and doing all he could to help put out the fire – but had he set it in the first place? It seemed unlikely, when he was making such an effort to help now.

Janna looked about. Was anyone missing? Who else might have fired the haystack? She had little doubt that this was no accident, but she was greatly fearful that Urk would be blamed for it. After all, he'd set fire to hay once before. Serlo would surely believe he might do so again.

She stepped closer to scrutinise the chain more carefully. Hugh was beside the burning haystack, his face illuminated in the blaze as he directed the villeins to throw the water where it would be most effective. Serlo was still beside the stream, keeping a watchful eye on the buckets moving up the chain, and also on the children, making sure they ran back to the haystack once they'd handed over the empty buckets to be filled. There was order amid the panic, for everyone knew how vital it was to keep the fire from spreading. Janna's glance narrowed as she tallied off the line of peasants labouring to pass along the heavy buckets without their precious contents being spilled. There was no sign of Edwin. Where was he?

She moved along the line to look for him.

'You! John! Get into the stream and help fill those buckets!' Serlo had seen her, and Janna knew that to disobey would invite his wrath as well as his suspicion. She hastened to do as she was told.

There was barely enough light from the flickering flames to make out the identity of her companions. But Edwin was not here, she was sure of it. She bent to her task, grabbing buckets from the children, sweeping them through the water to fill them, then heaving them up and into a pair of waiting arms. It was back-breaking work, but Janna had been toughened from her weeks in the fields and she knew she felt the strain less than the women who worked beside her. But they carried on without complaint, desperate to save the fodder that would keep their animals alive through winter, with meat on the table for themselves and their families.

'Give me a bucket.' She heard Edwin's voice beside her, and turned on him with a mixture of relief and fury.

'Where have you been?' she hissed.

He hung his head. She thought he looked guilty, and feared the worst. 'What's going on?' She grabbed his arm. 'Did you set fire to the haystack?'

'Of course not.' He wrenched his arm away. He didn't look at Janna but leaned over to fill a bucket as he said, 'I came to help as soon as I realised what was happening.'

'I hope no-one else noticed your absence! Don't you see, Edwin, we are the last to come here so we must be the first they will blame when they come to realise that these are not accidents but deliberate attempts to do harm.'

'Don't be silly! This was an accident, surely.' Edwin handed over a brimming bucket and grabbed another from a waiting child.

'How could it be an accident? Why would a haystack suddenly catch fire in the middle of the night?'

'Sometimes they overheat, especially if the grass is still green. It happens.'

It was true. Janna hadn't thought of that, but in her heart she was sure it hadn't happened that way. 'What about the dead lamb?' she asked. 'That wasn't an accident.'

'A fox? A wolf?'

Janna shook her head. 'A wild animal would have eaten the lamb, not killed it and left it for someone to find. Besides, its wounds were made by a knife, not teeth.'

'Yea, 'tis true.' Edwin's forehead creased into a frown as he thought about it.

'And the cows that got out and the fox that got in. And Hugh's lame horse. Do you really think all those things were accidents?'

'What happened to the horse?' Conscious that Serlo prowled about, watching them, watching everyone, Edwin hastily dipped his bucket into the stream.

His frown deepened as Janna told him what she'd seen and found at the stable. 'These things have all happened since my lord Hugh returned to the manor,' he interrupted her recital. 'It seems he's not as good at managing the farm as his reeve.'

So Mistress Tova was still spreading her poison. This time Janna was determined to defend Hugh. 'That's not true. You can't blame my lord for any of this.'

'I'm only saying what everyone says.'

Janna shook her head. 'These are not accidents, they're deliberate actions by someone wanting to cause harm,' she insisted.

'How can you be so sure?'

'The posies of rue left behind at the scene.'

'Rue?'

'For regret. That's what the old ones say, anyway. I wondered at first if the rogue felt regret for his actions after he'd done the deeds, but now I'm not so sure.' Without meaning to, Janna looked for and found Urk. He was coming their way, a bucket dangling from each fist. In spite of the gravity of the situation, his face creased into its customary cheerful smile as he thrust the buckets at Janna and Edwin.

'He looks happy enough. Maybe it's him,' Edwin commented.

'No, it isn't.' But Janna wasn't as sure as she sounded. 'I wondered if it might be you,' she said, deciding to voice her concerns.

'Me?' Edwin looked astonished. 'Why would I do something like this?' He gestured towards the haystack. 'What have I got to gain?'

The flames were dying at last. Smoke and the stink of wet, burnt hay tainted the air. Janna sighed with relief that the danger was past. 'I don't know. I just don't know anything,' she confessed.

SEVEN

ER WORRIES KEPT Janna wakeful and restless during the night. Her eyes felt puffy and pricked with tiredness when she finally rolled off her pallet and made herself ready to face Hugh. She was sure that she could smell herself, and she longed for a wash, but there was no privacy to be found unless she left the manor farm – and that she couldn't do, not without Serlo's permission. She certainly could not sneak out at night and plunge into the river, for if anyone saw her undressed they would know the truth. So she sighed, and wet her fingers and tried to smooth the singed stubble that covered her head, which was all she could do to make herself presentable. With a catch of alarm, she realised that her hair was growing long again. She patted the knife in its sheath. She must ask Edwin to cut her hair this very night.

With bread and ale consumed, she left Edwin to wait for the cook to assemble their dinner, and to chat to the serving maids while he waited, for he had become a great favourite in the kitchen. Her heart beat hard in fear and excitement as she first gathered soapwort, marsh mallow leaves and woundwort from the kitchen garden, then walked towards the stables clutching her bouquet of herbs.

There was no sign of Hugh, or anyone else other than a young boy. Janna frowned as she looked more closely. The youth was leading a small herd of nanny goats and their young through the yard towards the gate. Even as Janna watched, the boy raised his arm and aimed a pebble at one of the kids. It hit the goat on the rump and it jumped, bleating pitifully as it did so.

'Stop that!' Janna shouted. The boy hardly glanced at her before picking up another, larger stone. This time he aimed for the goat's head. The animal dropped, stunned, and lay in the dirt, kicking feebly.

Without thought, Janna raced towards the boy. Before he could run away, she had caught him, and she boxed his ears hard, packing all her new-found strength into the punch.

'Ow!' he shouted, wriggling and squirming in Janna's grasp. 'Let me go!'

'How dare you!' she panted. 'How dare you harm that little goat!'

'It's for our dinner.' The boy had turned sullen now. 'First finders of a dead animal gets to keep it, so Master Serlo says.'

'I'll wager Master Serlo doesn't say you can go out and kill it first!' Janna kept hold of the lad. She gave him a hard shake.

'There's no-one here to see me, 'cept you. Why should you care? Everyone does it.'

Somehow, Janna doubted it, but she wasn't prepared to debate the point with the lad. 'Then I'll tell Master Serlo what you've done. If everyone is doing it, he won't mind, will he?'

She felt the boy cower against her. He began to tremble with fright. Janna understood why when Hugh's cool voice interrupted them. 'What's happening here, boy? Why are you throwing stones at my goats?'

Janna let the child go. She stayed silent, leaving him to talk his way out of the situation as best he could. All bravado gone, he began to cry.

'Take the goats out and look after them properly, Eadwig,' Hugh said sternly. 'Be sure I will count them when you bring them in tonight. When you get home, tell your father he's to come to the manor house and bring you with him.'

The lad fled, leaving Janna alone with Hugh. She knelt to pick up the herbs she'd dropped when she'd grabbed hold of the goat's tormentor, feeling some relief as she watched the kid rise to its feet and stagger off to find its mother.

'I saw everything that happened,' Hugh said into the silence. 'I was waiting just inside the stable. I heard you shouting at Eadwig. I saw it all, Johanna.'

Janna froze.

'I'm right, aren't I?' Hugh continued softly. 'Your appearance might have changed, but your voice – and your manner – not at all!'

Janna stayed on her knees, not daring to move or say anything. Hugh put his hand underneath her elbow, and yanked her upright. 'I think you owe me an explanation,' he said, and began to propel her towards the stables. 'You can minister to Arrow while you tell me why you burnt your home to the ground and left us all to think that you were dead.'

'I did not burn my home, sire!' Janna was outraged that he could think such a thing.

He cocked his head to one side, studying her. 'The abbess is wrath, for the cottage was her property and now it is destroyed. And Godric, the villein, has told us that you died in the fire and that he has buried you in the forest. Why so many lies, Johanna, and to what purpose?' His voice lost some of its hard edge as he continued more softly, 'Was the fire an accident? You know, because I told you, that Dame Alice agreed to pay heriot to the abbess and mortuary to the priest after the death of your mother. If the fire was an accident, I doubt the abbess would hold you to blame, while the villagers would surely have helped you to rebuild your cottage and given you shelter until that was done. There was no need to flee, or to tell such lies.'

How little you know of the villagers, Janna thought, as bitter memories swelled up in her mind. She did not know what to say to Hugh, and so she stayed silent.

'In truth, I am disappointed,' he said then, as he snicked open the latch and led her into the stable. 'I had thought you more honourable, more courageous. I didn't take you for a coward, Johanna.'

'I am not a coward, sire!' Janna could stay silent no longer.

'And yet you have run from the village, and even disguised yourself as a boy to escape detection.' Hugh stalked on past a line of horses and stopped at Arrow's stall. The destrier blew a gentle greeting as Janna entered. She wondered if he remembered her. She stood awkwardly, uncertain how to make the horse lift his hoof so that she could inspect it. Hugh solved the problem by doing it for her. Janna clicked her tongue, distressed by the ugly wound which already was beginning to fester from the dung and dirt which had worked its way into the cut.

'I need boiling water and something to wrap the hoof,' she

said. 'I'll have to cleanse it first. Then I'll bind these healing herbs against the wound. You must not ride him, sire, or even take him from the stall.' She glanced down at the mud and dung on which the horse stood. 'It would be best if the horse stood on clean rushes for the while,' she added.

Hugh grunted. But he released the horse's hoof, and shouted for a stable lad to fetch what Janna needed. While they waited, he fixed his dark gaze on her once more. 'Who is Edwin? What is he to you?' he asked now.

'He's . . .' Janna was going to claim him still as her brother, but she was sure Hugh would not believe her. She decided to stick as close to the truth as she could. 'I came across him in the forest, sire, in Gravelinges. I was alone, and frightened, and he took care of me. It is true that he comes from Wales and that he has to seek his fortune after his eldest brother inherited both cot and land when his mother died.' Janna kept her fingers crossed behind her back against yet another lie. She hoped Hugh would not doubt her word as she added, 'Please believe me, sire. I did not set fire to the cottage. That was the work of the villagers, and that is why Godric seeks to protect me now.'

'The villagers burnt your home?' Hugh sounded horrified. 'Why would they do such a thing?'

'Because . . .' But even Janna's quick wits could not come up with a convincing enough story, other than telling Hugh the truth: that her mother had drunk the poisoned wine that Robert had given to Cecily, and that he knew Janna had found out his secret, which was why he'd incited the villagers to take action against her. She was sure Hugh would not believe it of his uncle-by-marriage, and so she stayed silent.

'I am sorry you did not bring your troubles to my aunt,' Hugh said, when it became clear that Janna would say no more. 'Dame Alice would have helped you, I am sure of it. She had great respect for your mother's skill, and yours too.'

'I am sorry too, sire,' Janna said softly. 'I was alone and frightened. With no home and no family, it seemed best for me to run away, and so I did.'

'You are safe now.' Hugh gave her a troubled glance. 'There is no need to disguise yourself any longer, Johanna. You could stay here and help Mistress Tova in the kitchen. I know she would be glad of an extra hand. And heaven knows we often have need of a healer for burns, and broken bones, and the pox if it comes again. You could be very useful to me, if you wish to stay.'

'I thank you for your offer, sire. Of course I am happy to help anyone in need of a healer, but I wish to stay as I am – at least as others think I am,' Janna said stiffly. She wanted to tell Hugh he was wrong; that she was no longer safe now that he knew her true identity. More than ever, she and Edwin needed to flee to Winchestre. She must talk to Edwin; they must leave that very night.

'You have nothing to fear from showing yourself as you truly are.' Hugh looked more puzzled than ever. 'In truth, your disguise does not become you.'

Janna felt a painful blush stain her face as she recalled how he'd once looked at her with admiration in his eyes. No more, not ever again. The thought stung. 'I beg you, sire.' She forced herself to look into his eyes, so he could see that she was in earnest. 'Do not allow anyone to punish the villein, Godric, for his lies. He told them for my protection,

127

just as I would ask you, sire, to keep the truth about me to yourself. I . . . I cannot explain to you why my life is in jeopardy, but I beg you to believe it, and keep my secret now if . . . if you care about my safety.'

Hugh stayed silent, still looking troubled.

'Please, sire!' In her desperation to secure his silence, Janna realised she'd grabbed hold of Hugh's arm. Quickly, she released it. 'Please, sire,' she said more quietly. 'I matter to no-one other than those who wish me harm. Please protect me with your silence.'

'Very well.' The promise was given grudgingly. It was clear Hugh was unhappy about the course Janna had urged on him. 'I know that the priest stirred up trouble against your mother, and that he might have influenced some of the villagers because of his refusal to bury her in consecrated ground,' he conceded. 'I have spoken to Dame Alice about the priest but she will not take action against him.' He stopped, and gnawed on his bottom lip. He seemed to be wondering how far he could take Janna into his confidence.

'You must understand that this is a difficult situation,' he said then. 'My aunt . . . married unwisely. Robert was her father's steward, and after her father died he wooed Alice. Being her father's only heir, and with all that property at her disposal, Alice was supposed to petition the king for permission to marry, but she was desperate to have Robert and no other. With a baby on the way, it became urgent to find someone who was prepared to wed them. This priest . . .' He broke off as the stable lad came clattering in, bearing a bucket of hot water and the bandage Janna had requested. But Hugh had said enough for Janna to understand the situation. Anger flamed anew as she reflected how worthless was the dame's husband. First, and to secure his future, he had seduced Dame Alice. Next, and for his own pleasure, he had seduced Cecily, the dame's tiring woman. Janna wondered how many others Robert had seduced – and abandoned – during his marriage.

'I want you to know that I petitioned the Abbess of Wiltune for a requiem mass to be said for your mother's soul, and for your own,' Hugh said now. 'I have to say that she was reluctant at first. It seems she knows something of your mother's past, but I managed to convince her of your worth, and so it was done.' Hugh surveyed Janna, his face grave as he added: 'Obviously a mass for the dead was not necessary on your account. I can only hope that you walk in the grace of God's blessing, and that you will continue to do so.'

'Yes, oh yes, sire, and thank you. From the bottom of my heart, I thank you for your kindness.' So he had kept his promise to her! Janna felt almost giddy with relief.

'Hmph.' Hugh looked as if he needed convincing that he'd done the right thing. 'And what are your plans for the future?'

To go in search of my father, Janna thought. But she wasn't prepared to take Hugh so fully into her confidence. 'To go to Winchestre, sire, to seek employment there.' It was part of the truth.

'With Edwin?'

'With Edwin.' Janna nodded confirmation.

'Why don't the two of you stay on here? I've already told you your worth to me, and Edwin is a good worker.'

'Thank you, sire. You are very kind.' Janna had no intention of accepting his invitation, but she wasn't going to tell

Hugh that she was proposing to run away that very night. Instead, she set to work, crushing the waxy green leaves of soapwort into hot water before bathing the wound. Hugh and the stable lad kept tight hold of the destrier so that it would not move, or kick out at Janna while she worked. She was grateful for the lad's presence, for it made further conversation difficult. Hugh had already given her much to think about, but she needed a quiet time alone to mull over what he had told her. For the moment, she concentrated on her task, feeling the great horse flinch as she set about binding its hoof, wrapping the hank of unspun wool tight to keep the healing herbs in place, and also to prevent any more dirt from entering the wound.

'Clean out this stall,' Hugh ordered, once Janna was finished and the horse was standing firmly on its feet once more. 'Then go and cut some clean rushes to lay on the ground.' As Janna made to do what she was bid, Hugh grasped her arm. 'Not you,' he said, angling his head towards the lad. 'Him.'

'I am capable of doing the work just as well, my lord, and it will go quicker with two of us.'

Janna felt a queer thrill in defying Hugh, and knew a moment's deep satisfaction when he said, with a smile quirking his mouth, 'I can see you haven't changed anything other than your clothes. You are still as independent as you were when you lived with your mother. Very well, then. Do as you wish.'

'Thank you, sire.' With difficulty, Janna kept a smirk of triumph off her face as she seized a besom and began to sweep the dung and dirt into a pile. When she next looked up, Hugh's silhouette blocked the light from the door; the next moment he had disappeared from view.

The stable lad didn't look at her as they worked together to clear Arrow's stall. Janna wondered how much of her conversation with Hugh he had heard. At least enough to let him know that Hugh regarded her so highly he'd arranged a mass to be said for her soul. Had Hugh said her name in his hearing? Janna cast her mind back over their conversation. No. With luck, the boy still thought of her as John. Perhaps he didn't trust her now. If so, she couldn't think of anything to say to make matters right, and so they filled and dumped their bucket loads in silence.

The lad went over to a row of implements then, and selected two scythes. He gave one to Janna. 'To cut the rushes,' he said shortly, and led the way out, heading down towards the river.

Looking up at the fields, Janna noticed the blackened remains of the burnt haystack. With a feeling of dread, she realised what she must do. 'Let's cut the rushes at the stream,' she said, pointing in the direction of the haystack. The stable boy frowned at her, seeming resentful that she was taking charge. 'It means we can carry the load downhill instead of uphill,' Janna pointed out.

He gave a grudging nod and changed direction. Janna followed him, veering off to the haystack as they passed. She bent to examine the ashy remains. The scene and the smell reminded her of the time she'd searched the burnt ruins of her own home, and how her search had uncovered her mother's secret cache with its clues to her father's identity, the clues she could not read and didn't know how to interpret.

Hugh's words came back to Janna. He'd said that the abbess knew something of her mother's past. Janna wondered now if, instead of fleeing in a blind panic, she should first have sought an audience with the abbess. Perhaps it was still possible? It would certainly be worth the risk of being seen by the villagers if the abbess could tell her where to begin her search for the truth about her mother – and her father. Janna pushed the thought aside for consideration later, and began her search.

She knew exactly what she was looking for and she examined everything very carefully, first the ruined remains of the haystack, then widening her search to encompass other haystacks nearby. It didn't take her long to spy it, the leaves a silvery green, the flowers a bright splotch of yellow tucked into the pale straw of a nearby haystack.

Janna snatched out the posy of rue, and ground it to shreds under her boot. Too late, she wondered if she should take Hugh into her confidence, if she should have kept it to show him or even brought him out with her to search the haystacks. Would he have believed her, or had she already stretched his trust too far?

It was too late, now, to think of it or to regret her action. Janna looked towards the stream where the stable lad was already hard at work cutting rushes for Arrow's stall. She hurried to join him. There was no sign of Edwin now, or her dinner either, Janna realised. With haymaking over, shearing had begun. The hurdles had been taken down and the animals were free to graze in the water meadows, but there was no sign of them or their keeper. She wondered where they were folded now, for it was there that shearing would be taking place and where she needed to search for Edwin if she wanted her dinner this day.

Janna was sweating, hot and filthy by the time she and the stable lad had finished cleaning out Arrow's stall and spreading armfuls of clean rushes over the bare earth floor. It seemed to her that the horse stood easier now. She knew Hugh's pride in his sleek black destrier and, having an affinity for all living creatures and in particular this one who had twice borne her on his back, she hoped that the cure was already working, and that the wound would heal without leaving any lasting harm.

With her task over, Janna hurried to the well, keen to slake her thirst. She sank the bucket down, then wound it up again. After splashing cool water over her hands to cleanse them, she cupped them and drank her fill. She was glad to get away from the sullen stable lad, glad to have a few quiet moments alone to think once more about her conversation with Hugh. She was mortified that he had recognised her, and found her out in all her lies, but she also felt an easing of her mind that she no longer had to pretend with him, that he knew the truth, or most of it at least. She hated lies; she hated deceit, and her anger flared anew at the memory of those who had made such a subterfuge necessary.

Her thoughts turned then to the abbess, who knew something about her mother. Hugh had indicated that the abbess thought badly of Eadgyth. She would also think badly of Janna once she found out that Janna was still alive, for she would believe that Janna had fled to escape the consequences once her cot had burned down. Was it worth braving the abbess's wrath in the hope she would relent enough to tell Janna what she knew?

With her thirst quenched, Janna sat for a few moments beside the well to rest and ponder the question, leaning her back against the rough stone wall with a weary sigh. But the shocks of the day were not yet over.

'Hello! My name's Hamo. What's yours?' A child's voice jerked her out of her reverie. She sat upright with a gasp, feeling giddy and disorientated. This had happened once before. Was she dreaming now, or was it happening all over again? She blinked as a little boy's bright face came into focus. She recognised him. Just so had he introduced himself to her at the manor house at Babestoche. She looked about her, recognising her surroundings as Hugh's manor farm, and breathed a faint sigh of relief that her mind wasn't playing tricks on her. But what was Hamo doing here?

He held tight to a piece of rope attached to a mangy dog. All skin and bones, with matted fur, it now limped over to sniff around Janna's toes. She backed away, her alarm increasing as she took in Hamo's companions with a quick glance.

They were just coming through the gate. There was no sign of Hamo's elderly and disapproving nurse. In her place, and still some distance away, came Cecily and . . . Godric? Janna blinked and peered more closely. Yes, there was no mistake. It seemed that Hamo had found himself a new nurse, as well as a guide to bring him through the forest. With an effort, she brought her attention back to the boy's questioning gaze.

'I know you,' he announced firmly, and then more questioningly, 'aren't you . . .?'

'My name is John,' Janna said gruffly, too alarmed by his unexpected arrival to worry about being rude and interrupting

134

the young lord of the manor. Her alarm increased as she noted Cecily's steps quicken to protect her charge. Cecily knew that Janna hadn't died in the fire, but Janna had sworn her to secrecy. Would she keep the secret even now?

And Godric, how could she face him? He had protected her so loyally, but he didn't know the truth for she'd stayed hidden when he came looking for her. She hadn't wanted him to see her, arguing to herself that she couldn't afford to become involved with him, or feel beholden to him, for he was tied to the manor whereas she was free to go – to run for her life, as it turned out. Her decision had seemed sensible at the time but now she could feel only shame at her mean spirit and lack of trust in not showing herself when he'd called her.

'My name is John,' she said again more firmly, and jumped to her feet, desperate to escape before anyone could challenge her identity. She'd forgotten about the dog. Startled by her sudden movement, it sank its teeth into her ankle and hung on, growling. The pain was sharp as a cut from a sword, and Janna stopped with a cry. 'Get your dog off me, Hamo,' she ordered.

'Bones!' Hamo dropped the rope. He tried to prise the dog's teeth apart, but it growled and sank them deeper.

'Be careful! Mind he doesn't bite you,' Janna said, automatically protective.

'Godric will help. He brought us through the forest and he found Bones. He'll know what to do.' And before Janna had a chance to protest, Hamo turned and shouted the villein's name. There was nothing else for Janna to do then, but wait for the shame of discovery.

'Bones! Let go!' Godric arrived in a burst of speed. He hardly looked at Janna. All his attention was on the dog as he bent and firmly prised open its jaw.

Janna felt the teeth withdraw, and wondered if she still had time to make a run for it. But Hamo had grabbed hold of her hand. 'This is John,' he said gravely, holding on tight. She had no choice but to stand still and face Godric.

'Thank you for getting the dog off me,' she said faintly.

His eyes widened. He said nothing, but he went pale. Janna knew she would never forget the look on his face as he studied her intently. Confusion gave way to elation, which immediately darkened into anger and utter rejection. His face closed into a bitter scowl, and he turned away. Cecily had reached them now, and she took in the situation in one quick glance. 'Janna! What are you doing here?'

Godric still said nothing. Janna wanted to find the words to reach him, to make him understand why she'd acted as she had, and to tell him what was in her heart. She tried, but she couldn't think of anything to say that might make the situation any easier. Stricken mute, she looked down at the ground.

'Janna?' Hamo queried.

'There you are, John! I've brought your dinner.' Edwin had come dashing into the yard, and he hailed Janna as soon as he spied her. As he noticed the still tableau beside the well, his footsteps slowed. He held out the sack of food to Janna as he advanced towards them.

With a muttered exclamation, Godric pushed past them all and headed towards the gate, moving at speed. 'Godric! Wait!' Janna said urgently. 'I can explain . . .' But he ignored her plea and increased his pace. The dog took off after him, moving as quickly as its maimed paws would allow.

'Bones! Come back!' Hamo made an effort to grab hold of the rope trailing behind his pet, but Cecily grasped him and hauled him back. 'You must stay with me, Hamo,' she said firmly, and looked at Edwin.

'Who is he?' she asked Janna.

A short silence followed Cecily's question, before Edwin cheerfully gave her his name. 'I am John's elder brother, mistress,' he added by way of explanation, and sketched a bow. Still no-one said anything, Janna because she was incapable of speech and Cecily because she was utterly confused. Edwin's worried glance moved between them both, and then he looked after Godric's disappearing figure. His frown deepened.

Cecily's glance followed his. 'Over here, sire!' She hailed a couple of strangers who were just coming through the gate. Seemingly Godric had guided the men through the forest along with Hamo and Cecily, for one of them put a hand on Godric's arm to restrain him. The other fumbled a coin from his purse but by the time he held it out, Godric had pushed past the pair and was gone.

In answer to Cecily's call they surrendered their mounts, including several heavily laden sumpter horses, to the waiting groom and paused to give instructions. As the groom led the horses away, Janna noticed that one of them had cast a shoe and was walking awkwardly.

'Shearing's started. I have to get back,' Edwin said hurriedly. 'You'd better come too, John, or you'll feel the sharp edge of Serlo's tongue.' He thrust the sack at Janna and disappeared around the side of the barn.

'John? Doesn't he know who you really are?' Cecily turned to Janna to clear up the mystery.

Janna sighed. 'Yes, of course he does. And so does my lord Hugh.' At the mention of Hugh's name, Cecily gave Janna a questioning glance, but she didn't say anything. 'I met Edwin while I was lost in Gravelinges,' Janna continued. 'He . . .' She was about to tell Cecily the truth of what had happened, but stopped herself in time. This was Edwin's secret, not hers, and his safety depended on her keeping it. 'He's from Wales and we're going to seek work in Winchestre,' Janna said instead, wishing there was no need to lie to Cecily, or anyone else. She was sick of telling lies, sick of having to hide the truth. 'We decided to travel together but, by greatest misfortune, we found work and shelter on this farm not knowing that it belongs to the lord Hugh.'

'To Dame Alice,' Cecily corrected Janna.

'But he manages the demesne for his aunt.'

'Yes, that is why we are here.' Cecily nodded thoughtfully. 'After my lord left Babestoche, Hamo fretted so much that Dame Alice decided to let him come here for a short visit.'

'How is ma dame? Is she quite recovered from . . .' Janna wasn't sure how to phrase the question delicately, but Cecily answered readily enough.

'In truth, ma dame still grieves over the death of her infant son. She is low in spirits and in health. She told me it would relieve her mind greatly to think that Hamo is here and happy with my lord Hugh.'

Janna surveyed the tiring woman, thinking it also a shrewd move on Dame Alice's part to remove Cecily from her husband's influence. Too much harm had already resulted from Robert's untoward interest in Cecily. Janna wondered how much Dame Alice suspected about their past liaison.

Cecily caught her hand. 'I know I said I would stay and watch out for ma dame,' she whispered, 'but I had no choice when she asked me to accompany Hamo. His own nurse is too old to make the journey and besides, Dame Alice believes Hamo needs someone closer to his own age to take care of him and amuse him.'

'I shouldn't worry about ma dame's safety,' Janna consoled her. 'That is, unless Robert has turned his affection to another young woman in your household?'

'No.' Cecily gave Janna a rueful smile. 'I think he has learned his lesson – as have I.'

'Then Dame Alice is in no danger. In fact, Robert will be trying to convince her that he has always had her best interests in his heart.'

'Pray God that you are right.' Cecily turned from Janna then, and swept a low curtsy. 'My lord,' she said hastily, greeting the two strangers who were now almost upon them. 'I hope you are not too weary after your journey? If you will come with me, I will take you to meet the lord Hugh, Dame Alice's nephew.' She turned abruptly away from Janna, at a loss to explain her earnest conversation with a lowly farmhand.

Janna came to her rescue. 'I'll see about finding the dog, mistress. And the young lord.'

'Hamo?' Cecily's hand came to her mouth. 'I didn't see him go! Where is he?'

'I'll set off in search of him right now, mistress.'

Leaving Cecily to take care of Hugh's visitors, Janna prepared to search the manor grounds, bringing with her the

sack of food that Edwin had thrust at her. She was hungry
and so, she was willing to wager, were the dog and its master.
If shouting didn't bring them into view, a sack of food well
might.

EIGHT

'HAMO! HAMO, WHERE are you?' Janna had searched the kitchen garden and orchard, as well as the undercroft and all the barns, workshops and other buildings that made up the manor's demesne. She'd even gone upstairs to peek unobtrusively into the hall, to make sure that he was not among the throng gathered around Hugh. Gytha was up there, she noted, with an instant pang of envy as she saw the beauty circulating among the guests, pouring wine into goblets and offering platters of food.

Hamo was nowhere to be seen, and Janna was growing anxious. The manor was close to stream and river. Could Hamo swim? She hurried downstairs and peered first into the well. 'Hamo?' she shouted, and listened to her voice echoing downwards. There was no reply. Wasting no time, she rushed out through the gates to check the manor's fish pool, but there was no sign of a child, drowning or otherwise. Janna's anxiety increased as she looked down over the stubbled water meadows to the swiftly flowing river beyond. Although it was quite shallow, the fast current could turn into whirlpools in the deep holes that pockmarked the riverbed. Even more dangerous was the water mill further downriver. Its great wheel churned in a thunder of foam with the force of the water channelled into it. She looked upstream towards the water-logged marsh, which was equally dangerous to a child who couldn't swim. Beyond the river and straight ahead was the solid green wall of the forest of Gravelinges. Might Hamo have crossed the river in safety at the ford, and be on his way home to his mother?

No, she thought, remembering Cecily's words. He'd pined at home; he wanted to visit his cousin Hugh. So why, then, had he run away?

She remembered the lame and mangy dog. Hamo seemed to have adopted it as a pet, and yet it had run after Godric when he left the manor. Had Hamo slipped away to find it? And if so, where might he have gone? She turned in a circle, trying to spot any signs of the boy and his dog. Behind the manor spread the fields, basking gold and green in the hot afternoon sun. The sounds of frightened baaing and bleating gave direction to the shearers, but there was no sign of Godric, or the dog. Would he go straight home? Had Hamo followed them into the forest? She shielded her eyes and peered across the water meadows once more, in case she could see anyone walking towards the forest. The thought of Hamo lost and alone gave her the shudders, until a new horror forced itself into her consciousness. Now she stood, icy cold in spite of the heat, and shaking with dread. Hamo's disappearance. Was this the next disaster to befall Hugh's manor? If so, whoever was behind what was happening must either have had advance warning that the party was arriving today, or have acted on impulse and with lightning speed to take advantage of Hamo's unexpected appearance. How likely was that? Fighting anxiety, Janna cast about for any signs of movement.

A couple of swans, followed by a line of fluffy grey-brown cygnets, paddled majestically upriver, labouring against the current that dragged them down towards the mill. There was no sign of any other living thing either in the water or beside it, but Janna couldn't see very much of the river's path for it was shrouded by trees. She forced herself to stand quietly, to think things through. There was no point in alarming herself needlessly, or rushing about looking in all the wrong places, she decided. Better, surely, to think of the most logical explanation for Hamo's absence: that he'd gone in pursuit of the stray dog, and Godric.

It was a hot day. Godric and his party would have had a long walk through the forest, might even have spent the night there. Neither Godric nor Hamo had taken water from the well to drink, or any food, so they would be thirsty and probably hungry too. Where might Godric or Hamo have gone for refreshment?

The river, Janna decided. Upstream or downstream? She shrugged. She had no idea, but there was no time to waste in indecision, not if she wanted to catch up with the pair.

'Hamo?' she shouted, as she hurried down towards the ford. 'Godric?' If Hamo was with Godric, why had he not brought the boy back to the manor? Her pace increased. If Hamo hadn't found Godric, he could be in the most deadly danger. 'Hamo!' she shouted. 'Where are you?'

A faint cry answered her, and she felt a momentary relief until she realised it was Godric's voice she could hear, not Hamo's. She couldn't see him, but his voice had come from the dense thicket of brambles and trees that lined the river's path upstream.

'Godric!' She broke into a run, the quicker to reach him. 'Hamo's lost,' she bellowed. 'Please, please help me look for him!' She pushed her way through trees and bushes, only to find her way barred by the mangy dog, which snarled and bared his teeth. 'Get out of my way!' Janna was too worried to be afraid. She aimed a kick in the dog's direction, and it backed off, barking furiously. 'Godric!' He'd been up to some illegal fishing, she realised, as she spotted a flash of silver on the river bank behind him.

'Where is he? Where's Hamo?' He'd come running, forgetting to hide the evidence of his poaching in his anxiety over the boy.

'I don't know. I thought he might be looking for you and the dog.'

'Bones.' Godric gave the dog a disgusted glance. 'Look at it! I tried to leave it behind, but the stupid thing kept following me.'

Even though the dog had given her grief, Janna thought Godric was being a little harsh. That the dog was in pain from its paws was evident. The dog had been lawed to conform to the harsh forest laws. Three claws had been cut off to the knuckle on each forepaw so that the cur could not chase after the king's game, but not enough care had been taken. Its paws were bloody, and full of pus. The dog was also half-starved, reasons enough for its antisocial behaviour. But Janna had no time for Bones now. Her anxiety overrode even the awkwardness she felt being face to face with Godric as she quickly explained the situation to him.

'You go on upriver and I'll go down towards the mill,' he said at once. 'Keep calling. If either one of us finds him, we must go in search of the other.' He glanced up at the sun. 'If neither of us finds him by the time the sun touches the tree line over there, we should retrace our steps and meet back here so that we can get back to the manor before it gets too dark to see.'

Janna nodded agreement, greatly relieved that he was prepared to help her search and that there were no recriminations – at least, not yet. 'Hamo!' Godric had already started off, following the river downstream. The dog limped behind him. Janna hastened off towards the marsh, also calling Hamo's name. Along the way, and just to be on the safe side, she quickly kicked Godric's illicit catch back into the river.

She hadn't gone far when she heard a shout. 'He's here!' Immediately she turned and raced downstream in the direction Godric had taken. After a few moments, she saw him. Her body went cold with shock as she saw that he carried the limp and dripping body of Hamo.

Pray he isn't dead, she thought, as she rushed up to Godric and fell into step beside him. He was striding up towards the manor, bearing his burden at the greatest speed he could muster. The boy was blue around the lips, and he hung lifeless in Godric's arms. Janna fought down her rising panic. She couldn't bear the thought that after all, they had come too late to help Hamo. There was a bloody gash across his forehead, but Janna noticed one of his eyelids twitch and felt a huge surge of relief.

She cast her mind back into the past, to a time when she and her mother had passed two villeins arguing over possession of a pig. As they'd passed by on their way to market, the argument had escalated over whose pig it was to sell. Punches were thrown, and finally one of the villeins pushed the other into the river. Hearing his cry, Eadgyth had turned and run back to aid the culprit rescue his victim, but the man was lifeless by the time they managed to get him out of the water. Janna remembered what her mother had done. 'Put Hamo down!' she told Godric.

'We have to get him back to the manor house.' Godric's pace didn't check.

'Put him down! On his stomach.' Janna grabbed hold of Godric's arm and dragged on him to make him do as she asked. 'We have to push the water out of his chest.'

Reluctantly, Godric laid Hamo down on a bed of soft grass. Janna turned his head to one side, then straddled the boy's back and pressed down hard. A gush of water erupted from Hamo's mouth. She lifted his arms to give him a chance to breathe in, then pressed down once more. She kept pushing and lifting until at last the boy began to cough and splutter. He took in a great whoop of air, and began to breathe on his own. But he was incapable of speech, so Janna turned to Godric. 'Where did you find him? What happened to him?'

'He was in the river, lying face down. Drowning.'

'I can see that,' she said impatiently. 'I mean, was anyone else there with him, anyone at all?'

'No.' Godric looked puzzled. 'Only me. If you hadn't sounded the alarm, if we hadn't gone after him, he would have died. It's lucky we found him in time.'

'How did it happen? Can you tell?'

Godric shrugged. 'He must have slipped and fallen into the river.'

'What about that wound on his forehead? Do you think he might first have been hit over the head and then pushed?'

'Why should anyone want to do that?' Godric squatted beside Janna, who had her arm around Hamo now and was helping him to sit up. 'What's going on? Why are you asking me these questions?'

'I can't tell you.' Janna wasn't done yet. She had one final question, but she dreaded hearing the answer.

'Did you notice any rue nearby? I mean a posy picked, not rue growing wild?'

'No. But I wasn't looking for anything like that.' Godric lifted a questioning eyebrow. 'Why should there be a posy of rue lying about?'

'It's for regret. Repentance.'

'I wish you'd explain yourself, Janna.' Godric lifted the boy into his arms once more. 'But I know that you don't care to explain anything to me, anything at all.' His tone was bitter as he strode off in the direction of the manor house, leaving Janna to scurry after him.

A great cry went up as they came inside the gate. It was clear Cecily had confessed to losing Hamo, for everyone came running from all directions to welcome them back. Hugh was at the forefront of the crowd. As Godric made to hand Hamo over to his cousin, Hamo wriggled free. 'I can walk by myself,' he announced with dignity, and bent to pat the mangy dog that had followed them in.

'What happened, Hamo?' Hugh asked the question that Janna most feared.

'Nothing.' The boy looked up, all injured innocence now.

'Tell me!' Hugh folded his arms and waited, hiding his concern with an appearance of exasperation.

'I . . . I wanted to find Bones.' Hamo made to take the dog in his arms but it bared its teeth and whined softly. Hamo backed off.

'I'm afraid the dog followed me when I left the manor, sire,' Godric admitted.

Hamo shot him a grateful glance. 'I saw Godric going towards the river. He didn't know I was following him,' he added, determined that Godric shouldn't get any blame for what had happened. 'When I got there I couldn't see him, or Bones, but I guessed he went downriver and that's where I went. But Godric must have gone the other way.'

Janna waited somewhat anxiously for Hugh to ask why Godric had gone up the river at all instead of crossing the ford and heading for home.

'What happened to you? Why are you so wet?' Fortunately for Godric, Hugh was much more interested in Hamo.

Hamo shrugged. 'I followed the path of the river a little way. I thought Bones might have fallen in but I couldn't see through all the reeds so I came close to the edge to have a look and . . . and I slipped and fell.' He touched the gash across his forehead, and winced when he saw the blood on his fingers. 'I s'pose I must have hit my head.'

It was possible Hamo's admission gave his dignity even more of a battering than his head and clothes had taken in the river, Janna thought. She heaved a deep sigh of relief as his words sank into her understanding. An accident, no more than that. 'Godric saved me.' Hamo looked at Janna. 'And also . . .'

'John,' Janna said firmly, before Hamo could say her name in front of everyone.

'And I thank you for it.' Hugh gave Janna a searching glance, then took Hamo by the hand. 'A hot bath for you, young man. Mistress Cecily!' He beckoned her forward, then turned to Godric. 'I'd like a word with you too,' he said, and hurried off. Godric exchanged an anxious glance with Cecily as they followed Hugh. 'I'll make up an ointment to put on the young lord's cuts and bruises,' Janna called after them, resolving to use some of the ointment to treat her ankle, where the dog's teeth had left their mark. Cecily lifted her hand to show that she'd heard, and kept on going. Ignored and forgotten, the dog trailed them up the stairs and into the hall.

With the drama over, the rest of the crowd began to disperse, the two visitors among them. Janna watched them leave. She wondered who they were and why they were visiting the manor. One was finely dressed. His tunic was richly embroidered and his boots were made of good leather, though scratched and stained with mud and muck. The journey through the forest had left its mark. His companion was more plainly dressed, and walked a pace or two behind his master. She looked about for Edwin to ask him who the lordling was. He was always quick to hear the gossip from the kitchen staff. There was no sign of him, but Gytha was still lingering, and as she caught Janna's glance, she smiled and came over.

'That boy will be in trouble for running away,' she observed, and wrinkled her nose. 'I hope he doesn't expect us to find shelter for that smelly, flea-bitten bag of bones he's found.'

Janna hid a smile. She was quite sure that Hamo had every intention of keeping his pet. She was also quite sure that the boy would prove more than a match for Gytha when it came to getting his own way. 'We have visitors, I see,' she responded.

'Master Siward and his manservant. They go to the great fairs to buy and to sell for their lord, but one of their horses is lame so they must break their journey here for a while.' Gytha shrugged, clearly uninterested.

'And have they travelled far?'

'They come from somewhere in the west.' Gytha yawned, and then brightened as a more interesting subject came into her mind. 'Master Siward paid me a great deal of attention when I served the wine and cakes. I do believe my lord Hugh was quite put out by his interest.' She gave a self-satisfied giggle. Janna wanted to hit her, but turned away instead, telling herself that her jealousy was unworthy. The girl was beautiful, and if Hugh wanted a dalliance with her it was none of Janna's business.

She remembered her promise to Cecily, and turned her steps towards the kitchen garden. Pangs of hunger reminded her that she'd dropped the sack containing her dinner while she'd tried to resuscitate Hamo. Should she go after it? She sighted the angle of the sun slanting across the downs. No, it would take too long. She would just have to go hungry. The thought contributed to Janna's misery as she bent to pluck the herbs she needed for the healing ointment.

She was on her way to the kitchen when Godric found her. 'I was going to leave without seeing you again,' he said curtly, 'but I thought you should know, Janna, that your running away has brought ill to my family, to my manor and to the village. I told a lie to Dame Alice and my liege lord, Robert of Babestoche. I told them that you were dead.'

Janna cast a quick glance around, making sure that no-one could hear their conversation. 'I know, Godric, and I am grateful to you, more grateful than I can say.'

'But I have been sore punished for the lie.' Godric spoke over her thanks. 'The priest has claimed mortuary from me, payment I cannot afford, and –'

'But why? Why claim mortuary from you?'

'Because I said that I had buried you in the forest, and because he claims that we were betrothed. He has taken my best goat in payment, even though the abbess has asked nothing from me. Nor has Dame Alice or anyone else. I told the priest he was mistaken about us, but he will not believe me.' There was such a depth of bitterness in Godric's voice that Janna couldn't bear it.

'I'm so sorry.' She put her hand on Godric's arm, but he shook it off and pulled away from her.

'That's not the worst of it,' he said. 'My mother took ill and died. There was no one to physic her as your mother did last time she had an attack and couldn't breathe properly. By running away, you've left the village without a healer, Janna.'

'I . . . but they drove me out!' Janna spluttered. Surely Godric knew that the villagers had burned her cottage down, that she'd had no choice but to flee?

'Everyone mourns your death.' He spoke sincerely.

'Everyone?' Janna's voice raised in anger. 'The villagers set fire to my cottage, Godric. They didn't care if I burned along with it. That's why I ran away. That's why I didn't dare show myself even to you!'

He glanced sharply at her. 'You should have trusted me,' he muttered.

Janna knew that he was right, but still she tried to justify her actions. 'I had to go! Don't you see, it wasn't safe for me to stay. I thought if I . . . That is, I didn't want . . .'

'. . . to see me. I know. You've already made that quite clear in the past.' Godric's mouth clamped down in a tight, hard line. Without saying goodbye, he turned and strode off towards the gate of the manor.

'I'm sorry about your mother. I'm so sorry, Godric,' Janna called after him. But he walked on, not acknowledging that he'd heard her words, or that he'd forgiven her.

There was still no sign of Edwin when at last, weary and hungry, Janna went to her bed. Although she felt concern, she told herself that Edwin was free to come and go about the manor as he pleased. What crowded into Janna's mind now were the events of the day. So much had happened to trouble and distress her. She felt great anger and impatience that she couldn't explain to Hugh, Godric and Cecily why she'd acted as she had, and great shame as she realised how they must view her now.

'It's not fair!' she muttered rebelliously as she turned and turned again, trying to get comfortable on her prickly straw pallet.

Restless, impatient for action, she lay and listened to the night noises, the snarks and snorts and mumbles of the sleepers. She had planned to leave the manor this very night. In the absence of Edwin, should she now go on her own? Yes, she thought, and half-rose from her bed. She subsided again as more careful thought advised against it. While she wanted most desperately to run away from Hugh, caution told her that she would do better to wait until Edwin could go with her. Alone, she was vulnerable, even if she was dressed as a boy. Edwin's presence, and their fabricated family history, would protect them both.

Janna passed an uneasy night. The faint light that heralded the dawn found her wakeful and anxious to rise. She scrubbed at her face with her hands and smoothed back her hair, feeling again its silky growth since the fire. She slipped quietly from her bed and pulled her knife from its sheath. She tested its edge with a cautious finger, and frowned. Then she remembered the great whetstone outside the black-smith's shop, left in position for the villeins to sharpen their scythes while haymaking. She was bent over the whetstone with her knife when Bertha walked past, carrying a small sack. Janna greeted her cheerfully.

Bertha stopped short, looking startled. 'What are you doing out here so early, John?' she asked, not returning Janna's greeting.

'Sharpening my knife.' Janna wondered if she could take advantage of Bertha's good nature. 'Are you any good at cutting hair? Will you cut mine?'

Bertha's attention came full onto Janna then. She hesi-tated. 'Does it have to be done now?'

Janna nodded. 'Yes, if you please, mistress.' She didn't want to delay, and the alternative was to cut her hair herself. Without being able to see anything, she knew she'd make an awful job of it.

Bertha sighed. She dropped the sack she was carrying and held out her hand for Janna's knife, while Janna settled herself down on the stone block within easy reach of Bertha's hands.

'How does your family, mistress?' she asked, to make conversation while Bertha set about hacking at her hair. She tried not to wince as snippets fell about her feet, curled round like small golden snails.

'What?'

'Your family. Are they well?' Janna wondered what pre-occupied Bertha, and why she was abroad so early. The sun had not yet arisen. Mist shrouded the cots and turned trees into many-armed ghosts in the pearly light.

'Yes, my family are well, thank you. And you? Are you well?'

'Yes, I thank you.' There seemed no more to say on that topic. What else could they talk about to pass the time? Janna's thoughts turned to the missing Edwin. 'I wonder if you've seen my brother at all, mistress? He was not in his bed last night, and I'm wondering what has become of him?'

'Edwin?' The knife slipped in Bertha's hand, nicking Janna's scalp. Janna stifled a cry. She shifted uneasily on her stone seat, wondering at Bertha's clumsiness. 'No, I haven't seen him,' Bertha continued snappily. 'Why should you think I have?'

'No reason,' Janna said hastily. 'I'm concerned about him, that's all.'

'I expect he'll turn up soon enough. There!' Bertha slapped Janna's shoulders in a hasty dust-up, sending bits of hair scattering in all directions. 'You look like a boy again, John.'

And what did Bertha mean by that last remark, Janna wondered. Had her disguise worn thin, or had Edwin told her the truth about both of them? Was that why she seemed so anxious for Janna to be gone?

No. Janna dismissed the notion. Edwin's truth was too dangerous to be told. She was just imagining the worst.

'Thank you, mistress,' she said. As she walked past the last of the little cottages towards the manor, she looked back, curious to know where Bertha might be going, but the carpenter's daughter had already vanished. Hunger drove Janna on to the kitchen, and also the hope that she might find Edwin there, ravenous after his night out and ready to break his fast. She had to jump sideways to avoid the sharp teeth of Bones, who was tethered nearby, before she could enter the door.

'So there you are,' Mistress Tova greeted her. 'And where is your brother?'

'I know not, mistress. I thought he might be here, having something to eat.'

'I haven't seen him since yesterday afternoon.' The cook poked her long nose into the air, and sniffed.

Janna tried to hide her disquiet by stuffing a hunk of bread into her mouth and chewing vigorously, before washing down the mouthful with a gulp of ale. Once her appetite was satisfied, however, she took the chance to question the rest of the kitchen staff. To her alarm, no-one had seen Edwin.

'Run away and left you to face Serlo alone, most like. I always knew he was no good.' The cook dusted her floured hands down her apron before adding a final word. 'Just wonder what he's taken with him,' she muttered darkly.

'Nothing! He's as honest as I am!' Even as Janna leapt to Edwin's defence she remembered how he'd tried to steal her purse. She also remembered all the lies she and Edwin had told. 'Master Serlo has probably found work for him to do elsewhere about the manor that's keeping him busy,' she said, conscious of the rising tide of heat that coloured her face with shame. Yet she had to defend Edwin, and herself, lest the burning of the haystack was laid upon their shoulders, along with the other disasters that had happened recently.

Mistress Tova sniffed again. 'Master Serlo will keep good watch over your brother. He won't be able to cause any more trouble while the reeve is there.'

Janna knew what she was thinking, what everyone was probably thinking. She was about to tell the cook off for spreading malicious lies, but stopped herself in time. In the past her hasty words had often caused her trouble, but she was learning from bitter experience to put a guard on her tongue, to think before she spoke.

'Master Serlo is a good reeve,' she agreed instead. 'And a good catch for any girl – even if Mistress Gytha doesn't want him for a husband,' she added, hoping to divert the cook from her suspicions.

The cook shot her a sharp glance. Janna tried to look demure, but her eyes twinkled with mischief. ''Tis true,' Mistress Tova acknowledged grudgingly. 'My lord certainly knows Serlo's worth, for he treats him well. Serlo has a good-sized cottage, and he was given the gore acres to cultivate for himself. I've seen the cartloads of goods that Serlo takes to the big fairs, his own bounty as well as my lord's, and good quality, all of it. Fetches a good price too, I'll be bound.' The cook tapped a bony finger against her long nose. 'There'll be no shortage of pretty girls waiting in line when he decides to take a wife. Of course, he'd marry Gytha tomorrow, if she would only have him. I've told her she could do a lot worse for herself than marry Serlo, for once young Hamo comes of age . . .'

She shrugged thin shoulders, leaving unsaid her wish that her daughter would secure her future with the reeve rather than trying to seduce the reeve's master who, at the end of the day, might be left with nothing. Janna wondered whether to encourage the cook to urge her daughter to see sense, but decided it was wiser to keep out of their affairs. Instead, she thanked the cook for the sack of dinner she'd provided, and asked after Hamo.

'Staying in his bed today, at Mistress Cecily's insistence, but there's nothing wrong with his appetite.' The cook's words set Janna's mind at rest that Hamo was none the worse for his ducking. She remembered the tethered dog beside the kitchen door.

'And Bones?' she asked. 'What is to become of the dog?'

The cook scowled, and jerked a floury thumb over her shoulder. 'I'm to give it vittles and water.' Janna saw a bright eye peer hopefully around the doorway at them.

'If the young lord is to keep his pet, then I'd like to put some medicament on its paws,' Janna said. 'Hopefully, the cur's temper will improve once it is out of pain.'

'Get the skivvy to muzzle it,' the cook advised. 'It'll have a piece of your breeches, otherwise.'

Janna laughed. 'I know all about that,' she said cheerfully, and put down the sack of food while she went off to pluck some herbs.

Her hands stank from the juice of ragwort as she brewed a lotion with sanicle to put on the dog's paws. Conscious that time was passing, but feeling slightly guilty that she was getting out of the difficult part of the treatment, she gave some of the astringent mixture to the skivvy with instructions to first cleanse the dog's paws and then wrap them tight to protect them from becoming dirty and infected once more. 'Keep Bones tied up and out of trouble,' she said, adding, 'and get someone to hold the dog's jaw tight so he won't bite you.' Ignoring the skivvy's horrified expression, she gathered up a fresh paste of healing herbs for the big, black destrier that awaited her in the stable.

She was pleased to find no sign of Hugh, while his mount seemed much better. She summoned the surly stable lad to hold up the hoof while she unwound the bandage to check. The wound was healing nicely, and she felt a sense of satisfaction as she washed it with lotion and applied the new paste. Human or animal, it mattered not who or what she treated so long as she could heal them, she thought, as she bound up the horse's hoof once more.

Bright sunshine had burnt away the early morning mist. Janna emerged from the dimness of the stables and stood blinking in the sunlight. Shearing was still underway and she knew she should go down to the fold to help, but for a moment she lingered, enjoying a moment's rest in the warmth of the sun.

A flock of geese disturbed her reverie. Honking and hissing, they swarmed around her. Janna drew back, alarmed by the close proximity of the big birds with their sharp, serrated bills. The harassed goosegirl flapped her arms and shouted at them, doing her best to round them up and drive them on through the manor gate and down into the stubbled water meadows to feast on frogs and grasshoppers. Janna kept quite still until they had moved on before following them through the gate.

Her path to the sheepfold took her past the young goatherd. She was surprised he was still in charge of the little flock but then noticed how subdued he looked. Even if Hugh hadn't taken a switch to the boy, his father probably had. In fact, the boy might have had a beating from both of them. Janna felt a little sorry for the lad. It was clear that he'd learned a hard lesson from it all. She gave him a smile as she walked past, and earned a scowl in return.

Dogs yipped and barked as they circled the sheep penned into the fold. All was chaos and confusion. Frightened lambs and sheep baaed in protest as they were caught and thrown to the ground, while the villeins cursed as they fought to hold them still long enough to bind their feet so that they could be shorn. The shearers also cursed the struggling sheep, and tried not to nick the animals' skin as they clipped the wool with heavy, one-handed shears, for the skin could be used as vellum for writing on and was therefore valuable. Excited children laughed and ran about and got in everyone's way, harried by the irate shepherd who was trying to bring some order to the proceedings. Janna looked around, without much hope, for Edwin, but there was no sign of him.

Undecided what she should do, and whether she had the strength to wrestle even one sheep to the ground, she looked to the shepherd for guidance. He surveyed her with a critical expression, obviously sharing her doubts. 'You, John,' he said. ''Tis said you have the healing touch. Some of my flock have fly sores. They're over there.' He jerked a thumb at a small fold which had been hastily erected out of hurdles roped together. It was packed with shorn and shivering sheep. 'Get one of the children to help you.' He beckoned Urk to come forward. The boy smiled happily at Janna, pleased to be singled out for such an important task.

'Take each sheep out of the pen and bathe the sores with that mixture.' The shepherd waved a hand towards a large wooden trough propped beside the fold. It was full of a yellow liquid. Janna sniffed the air, picking up what she'd missed before among the stink of animal dung and dust: the distinctive stench of ragwort.

She nodded and let herself into the small fold, followed by Urk. Sheep pressed around her, baaing lustily and pushing at her from all sides. Urk grabbed hold of a ewe and marched it out and over to the trough. He looked at Janna, awaiting instructions.

'Well done, Gabriel.' She hastily followed him out of the fold. 'I'll bathe its sores if you'll stay in the pen and bring the sheep out one by one?'

The boy nodded acceptance and handed over his charge. Janna held onto the ewe by its horns. After a moment's thought she picked up the handful of wool that stood next to the trough and dipped it in, wrinkling her nose at the stink as the liquid swirled about. There were a few nicks and smears of blood on the animal's skin. Janna bathed them first to get rid of the flies which were already harassing it. Wincing at the sight of the ulcerated flesh on its nether regions, Janna gave the sores a thorough wash. The stinking ragwort would cleanse them and kill any maggots, but she thought she detected also the aromatic tang of tansy to repel the flies that had caused the problem in the first place.

Urk had been watching and, as Janna finished her ministrations, he dragged another ailing sheep out of the small fold and handed it to Janna in exchange for the ewe.

'You can take that one back to the big pen, then bring me another,' Janna told him. 'And thank you, Gabriel. You're being a great help.'

One by one, the sheep were washed and released into the fold, under the watchful eye of the shepherd, who moved about, supervising his flock. Janna was hot, tired and sweaty by the time the last sheep was bathed. Urk came out of the fold to take the animal from her, but it broke free before he was close enough to clutch hold of it. With the alluring prospect of rich grazing in the water meadows ahead, the ewe bumped past Janna and set off at speed, followed by Urk in hot pursuit.

Knocked off balance, Janna fell against the edge of the wooden trough. It tipped, splashing its contents over her smock and breeches. Janna surveyed the damage in dismay. Her clothes were filthy, and she stank. She saw that Urk had managed to capture the absconding animal and was bringing it back to shut in with all the other sheep. Her task was over. She looked towards the cool, flowing river, and got to her feet.

'By your leave, I'm going to rinse this stinking mixture off my smock,' she told the shepherd. Not giving him a chance to argue, she hurried on down to the water. She untied her girdle and laid it and her purse on the river bank before leaning over to wash the stain from her smock. She sneaked a quick look around to see if anyone was paying attention then leaned further until she overbalanced into the river. The shock of the icy water on her hot skin took her breath away for several long moments. Recollecting her purpose, she began an opportunistic floundering, determined to make the most of this chance to give herself and her clothes a hasty rinse. She also took a long drink of water, relishing its coldness as it slipped down her dry throat. Finally, she regained her footing and emerged from the river. She made her way towards the place she'd dropped her belongings, wringing the water from the front of her smock as she walked.

The last of the sheep were being tied and shorn, while other villeins carried the fleeces back to the manor. There, women were already combing the fleeces smooth with the dried heads of teasels, which were prickly as hedgehogs. The best fleeces would be sold at the annual fair at Wiltune. Janna had been to the fair once, and still remembered the excitement of it all. It was the high mark of the year, both because it was a holy time to commemorate the death of St Edith, but also because merchants and travellers came from miles around to sell their wares.

Revelling in her clean skin and clean clothes, Janna picked up her girdle and purse and tied them safely around her waist.

'Where is your brother, John?'

Janna jumped. She hadn't noticed Serlo's approach. His gaze rested quizzically on her wet smock. She quickly crossed her arms over her chest lest he see the shape of her breasts mounded beneath the fabric. 'He must be working elsewhere about the manor, Master Serlo. Perhaps my lord Hugh has given him a task?' she improvised quickly.

Serlo frowned. 'He should be here, helping with the shearing,' he said.

'And so I shall tell him, just as soon as I see him.' Janna gave an exaggerated shiver. 'I fell into the river and I'm cold. May I have your leave to run in the fields until I am dry?'

With a reluctant nod, Serlo waved her away. Feeling relief, Janna retraced her steps to the sheepfold to retrieve the sack of food, and took off up into the fields. She kept up the pace until she was hidden from his sight by a field of growing wheat. She slowed to a walk and looked about for somewhere to eat her dinner, while she pondered what to do next. Edwin had seemed so keen to stay at the manor. What had happened to change his mind? If he'd run away, why hadn't he asked her to go with him? He knew she wanted to leave, and that it was only his wish to stay that was keeping her here. It didn't make sense. Even if he'd left without her, he could at least have said goodbye.

If Edwin really had gone, she might as well leave too, she concluded. There was certainly no future for her here, in spite of Hugh's kind offer. She sat down in the shade of a patch of brambles, and opened up the sack of food. She munched on some bread and sheep's cheese while she considered what had been happening here on the manor. Years of standing about and watching Eadgyth treat her patients had taught Janna to look, to listen and to learn. As she ate her dinner, she thought through the incidents she'd witnessed, racking her brains to make sense of it all. Was there anything to link the incidents together, other than the posies of rue?

No, there was not, she concluded. Perhaps she should approach the problem from another angle. Why the rue? What was the reasoning behind the incidents?

Janna cast her mind back to everything her mother had told her about the herb. 'It's known as "herb of grace" to Christians, for they believe rue is a symbol of the true repentance that leads to God's grace,' Eadgyth had said. But it was clear to Janna that the culprit repented nothing, for the incidents kept on happening. Not repentance, then. What else had she been told? 'The Romans thought they'd gain a second sight and see visions if they took the herb, but others have used it to curse their enemies.' Eadgyth's eyes had twinkled as she'd continued. 'You can also wear rue for luck, for protection, or as a cure against disease. In fact, daughter, it seems the ancients couldn't quite make up their minds whether the herb should be used for good or ill. For myself, I believe the herb has many good uses, and these I will show you.' And so she had, Janna thought, remembering the many medicaments to which rue could be added.

She sighed. She was no nearer to working out the truth of the matter, but she was sure that something else was going to happen, perhaps worse than all that had gone before. She wondered what the next disaster would be, and felt a shiver of premonition.

Something niggled at the back of Janna's mind; something she'd seen, something important that perhaps could tell her who was responsible. She closed her eyes, the better to recall what she'd seen or heard, but the memory remained elusive.

She was thoughtful as she walked back down to the fold, where the last of the sheep were being sheared. If Edwin was gone, she should leave too. But not now; she couldn't risk Serlo seeing her go. He was already suspicious enough. If she left, it would confirm Serlo's belief that she and Edwin were behind the so-called 'accidents'. They would be pursued, and by the forester too. Janna had no doubt Serlo would carry out his threat to raise the hue and cry. Nor would he willingly let her go if she asked to leave, not when she was one of his suspects; not when it was his intention to get more work out of them in return for his silence. Uneasy and afraid, she wondered if she should make a run for it anyway. Whatever her decision, Janna knew she must wait until nightfall. If there was no sign of Edwin by then, maybe she could sneak out while everyone was snoring. But in which direction should she go?

Janna resolved that whatever she chose to do, she must first find out the way to Winchestre. But as she asked her question, she found herself more confused than ever by the responses.

'Winchestre lies that way.' One shearer stopped clipping to point downstream. 'No, you'll find the road over there,' said another, and jabbed a finger in the opposite direction. 'It's behind us,' said a villein, who was busy making his mark on his own sheep. He took time to poke his thumb back towards the fields.

She would go over the fields and see what lay beyond them, Janna decided, as she picked up an armful of rolled-up fleeces and laboured back to the manor with her burden.

Even if the road took her in the wrong direction, it would lead her away from the manor, and also from Babestoche where Dame Alice and Robert lived. It would lead her to safety. She could always ask about Winchestre along the way, and change direction at a crossroads, if need be.

All these thoughts left Janna's head as, with the day drawing to its weary end, she suddenly heard a bell begin to toll. She recognised the sound. It came from the church at nearby Wicheford and, on Sundays, it summoned the faithful to mass, including those villeins from the manor who felt like making the journey across the downs. But today was not Sunday, and the bell rang on and on, clanging its urgent appeal long past its usual recording of time or occasion. The villeins hurriedly gathered up the last of the fleeces and hastened to the manor to find out the cause of the summons, Janna among them.

'Hamo.' She heard the boy's name mentioned several times as they came closer to the confusion and bustle in the yard. It was said with annoyance, impatience, and also with anxiety. Janna's steps quickened. Surely he couldn't have gone missing again after such a narrow escape last time? But it seemed that he had. A cry of alarm had gone out and everyone was being pressed to search for him. The yard was full of servants and labourers, all milling around and discussing what to do. At their centre, trying to organise the comings and goings, and looking distraught, was Hugh. Janna noticed several unfamiliar faces amid the throng, strangers from neighbouring Wicheford. United in adversity and drawn by a sense of community, they too had come to join in the search for the missing boy.

Hugh raised his voice. 'Hamo was last seen playing with his ball here by the undercroft,' he shouted above the hub-bub. 'I want the women and children to search the gardens and all the buildings of the manor. The rest of you will comb the fields and search along the river, up and down. Pay careful attention to the mill, and also the marsh. I, myself, will take a small party into the forest. Although the fence-month has passed, the does will still be guarding their young. Should any of them stray into the fields do not, on any account, do anything to startle or harm them, or the forester will call you to an accounting before the king.' With chopping motions of his hands, he began to divide the villeins into groups, ready to send them off in different directions.

Janna hurried up to him. 'Where is the dog, my lord?' she cried. 'You should also look for Bones.'

Hugh glanced down at her. 'I haven't seen it, have you?' Janna shook her head. Hugh raised his voice once more to shout: 'Look out also for a stray dog.' His face was tight with worry as he continued to issue instructions to the villeins.

'I hope you find him soon, my lord.'

Hugh nodded. Janna stood back, and waited to be told where to go. A sudden thought came into her mind, and she sidled forward once more. A quick glance confirmed her fears and struck dread through her heart. A small posy of rue lay on the doorstep of the undercroft.

NINE

JANNA BENT DOWN and picked up the posy. Her first thought
was to show it to Hugh, and tell him what she thought it
meant. Her second thought urged caution. The posy, in
itself, proved nothing, for all the other posies were either
gone or had been destroyed, some by Janna herself. She had
nothing, now, to prove that these acts were deliberate and
that Hamo had not wandered off by chance. This time he
must have been taken, and by someone who wished him
harm.

Janna felt sick. She longed to spill out her worries to
Hugh, but a question stopped her even as she opened her
mouth. Who stood to gain by Hamo's disappearance –
perhaps even his death? The answer had been spelled out to
her, only too clearly, on her first meeting with Hamo.

'All my mother's property and wealth will be mine when
she dies,' he had told her. 'I am the first-born son, you see.'

Hamo, as the first and only surviving child born to Hugh's
aunt, Dame Alice, would inherit everything on her death.
In the interim, Hugh kept this manor for his aunt, but he
would be expected to vacate it once Hamo married. Unless,
of course, the child died before then?

Janna swallowed hard. She cast a glance at Hugh, hating what she was thinking yet understanding that she could not deny the truth of his situation. Only Hamo stood between him and a vast inheritance from Dame Alice. All the evidence could easily point to Hugh. These incidents had only started on his return to the manor. He, more than anyone, was free to come and go as he wished; no-one would dare to challenge him. Had he set up a pattern of accidents to convince his aunt that Hamo's disappearance – even his death – while regrettable, was just another accident?

Rue for regret. Repentance. Yes, Hugh might well regret the circumstances that forced him to act in this way. And he might well feel repentance for his actions.

It was still no excuse for murder! Janna continued to watch Hugh direct proceedings, meanwhile berating herself for letting her thoughts run away with her. Hugh murdering Hamo! It was laughable, quite out of the question. She herself had seen his fondness for his cousin when they'd played ball together. And Hamo wouldn't have fretted after Hugh left the manor if his cousin hadn't shown him genuine kindness. Nor did it seem likely that Hugh would have tampered with his own destrier's shoe to lame the horse, for his anger had been apparent and his concern quite real.

No. Janna tried to laugh off her fears. There must be some other explanation. If not Hugh, then who? Edwin? Janna shook her head. His absence might indicate guilt to some, but he'd gone missing before Hamo's disappearance. Unless that was to cover his actions and avert suspicion? Janna remembered that this wasn't the first time Edwin had gone missing. He'd been absent on the night of the medale, when the haystack had caught fire and the villagers had come together to put it out. Had he gone off to fire the haystack, and come back later pretending innocence? Was that what he intended to do now? But that was assuming Hamo had vanished for a reason, perhaps for ever, and she couldn't bear to believe that. She sighed with exasperation. Her imagination was taking her into all sorts of places she didn't want to go.

Where was Edwin? She had to find him in order to clear his name. Yet it was also true Edwin had a bad side to his character, she conceded. After all, he'd tried to steal her property. Janna's hand went automatically to her purse. She heard the coins clink at her touch, and felt the shape of the small statue she had found, the mother clasping her child. Her fear eased slightly, and she smiled at the notion that the statue had brought comfort.

Mother and child. She felt a sudden pang of deep distress as she recalled Dame Alice. The lady was utterly cast down by the death of her newborn babe. She would surely go off her head with grief if her only surviving son also died.

This won't do, Janna told herself sternly. It's too early for despair. Hamo's missing, not dead. And he hasn't been gone for long. She remembered the mangy dog. Hamo must have gone in search of it once more. He would surely soon be found.

By now, everyone had been summoned by the urgent, clamouring bell. Although she'd been ordered to search outside the manor with the men, Janna decided instead to hunt for Bones. Instinct told her that if she could find the dog, she would probably find Hamo too. Regardless of what the rue might mean, it was too great a coincidence that boy and dog should both be missing. So she tried the kitchen first, where she'd last seen Bones. She searched within and without, but there was no sign of dog or boy. She widened her search then, calling as she went, but there was no answering bark or shout for help. It seemed she was right: both of them had vanished. So where had they gone, and with whom?

'You! Boy!' Serlo had his horse on a rein, ready to mount, but now he stopped and beckoned Janna to come to him. His face set in a thunderous frown as he waited for her to draw near. 'Where's your brother?' he barked. From the hostility in his tone, Janna understood that she and Edwin were under suspicion for this too. It took all her courage to face the reeve.

'I don't know where Edwin is, Master Serlo,' she answered politely. She became aware she was still clutching the posy of rue, and hastily secreted it behind her back.

'And the young lord? I don't suppose you know where he is either?'

'No.' Janna hesitated, wondering if she had the nerve. 'But I do know he's not with Edwin,' she added boldly.

'And how would you know that if you don't know where your brother is?'

'I know Edwin, Master Serlo.' Janna hoped that, indeed, she did. 'I know he wouldn't take the boy away for any reason, even in fun.'

Serlo's frown deepened. 'What makes you think there's any reason behind Hamo's disappearance other than that the silly child has wandered away and got lost?' he snapped.

Janna kept silent. Hamo was anything but silly. He'd run after his dog and got into trouble for it. While he might go in search of the dog once more, it seemed unlikely he'd go to the river again, or even stray far from the manor unless enticed away by someone he trusted. But she couldn't blame Serlo for trying to put a good face on things. Besides, it was perfectly possible she'd read the situation wrongly. The fact that there was a posy of rue on the steps of the undercroft might not have anything to do with Hamo's disappearance; it might be a sign of something quite different, something relatively minor. Up until now the incidents had caused harm, but they were not too serious for all that. Kidnapping a child, the heir to this manor farm, on the other hand, was a very serious crime indeed.

'Get out and look for Hamo,' Serlo growled. 'I don't want to see you back here before dark. And make sure you bring your brother with you!' With a scowl he mounted his horse and rode out through the gate.

Janna pulled a face at his departing back. 'I'm already looking for Hamo,' she muttered. 'What do you think I'm doing? Walking about for my health?' Nevertheless, she linked up with a group of women who were busy searching through the manor grounds. Although she joined them in calling out Hamo's name, she also called for Bones. But only silence answered their calls.

The bell began to toll again, a low and mournful sound. A shiver ran through Janna as she came to understand its meaning. The sound was to guide the lost child home to safety. It would continue to toll until Hamo was found. And if Hamo didn't come running home, it would mean that he could not; it would mean that he was dead.

Partly following Serlo's instructions, partly to avoid Serlo himself, but mostly because she was worried sick, Janna left the manor grounds to search along the length of the river. She stayed out until it grew too dark to see properly. In twos and threes, the villeins began to return, shaking their heads in hopeless despair as they asked each other for news. Hugh called for resin torches to be fetched. With flames held high to light their way, some of the men streamed out of the gate to continue their search once more, a few on foot and some on horseback to ride further afield. Janna was relieved to see that Serlo was among them. The women and children, meanwhile, went off to their own cots to see about an evening meal and a night's rest.

Not wanting to encounter Mistress Tova's gossiping tongue, or questions about Edwin's whereabouts and sly innuendoes about his reliability, Janna wearily climbed the stairs to the hall and settled down onto her pallet, determined to continue her search as soon as dawn lightened the sky. Momentarily, she wondered what had become of Edwin. But her thoughts soon returned to Hamo. She pictured him falling into the river and being crushed by the mill wheel, or blundering through the forest, lost and frightened, not knowing which way to turn. There were wolves out there, and wild boar. Having no weapon, or anything to defend himself, Hamo would be easy prey.

Janna screwed her eyes tight shut, trying to block out the pictures she'd conjured up. With so many people out looking for him, how could Hamo stay lost – unless someone was determined that he shouldn't be found? She tried to push the thought from her mind but it lay there like a stone, too heavy to shift, too heavy to ignore.

Janna passed a restless night. Nightmares frightened her awake, so that she lay, heart thudding, listening to the snores of the sleepers and, at regular intervals, the lonely sound of the clanging bell. In the end, she fell into a deep sleep and didn't wake until one of the villeins gave her a hard shake. 'You'd best get up, John, if you want time to break your fast,' he said. 'Master Serlo wants us out at first light to look for the young lord.'

Janna hurriedly did as she was bid, but she was still yawning and only half awake as she munched on a chunk of bread and tried to come up with a plan. The first thing, she decided, was to give the undercroft a thorough search, just to satisfy herself that the posy of rue was in no way connected with Hamo's disappearance.

'Where's your brother, John? I want a word with him,' Serlo said sternly. Startled, Janna whirled to face the reeve. She hadn't seen him come in to the hall but, judging from the thunderous frown on his face, he was in a temper and determined to take it out on someone.

'I . . . I know not where Edwin is, Master Serlo,' she confessed miserably, sure now that she would be punished in Edwin's place.

'I judge him responsible for the young lord's disappearance – and you will be suspect too, if you cannot bring

Edwin to account. I'm out of patience with you both, but there's no time to waste on you now. If you don't have Edwin here by nightfall, I'll raise the hue and cry after him. I'll call in the sheriff. Be sure that I'll also urge the forester to tell all he knows. There'll be no place for you to hide after this, John, you or your brother. Just think on that.'

'I swear we know nothing about the young lord's where-abouts, Master Serlo,' Janna said hurriedly. 'But I will go in search of Edwin. And the young lord, if you'll give me leave to go?'

Serlo nodded curtly, and turned away to deal with a group of women who awaited further instructions. Gytha was among them, and in spite of her anxiety Janna felt a twitch of amusement. Serlo couldn't keep his eyes off the girl. All his remarks were addressed to Gytha. She stood before him, hardly responding to his attention, while Serlo watched her as a starving man might watch his last crust disappearing down the mouth of a rival.

Janna turned and walked quickly down the stairs. She had more pressing problems to think about now: was it more important to find Hamo or Edwin? Could they even be together?

Another possible companion for Hamo came into Janna's mind. Urk was older than Hamo, but he was about the same age in his reasoning. Hamo would think nothing of running free on his cousin's property – his own property – while Urk had already shown that he wasn't aware of, or didn't under-stand, the rules that bound the villeins living on the manor farm. He would be delighted to go searching for Bones, or even play a game with Hamo if the young lord still had his ball with him.

Where might the two of them go? After a moment's reflection, Janna thought it most likely that they'd stay right here within the confines of the manor, where the ground was cleared and suitable for play. In which case they must soon be found. On the chance that they'd strayed further, Janna decided to search for them in the villeins' cots that spread beyond the manor. Not understanding the differences in their station, perhaps Urk had taken his new friend home with him.

She hurried outside the timber palisade, making straight for Mistress Wulfrun's cottage. There was no sign of Urk, or Hamo, but Janna decided to stay and check all the cots while she was there. Most everyone had already joined in the search for Hamo, but Janna alerted a mother who had just been brought to bed with child, and also an elderly and infirm grandmother, and bade them keep a careful watch out for him. The rest of the cots were empty. Remembering her earlier idea, Janna headed back to the manor house. She could hear the villeins' voices calling Hamo's name as they hunted for him up and down the river. If Hamo was there, dead or alive, he would certainly be found.

Several riders flashed past. Janna stared after them. She didn't recognise the horses, but she knew at least one of the horsemen. Hugh. He had donned his green cloak for the journey and it sailed out behind him, given wings by the wind. She wished him a silent 'God speed', pleased he wasn't riding his own destrier, that he was giving the horse's hoof a chance to heal. They must be widening the search, she thought.

Women and children now moved about with a steady purpose, methodically inspecting once again every nook and cranny that might provide shelter for a small boy. The men fanned out beyond the manor walls, some to continue the search up and down river, looking especially at the mill and the great marsh; the rest to walk through the tall corn or search the meadows on either side of the river, and the outskirts of the forest beyond.

Janna wondered if she should go with the men, but investigating the undercroft was on her mind now. She would rather know the real purpose behind Hamo's disappearance. She hoped to set her mind at rest. So she walked into the undercroft below the hall, and began a systematic search for anything, anything at all, that might explain the significance of the posy of rue left lying on the doorstep. What was she looking for? She wished she knew.

She kept her mind and eyes focused on the scene in front of her as she poked about. She was looking for something out of place, or something spoiled, perhaps. Even something missing – but how would she know if that was so? She sorted through the few poor possessions stored by the servants who shared her sleeping quarters in the hall, then moved on to the rest of the undercroft where food and grain were kept. Being the hungry month, the time just before harvest, the sacks of grain were few; most were empty. One of the sacks was ripped and Janna checked it carefully. Precious grain spilled out of it. Mouse droppings confirmed that it was mice rather than a human hand behind the deed.

There were also barrels, and several chests. She tried the lid of one of the chests, but found it locked. So were most of the others, she found, as she tried them all. Only one opened to her touch, but a quick riffle through its contents

confirmed that there was only a woollen blanket, worn thin
and perforated with moth holes, and some chipped pots and
jugs inside it. Nothing in the undercroft appeared to have
been tampered with; everything seemed in order. Just to be
sure, Janna tapped on each one. 'Hamo?' she called softly,
but there was no reply. She didn't know whether to be glad
or sorry.

With her inspection over, Janna walked outside and
paused for a moment while she worked out where to look
next.

She was hot, thirsty and tired. And hungry. There were
apples growing on the trees that bordered the kitchen
garden. As Janna visualised the juicy fruit, her mouth began
to water in anticipation. She hurried towards the fruit trees,
hoping that the apples were ripe enough to eat, and that
no-one was around to watch her steal one. A movement
caught her eye and she stopped, wondering what it could be.
It looked like a long brown snake. The frayed end told Janna
what she'd seen. Curious now, she traced its source to a large
wooden barrel. She peered over, and found Bones cowering
behind it.

'Come here!' she ordered. She tugged hard on the rope.
The unwilling creature skidded around and came into full
view.

'Where's Hamo?' Janna demanded, then felt silly as she
realised she was talking to a dog. But so had she talked to the
animals she and her mother had kept at their cottage. 'Do
you know where he's hiding?' Her words seemed to soothe
the dog, for it stopped cringing away and baring its teeth
at her and, instead, sat down and looked up at her with

pleading eyes. Janna was incensed to see that its paws were still untreated by the kitchen skivvy. She chided herself for passing on the task rather than taking care of it herself.

'Poor old Bones.' She dragged the dog inside the empty kitchen and set about finding it some scraps, hoping to bribe it into good behaviour so that she could put the medicament on its paws. Perhaps the dog knew something about Hamo's disappearance; perhaps it could even lead her to Hamo? First, though, Janna wanted to take care of its wounds so that at least it could walk properly with her when she went searching.

Once the dog was busy chomping its way through a piece of raw meat, Janna poured water into a basin and set about cleansing its front paws. As she suspected, the claws had been cut off without care, and the wounds were dirty and full of pus. The dog growled at her as she probed deeper. 'Have a bone, Bones,' she said, and hurriedly stuffed one of the cook's soup bones into its mouth.

It dropped the bone and began to shiver and whine softly as Janna first cleansed then bound its paws with scraps of wool smeared with the cream she'd made up earlier. It seemed to sense that she was friend not foe. It even managed a feeble wag of its tail when she was done, while it wasted no time getting back to the feast she'd provided. 'You realise I'm going to blame you for stealing this food,' Janna told the dog as she scoffed up a cold meat pasty while she waited for it to finish eating. She was only half-jesting. Mistress Tova would be incensed when she realised what was missing.

Hastily, she drained a mug of ale to slake her thirst. 'Come on,' she said, feeling slightly more cheerful after her repast. She pulled on the dog's leash once more. With a last look of longing at a ham that hung enticingly beside the cooking fire, the dog trotted after Janna, still limping slightly.

Holding on to the rope to keep the dog with her, Janna crossed the river. If Hamo wasn't within the manor walls, neither was Edwin for he, too, would have been found in the search. With Serlo's warning sounding in her ears, she went first to the sheep shed where once they'd taken shelter from the forester. As she'd suspected, it was empty. She peeped behind the rough wooden feeding trough, and felt a great relief when she espied the rusty sword she'd secreted there, along with Edwin's pot and jug. If Edwin had left the manor to go adventuring, he surely would have remembered to take everything with him. Wherever he was, he couldn't be far away. Hunger must surely drive him home, and soon.

A group of peasants beating through the edge of the forest beyond caught Janna's eye. Urk's mother was among them, and Janna hastened to join them. Edwin could take care of himself; it was Hamo who occupied her thoughts now. A quick glance confirmed that Urk was not part of the group. She made a beeline for Mistress Wulfrun, hoping her suspicions might prove correct.

'Mistress,' she greeted her. 'I've been looking for Urk . . . Gabriel. Do you know where he might be?'

Urk's mother nodded. 'He went off with the other children to search the barn,' she muttered, looking worried.

'Was he alone, do you know?'

'No, I told you. He was with the other children.' Mistress Wulfrun shot a suspicious glance at Janna. 'Why do you ask?'

'I wondered if he might have gone somewhere to play ball with a special friend, perhaps?'

'Ball?' Mistress Wulfrun couldn't have looked more confused if Janna had asked whether Urk had grown wings and flown up to the moon.

Janna nodded thoughtfully. Hamo might have the leisure to play ball games, but it seemed that Urk did not.

'And did Gabriel sleep in his bed last night?'

Mistress Wulfrun drew herself up to her full height and glared at Janna. 'He was not out setting fire to a haystack, if that's what you're trying to suggest.'

'No!' Janna was sorry to have offended Urk's mother. She wasn't sure how to put things right. 'It's just that the young lord loves to play with his ball. I wondered if Gabriel had gone off to play a game with him, that's all.'

'Gabriel has no time to play games.' Mistress Wulfrun strode on, calling out Hamo's name as she went. Janna clicked her tongue impatiently as she realised she hadn't had an answer to her question. She left the villeins to their search and went back to the manor, dragging Bones on the rope behind her. The clanging tones of the bell followed her passage. Janna scrutinised the knots of people coming and going, wishing more than anything to recognise Hamo among them. Although several small figures brought her to a heart-thumping halt, closer inspection always revealed them to be some other child. She hurried inside the gate and went looking for Urk and his friends.

Oblivious to the urgency of their task and the real danger to Hamo, the children were having a game, throwing hay about and shrieking with delight. Urk was by far the oldest, but he also seemed to be having the most fun. She drew him aside. 'Have you seen Hamo, Gabriel?' she asked.

He shook his head. 'Hamo's lost,' he said helpfully.

'I know. I wondered if you'd seen him. Did you maybe go somewhere to play ball with him?'

'Ball?' Urk looked just as puzzled as his mother.

'Did you see Hamo today? Do you know where he is?' Janna tried again.

'No. Hamo's lost.' Urk bent down to pat Bones. 'Nice dog.' Bones's tail twitched in acknowledgment.

Janna sighed, feeling discouraged. 'Go on then and look for Hamo,' she said, and gave him a gentle push in the direction of the younger children. Urk ambled off, giving her a bewildered glance as he left. Janna looked up at the sky. The sun had begun to fall towards the earth; it would be dark within a few more hours, and then Serlo would demand an explanation of Edwin's absence. She felt like a watermill in a dry river bed, churning around uselessly and achieving absolutely nothing. She'd been rushing about everywhere, but she still had no answers to give Serlo, and no idea where to find them either. What was she to do? With dragging steps, she went back to join the searchers at the forest's edge.

She looked across the water meadows to the manor beyond, with the small cots of the peasants clinging to its side like ticks to a dog. Behind the manor stretched the cultivated fields, stripes of ripening corn interspersed with patches of dark, fallow earth. A small copse of trees stood to one side, jutting into some of the strips and cutting the field into an awkward shape. From the height and distance of her position, Janna could see now that the copse hid a solid, stone-built cottage.

'Who lives there?' she asked, while beside her, Bones began to whine. 'Sshh.' She smacked his muzzle gently to shut him up so that she could hear Mistress Wulfrun's reply.

'Master Serlo. The cottage and those gore acres around it belong to him.'

Janna gave a long, low whistle as she quickly revised her opinion of the reeve. Mistress Tova had mentioned Serlo's cottage and fields, but Janna hadn't realised the full extent of his holding. Gytha would do well to encourage him, Janna thought now, for her chances of improving her station were far greater with Serlo than they could ever be with Hugh. As Serlo's wife she would have a certain status; she would also become a woman of property. Yet as she mentally compared the two in her mind, she had to admit that in Gytha's position she'd also be hoping for a future with Hugh rather than plighting her troth with Serlo.

With an effort, she dragged her thoughts back to the more pressing matter of the missing boy. 'Has anyone looked in Serlo's cottage for Hamo?' As she spoke, Janna gestured towards it. Bones strained on his leash beside her, still whining.

'Yes, indeed.' Mistress Wulfrun caught hold of Janna's arm. 'Don't think to go searching there, John. Master Serlo will not take kindly to anyone trespassing on his property. Besides, I saw him go in for his dinner at noon. Wherever Hamo may be, you can be sure he's not there.'

Janna nodded, accepting that the woman was giving her good advice. 'You know the manor farm better than I do, mistress,' she said. 'Where do you think Hamo might be?'

'I wish I knew.' The woman scratched her nose, looking thoughtful. 'They say my lord Hugh has gone to break the bad news to Dame Alice, but in his absence Master Serlo will continue the search until the boy is found. Conscientious as he is, he knows every rock and tree on the manor farm. Wherever Hamo is, alive or dead, Master Serlo will find him.'

'Then let us pray that Master Serlo finds Hamo alive!' The alternative was too horrible to contemplate. As Janna walked on, calling Hamo's name in the silences left between the clanging tones of the bell, she wondered how Cecily was faring and what she was doing. Newly in charge of Hamo and wanting only the best for Dame Alice, she must be beside herself with anxiety. And self-blame. How had Hamo managed to escape Cecily yet again? It was something she should have thought to ask right from the start.

Janna turned abruptly and hurried back to the manor, tugging Bones, who continued to bark and pull on his rope to get free.

Janna was just crossing the yard when she saw Cecily vanish through the line of pear and apple trees that hedged the kitchen garden. At once she followed, curious to find out what Hamo's new nurse sought there. But it seemed that Cecily had merely escaped to find some privacy, for Janna found her sitting hunched under a pear tree, weeping as if her heart would break. Her head was buried in her lap and her arms were wrapped around to muffle the sounds she was making. She didn't hear Janna approach.

'Cecily.' Janna put an arm around her shoulders to comfort her. At Janna's touch, the tiring woman leapt in fright and shied away. 'Oh, it's you, Janna,' she said then, and subsided onto the ground once more. She wiped her eyes on her sleeve, and gave a mournful sniff. 'What am I going to do?' she burst out. 'My lord Hugh has gone to tell Dame Alice that Hamo is missing. Ma dame will never forgive me if harm has come to him. I'll never forgive myself. Oh, Janna, I have caused such trouble to my lady and her kin!' She burst into a storm of weeping once more. This time she didn't pull away when she felt Janna's embrace, but leaned into Janna and wept even harder.

No wonder Cecily was hurting, Janna thought. She had loved Robert once, loved him enough to forget all honour, and all loyalty and gratitude to Dame Alice, Robert's wife. That he'd proved so base, so unworthy of her sacrifice, must double both her sadness and her shame. And now there was the added blame of the disappearance of Dame Alice's beloved only child. There was nothing Janna could say to ease Cecily's pain or make things right for her. All she could do, all anyone could do, was look for Hamo and pray that he'd be found before it was too late.

Janna continued to hold Cecily, patting her arm as she did so. 'Hush,' she said at last, offering what little comfort she could. 'Everyone's out searching for Hamo. I'm sure he'll be found soon.' She wasn't sure, but she wasn't prepared to give up hope either. 'Maybe we can put our heads together, and see if we can make some sense of all this?'

Cecily nodded, and gave a forlorn sniff. Encouraged, Janna asked, 'When did you last see Hamo, Cecily? How did he come to run away?'

'I know not.' Cecily gave her eyes a fierce scrub on her sleeve, and sniffed again. 'I was called away to the kitchen to speak to the cook about Hamo's meals. I asked him to come

185

with me but he didn't want to, and so I left him playing with his ball.'

Janna reflected, with bleak amusement, that Hamo's new nurse didn't yet have his measure. Telling, not asking, would be far more effective if she wanted the child to obey her. She remembered what Hugh had said. 'He was playing by the undercroft?'

'Yes. He was throwing his ball at the wall and trying to catch it. Actually, he's very good at it.'

Having played ball with Hamo herself, Janna knew just how accurate was his aim, and how skilful his catching. She also knew that Hamo loved to play ball and realised she could hardly blame Cecily if the boy resisted her efforts to drag him away.

'How long were you gone?' she asked.

'Only long enough for the cook to show me what she had in her stores, and for me to give her some directions regarding Hamo's likes and dislikes. She was willing enough to listen and to learn, there was no argument there. But when I came out again and looked for Hamo, he was nowhere to be seen. I swear to you,' Cecily clutched Janna's arm in agitation, 'I was not gone for long. Moments only!' She began to cry once more.

'Was the dog with Hamo while he was playing with his ball?' It was a chance question, but Cecily's answer reinforced Janna's certainty that the two were linked together somehow.

'No,' she said. 'We'd been looking for the dog everywhere. Hamo couldn't find it. He was very upset.' She looked down at Bones, now sitting placidly beside Janna. 'Where did you find it?' She brightened momentarily. 'Maybe Hamo . . .?' Her voice trailed off as Janna shook her head.

'Bones was here, in the kitchen garden,' she said. 'There was no sign of Hamo.'

'But Hamo and I looked here just before he disappeared. Bones wasn't here then.'

'I saw the dog outside the kitchen when I broke my fast yesterday, but I didn't see him after that until I went looking for Hamo earlier today, and found the dog cowering behind those barrels over there. He seemed very frightened, I don't know why.' It was something to think about later, but for now she was anxious to question Cecily further. If Hugh was somehow implicated in Hamo's disappearance, then Janna vowed to find it out. 'Tell me about my lord Hugh. Where does he go? Does he spend much time with you in the hall and in the solar?'

Cecily frowned at Janna, and remained silent.

'Mistress Gytha is very attractive, is she not?' Janna prompted, hoping to goad Cecily into speaking by throwing in a snippet of kitchen gossip. 'I know she cares for my lord. I wondered if he might spend time dallying with her?'

'Gytha?' Cecily's eyes widened. Too late, Janna remembered that at one time she'd wondered if Cecily herself was enamoured with Hugh. She wasn't then, but perhaps that, too, had changed in the time Janna had been gone. Janna wished she could undo her question.

'Gytha?' Cecily echoed again. She gave a short laugh. 'I think my lord might wish to do better for himself than the cook's daughter.'

Although Cecily's words echoed what Janna herself had

thought, still she couldn't help feeling sadness at being reminded that if Gytha was beneath Hugh's attention, she herself must come even lower. Then she remembered the purpose of her questions. If Hugh was guilty, as she feared, he could have no place in her heart, none at all.

'I doubt that my lord has spent much time with Gytha or any other pretty woman who might take his fancy, for he has been very busy since his return.' Cecily's voice broke into Janna's thoughts. 'He goes out every day to inspect the fields, and see what's to be done about the manor, and make sure that all is as it should be. He's told me of his concern that the manor isn't more productive. I believe there have also been several unfortunate accidents recently. Although my lord Hugh pays tribute to Master Serlo, whom he says is an excellent reeve, I suspect his main aim is to convince his aunt of his own good stewardship, and to stay in her favour so that she will let him keep the manor for himself after young Hamo comes of age.'

So Hugh could have gone anywhere and everywhere, with no-one to check on his movements. Janna knew she could push Cecily no further. It was clear she had little real knowledge of how Hugh passed his days. But she might yet have some useful knowledge for Janna.

'Who are the visitors that travelled with you through the forest? Where are they bound?' she asked, feeling sure Cecily would have taken more interest in them than Gytha, and that she'd be able to give a better answer. It might be, she thought hopefully, that the travellers could tell her the way to Winchestre. They might even be going there themselves. If that was the case, maybe she could follow them.

A sudden memory troubled her. Edwin had been present when the travellers arrived – and he'd been missing ever since. Had he already interrogated them about Winchestre? Was that why he'd vanished? Or had he disappeared for another reason entirely? She became aware that Cecily was watching her, eyes narrowed in suspicion.

'You're always asking questions,' Cecily observed, 'and always to a purpose. What's on your mind, Janna?'

Janna was tempted to trust Cecily with her plans but knew that she should not, for she could do nothing nor go anywhere until Hamo was found. 'Nothing in particular is on my mind,' she lied. 'I'm just trying to work out who Hamo might be with, or where he might be. I'm trying to help, mistress.'

'I doubt Hamo's gone anywhere with the visitors.' Cecily thought for a moment. 'In fact, I know he hasn't, for I saw them with Serlo, taking part in the search.' Her voice shook; she fought for control.

'Who are they? Where are they from?' Janna asked again. It seemed unlikely that strangers could be responsible for Hamo's disappearance for they would have no reason to wish the boy harm, nor would they have the local knowledge to keep him hidden. Yet their identity was of interest to her, for in that might lie the answer to another disappearance and a solution to at least one of the mysteries that plagued her.

'They come from near Tantone. I think 'tis in the next shire from ours.'

Tantone. Janna nodded as her suspicion was confirmed. 'Why have they come here?' she asked carefully.

'They stopped to break their journey because one of their horses is lame. Their destination is Winchestre and they plan to be there in time for the annual fair of St Giles.' Cecily sounded troubled as she added, 'But I think there might be another purpose to their travels. I heard them ask my lord Hugh if he'd seen or given shelter to any outlaws over the past few months.'

'Outlaws?' Janna's voice squeaked upwards in horror at the realisation that Edwin's secret must be known to Hugh. With an effort, she tried to control her agitation. 'What did my lord tell them?'

'He asked if the outlaw was travelling on his own. When Master Siward said "yes", my lord replied that he had not come across any man travelling alone. Oh!' Cecily caught her breath. 'Is that . . . is he Edwin? Is Edwin him?'

Janna was sorry, now, that she'd questioned Cecily. She was sure the tiring woman would not have worked it out if she hadn't prompted her to it. But it was too late, now, to take back her words. She nodded.

'Oh, Janna!' Cecily clutched her arm, her own woes forgotten at this new threat. 'We might have been murdered in our beds!'

'Nonsense!' Janna could understand Edwin's disappearance now, but she wished he was here to argue his cause and state his innocence. More than anything, she was grateful to Hugh for keeping both her secret and Edwin's. She felt mean and unworthy when she remembered her suspicions about him, yet she knew she must not trust him unless and until she could prove him innocent of any knowledge of Hamo's disappearance.

'If my lord Hugh has kept Edwin's secret, and mine, I beg you to do the same,' she pleaded. 'Besides, Edwin has left the manor. I think those men have frightened him away.' For all she knew, it was true.

'Thank goodness for that.' Cecily breathed a soft sigh of relief. She climbed to her feet, and stretched out her hand to Janna to pull her up. 'I must get back,' she said, and looked suddenly awkward. 'Janna, I hate to see you as you are. I wish you —'

'It's all right. I don't mind.' Janna brushed dust and grass seeds from her breeches. 'You go on ahead. You shouldn't be seen with me. It might cause talk.'

Cecily hesitated. 'Go on.' Janna gave her a push. 'I'll follow you.'

A mournful tolling spoke the message that Hamo still wasn't found as the villeins returned to the manor, the women and children parting from their menfolk at the gate to make their way back to their own cots. Janna could see the leaping flames of smoking torches. The men had returned only to fetch them so they might continue the search. She could hear Serlo's voice bellowing out above the confusion, and she lingered a little longer, watching as the lighted flares streamed out and disappeared beyond the manor walls. She noticed that the forester had joined the search, and shrank back into the shadows. She must make sure to keep out of his way if he was still around in the morning.

The bell commenced its mournful tolling once more, calling out to the lost boy, summoning him home.

A wave of desolation swept over Janna. She was sure now that Hamo was not lost, but had been taken by someone and hidden somewhere. If he was lost, or had met with some misadventure, he would have been found. Could that mean that he was still alive? Janna took some comfort from the thought, even while she struggled against naming the only man who could wish Hamo harm.

Yet Hugh was absent from the manor. He had gone to fetch Dame Alice, which meant that there was no-one here to take care of Hamo while he was held captive. Perhaps, then, the boy must be dead after all?

No! Janna pushed the thought away from her. She couldn't give in to despair. She wouldn't!

Something else was bothering Janna now. Intent on clearing it up, she set off after the tiring woman, walking with long free strides. Cecily had said that Hamo was playing ball against the manor wall when she'd been called away to the kitchen to talk to the cook. Who had called her away? And where was Hamo's ball?

Cecily was about to climb the stairs up to the hall. She'd stopped to pluck an armful of flowers from the garden, perhaps to brighten the chamber in time for Dame Alice's arrival or perhaps just to cheer herself up. Janna had almost caught up to her when a sudden roar stopped them both.

'John!' Before Janna could move, could run, Serlo was upon her. He grabbed hold of her smock in one big hand, and began shaking her as a dog would a rat.

'Stop it! Stop that!' Cecily said sharply, and bent to calm Bones, who'd begun to bark hysterically.

Serlo gave her one startled glance. 'He is a thief, just as his brother is a thief!' He gave Janna another hard shake. Janna jerked her chin at Cecily, trying to tell her to go away and leave them. But Cecily stayed. 'What evidence do you have for such an accusation, Master Serlo?' she asked calmly.

'A length of fine woollen cloth is missing from a storage chest in the undercroft.' Serlo kept tight hold of Janna. 'Two silver goblets are also missing.' He thrust his face into Janna's, scowling ferociously. 'Where are they?'

TEN

JANNA'S FIRST FEELING was overwhelming relief. The posy of rue must have been to mark a theft, not the taking of Hamo. In spite of her situation, she felt almost light-hearted.

'I know nothing of these articles,' she said steadily, pitching her voice louder to be heard above the noise Bones was making. The dog had tried to sink its teeth into Serlo's ankle, and had received a kick for its efforts. Now it kept a wary distance, but it continued to bark and growl at the reeve. 'I have no possessions for you to search,' Janna continued, 'but I warrant that no matter where you look, you will find nothing to link either me or Edwin to the missing objects.' The storage chests had been locked, she remembered now. Whoever had the key must surely be responsible for the thefts. She opened her mouth to voice her thoughts, and quickly closed it again. It could only increase Serlo's suspicion if she confirmed she'd already investigated the chests.

'What about your thieving brother?' Serlo gave her another shake. 'I gave you until nightfall to find him – and the young lord. Where are they? What do you know of them?'

'Nothing, Master Serlo. I don't know where they are. I wish I did.'

'There, Master Serlo,' Cecily said, 'You have your answer. She knows nothing.'

Janna closed her eyes and groaned inwardly. Had Serlo noticed Cecily's slip? If so, he gave no sign of it.

'You will stay here under lock and key until your brother returns,' he said sternly.

And if he doesn't return? Janna dared not ask the question.

'Master Serlo, may I suggest you consult my lord Hugh before locking up this . . . this youth,' Cecily said quickly, trying to make up for her mistake.

The reeve frowned at the tiring woman, seemingly puzzled by her intervention. 'With respect, ma dame, this matter does not concern my lord or you,' he said coldly.

Cecily looked at him with dislike. 'Nevertheless, I will put this matter before my lord as soon as he returns with Dame Alice,' she said firmly.

In spite of her precarious situation, Janna's mouth twitched up in a smile. It seemed the tiring woman had some iron in her spirit in spite of her fragile appearance.

Her smile vanished as she heard Serlo's reply. 'And I will keep this villein safe under lock and key until that time'.

Despite Cecily's continued protests, he dragged Janna across the yard and pushed her into the barn. His shove sent her flying into the darkness. She fell against a pile of hay, feeling the hard ground graze her knees through the rough fabric of her breeches. She heard the snick of the latch as it came down to hold the door fast, and then a frantic howling. Bones was shut outside, and not happy.

'You'll be sorry for this!' Cecily's threat came loud and clear through the wattle and daub walls of the barn, and so

did her next words: 'Come on, Bones, you come with me.'
The sounds of whining faded into the distance. Janna kept
silent. She didn't know if Serlo was still outside, but she
knew that calling out wouldn't change his mind. She would
not demean herself further in his eyes.

It was pitch black inside the barn. Janna couldn't see at
all. She scrambled to her feet and stretched out her hands,
ready to explore her prison. But the barn was crammed full
of hay and she quickly found there was nowhere to go. She
sat down to consider her situation. While she hoped that
Hugh wouldn't suspect her of theft, it was perfectly possible
that he would lay the blame on Edwin. Thanks to the
travellers, Hugh now knew Edwin's circumstances. Janna
was the only one who could speak up for him and try to
clear his name. In all conscience she wondered if she could
or should, when Edwin had been so quick to help himself
to Janna's own possessions.

A sudden realisation brought a hot wave of shame to
Janna's cheeks. She was ready to believe the worst about
Hugh's intentions towards his young cousin, while expecting
him to believe the best about her. But, whatever he thought,
she knew she couldn't count on him to interfere with Serlo's
decision. It was really up to her to help herself. Meanwhile
there was Hamo to consider. As she was not going anywhere
soon, she might instead ponder where the child might be.

Try as Janna would, she could think of no place that
hadn't already been searched. Her thoughts took a different
tack. Was she making too much of Hugh's relationship to
Hamo? Did the theft prove that no-one wished Hamo any
harm? While Janna tried to tell herself that the child had

merely run away once more in search of his dog, and that he'd become lost, she was filled with dread that he was lying somewhere, bound and gagged, or even worse, already dead.

She shook her head, trying to dismiss her fear. Worry over Hamo was taking her nowhere. Once again, at the back of her mind, came the thought that she knew something, had seen something that might shed some light on Hamo's disappearance. She sat quietly, trying to free her mind of all her worries so that the missing memory might take their place. But nothing came to her. The knot of anxiety tightened in her stomach. She was trapped here and, if Serlo kept his word, she would face the forester, and maybe even the sheriff, in the morning. Face them alone, without Edwin.

Suddenly angry, she pounded her fist into the hay. It wasn't fair that he'd run off without a word, leaving her to face this mess on her own. Where could he be? Once he'd recognised the travellers, would he have hurried off to Winchestre on his own, not knowing that the travellers themselves planned to go there? It seemed unlikely. Edwin knew she wanted to go to Winchestre. He would have told her his plans; he would have taken her with him because his own safe passage lay with her and with their story.

He must be lying low then, waiting for the travellers to leave so that he could safely show his face again. The forest? Was he hiding there once more? It was possible. Even so, Janna found it hard to believe that he would not have got word to her somehow. Who else could he trust if not his travelling companion?

A name came into Janna's mind, and she frowned and sat straighter as she recalled Edwin's earlier disappearances. She hugged her knees to her chest and rested her forehead against them as she began to sort out the arguments both for and against the one person to whom Edwin might turn for help, and trust with his safety. She found that she could think of no arguments against; everything confirmed her new suspicion.

She jumped up, anxious now for action. She had to get out of here, she had to go and find Edwin. She looked about her, realising that her eyes had become accustomed to the darkness. A thin sliver of twilight filtered between the over-hanging thatched roof and the top of the sturdy wooden walls, faintly illuminating the contents of the barn. She peered at the hay piled behind her and then, with quickening interest, at the solid shapes of farming implements stacked beside the stout door that shut her in.

She hurried to inspect them, hoping to find a sturdy axe to hack her way through, but there were only some curved sickles, which were the wrong shape for an attack on some-thing as solid as the door. She turned next to a wooden plough with its iron cutting parts. She felt the coulter and share carefully, but they were fixed firmly into place and no good for her purpose anyway. She looked to see what else might be helpful, and saw several flails for threshing corn once the harvest was in.

Janna picked up the long shaft of a jointed flail, and jiggled it experimentally. Yes, it might work. It was certainly worth a try. If Serlo meant to keep her locked up, he should have given more thought to his choice of prison. He certainly should not have underestimated her need to escape! She tucked the flail under her arm and began to climb the pile of hay, sneezing ferociously as dust swirled and eddied around her. Her foot slipped; Janna grabbed a handful of hay to save herself. It came away in her grasp and she crashed down into a heap on the hard ground. Hampered by the flail, she tried again, scrambling up and slipping down just as she'd almost reached the top of the stack. Once more she tried, and once more after that. She was utterly determined that Serlo would not find her here in the morning. At last she managed to reach the thin crack of light that marked the division between the wall and the thatched roof. Janna knew she had to hurry for, once the sun set, the villeins would all go to bed rather than waste a precious rush light. Before that happened, there was someone she needed to see, and much for her to do.

She pulled the flail from under her armpit, and thrust the long handle into the thin crack between wall and thatch. Using all her force, she began to push against reeds and straw, levering the stick up and down so that they began to loosen. She sneezed and sneezed again as dust, spiders and earwigs sprinkled down onto her hair and shoulders, but she kept on working until she had dislodged enough thatch to form a small hole. A quick slide down the hay to the farming implements, and this time she climbed with a sickle in her hand, hooking it through the hay to give her extra purchase on her way up again.

The small curved blade cut away the loose reeds one by one until there was a hole large enough to wriggle through. Wasting no time, Janna dived halfway through and peered out into the night.

A quick glance was all she needed. Plunging to the ground head-first would only achieve a broken neck. She wriggled backwards until her feet rested once more on the piled-up hay, and turned around. Balancing on her elbows and stomach, this time she thrust her feet first through the hole she'd made. She eased herself through, pushing until she could hold on no longer. With a cry, quickly stifled, she fell to the ground, landing awkwardly so that an ankle twisted painfully beneath the weight of her body.

At least she was free! Janna stood up carefully, and took a cautious step on her sprained ankle. She sucked in a breath at the sharp pain and quickly shifted her weight to rest on her other foot. What she needed was a stout stick to lean on. She peered anxiously into the dusky darkness, half-expecting Serlo to pounce on her once more. But everyone who was not out on the search had gone indoors for supper and to bed. Keeping to the shadows, Janna left the manor and hobbled towards the carpenter's cottage as fast as her sore ankle would carry her.

She knocked on the door. It was opened by Bertha herself. Janna watched her closely, looking for any signs she might have missed when she'd questioned her once before. 'I give you good night, mistress,' she said in a friendly fashion.

'God be with you.' Bertha looked out past Janna's shoulder, scanning the track that gave access to the villeins' cots. 'What are you doing here?' she asked curiously, bringing her attention back to Janna.

'I'm looking for Edwin.'

'Why should you think I know where he is?' A scowl masked Bertha's pleasant features. Janna wondered if she was going to have the door slammed shut in her face. She quickly leaned against it to prevent the possibility.

'Several reasons,' she said cheerfully. 'I always thought Edwin was shy with girls. I also know he kept away from them because, with no home and no prospects, he has nothing to offer a wife. He told me so himself. But now I'm not so sure.' She peered at Bertha in the pale light of the rising moon. 'You're in love with him, aren't you?'

'Why should you think so?' Bertha cast a quick glance over her shoulder, perhaps to check on her family's where-abouts. She stepped outside the cottage, forcing Janna to move away from the door.

'Because you came over and sat with Edwin and me instead of with your family at medale.' Janna noticed Bertha hadn't denied the claim. It gave her the confidence to continue. 'Because Edwin knew that your sister wanted to dance with me, which meant that he must have met your family already. Because he wasn't around when the haystack was fired and we were trying to put out the blaze. Was he off dallying with you, mistress?'

Bertha's lips clamped firmly together. Janna waited for her denial, but it still didn't come. 'Also,' Janna continued, wondering if she was being rash, building too much into Bertha's parting remark after she'd cut her hair, but deciding to take the chance anyway. 'You know who – or what – I really am. Edwin would not have told you that unless he trusted you.'

Silence greeted Janna's remarks.

'If it's any help, I think Edwin cares for you too, mistress,' Janna continued, remembering how angry Edwin had been when she'd passed on the cook's gossip concerning Bertha. She'd misread the situation at the time, thinking he was upset about Gytha. But she was quite sure she was on the

201

right track now. 'You were carrying a small sack when I asked you to cut my hair. That was food for Edwin, wasn't it? You're hiding him somewhere.'

Still Bertha remained silent. Janna began to lose patience with her. 'You can trust me,' she snapped. 'Edwin does. We're in this together, you know.'

Bertha blinked. She opened her mouth to speak, and closed it again, looking undecided. Janna decided to help her out. 'Do you know that Edwin and I are being blamed for the theft of some woollen cloth and two silver goblets? Have you seen any such things, mistress?'

'No.' Bertha licked dry lips. 'No, of course not!'

'Then it would be good if Edwin came out of hiding to speak his innocence. As it is, I've been locked up in a barn for the theft.'

Now Bertha looked thoroughly bewildered. 'But I escaped,' Janna explained, continuing earnestly, 'Mistress, if you know where Edwin is, and if you value truth and justice, I beg you to take me to him now.'

Still Bertha hesitated. Janna itched to give her a push, just to get her moving. She restrained herself with difficulty. 'Did Edwin tell you about the visitors to the manor?' she asked instead, wondering just how much he had taken Bertha into his confidence. She was fearful that she might be jeopardising his safety with her question, but she also needed something to convince Bertha to help her.

It was some relief when Bertha nodded slowly. Janna decided to put her mind at rest if it would help her cause. 'It is true that the travellers look for Edwin, but that is not their main purpose for being here. They are on their way to trade goods at the fair in Winchestre, and have only delayed their visit while their horse is lame. And they are also helping in the search for Hamo.' The thought diverted Janna for a moment. 'You don't know where Hamo is, do you?'

'No.' This time the answer came bold and clear.

'No. Well, I am sorry for that. But we can both reassure Edwin concerning the travellers, for they have asked the lord Hugh about him, but he has kept our secret.'

Now Bertha looked startled. Janna smiled grimly to herself. 'Please,' she begged. 'Please, mistress, tell me where Edwin is, for my sake and for his.'

Reluctantly, Bertha stepped aside, and beckoned Janna to come in.

'He's here?' Janna could hardly believe it.

Bertha nodded. She put a finger to her lips, warning Janna to silence, then led her through the carpenter's workshop and into the room beyond. While Janna greeted Bertha's surprised family, Bertha picked up a bucket of slops containing vegetable peelings and assorted greens, and a small sack of grain. She walked on through to a pen adjoining their cottage. In it were a pig and three small piglets, two goats and several hens. They crowded around Bertha as she walked in, clamouring to be fed, but she pushed past them and walked on to a small thatched cover at the back of the pen. A pile of wood was set under the thatch out of the weather. Janna's confusion grew.

'Edwin?' Bertha called softly.

He peered around the wood pile with a cheerful grin, which quickly turned to a frown of concern when he noticed that Bertha had company.

'Have you been here all the time?' Janna asked, astonished.

'No,' Bertha answered for Edwin. 'He told me he was leaving the manor, and he showed me where he'd be – up a tree in the forest. You were right, John – Janna – I brought food to him there. But when Hamo went missing, I knew Edwin was in danger of being found, and so I went to fetch him as soon as it grew dark.'

'I watched you all go out to search for the boy.' Edwin's tone was regretful as he added, 'I wanted to help look for him too, but I dared not come out of hiding, for the travellers were part of the search party. You know who they are? You know why I had to run?'

'Yes, I know,' Janna reassured him.

'And the boy? Hamo? He is still not found?'

'No.' The bell began to ring out its lonely message once more, confirming that the search continued. Edwin's words reassured Janna that he really knew nothing about Hamo's disappearance. But that left the problem of the missing length of woollen cloth and the silver goblets. 'Some things have been stolen from the storage chests in the undercroft,' she said now. 'What do you know about it, Edwin? And don't lie to me, either. You stole my purse from me, I haven't forgotten that.' A shocked gasp, quickly suppressed, told Janna that Edwin hadn't been entirely honest with Bertha.

'I don't know nothing about stealing goods from the undercroft,' Edwin blustered, angry that Janna had shown him in a bad light. 'What's missing? And why should you think I had anything to do with it? I haven't even been at the manor, I've been up a tree!'

'Sshh, keep your voices down,' Bertha warned. 'I'll leave

you two to argue while I feed the animals.'

Watching Bertha empty the bucket of greens and slops, and throw grain to the hens, hearing the clucking, grunting and bleating as the animals fought one another to get to the food first, reminded Janna of her own chores when she'd lived with her mother. She felt a sharp pang of sadness. Their lives had been hard, but she'd been happy enough. She felt so much older now; she'd lost her childhood innocence the day her mother had died and she'd come face to face with evil. She would never be the same again.

Janna shook off her dark thoughts with an effort. While Bertha squatted to milk the goats, Janna began to tell Edwin what had been happening in his absence. Bertha joined in, ranging herself on Edwin's side until Janna was convinced that they knew nothing about either the stolen property or the missing Hamo. They continued then to confer in low voices, with Janna trying to persuade Edwin to show himself while he and Bertha fiercely resisted all her arguments.

'You've turned me into an a fugitive!' Janna said hotly, when she saw he would not be persuaded.

'You were a fugitive when I met you,' Edwin reminded her.

It was true. But that fact didn't help Janna now. 'I'm supposed to be locked up in the barn. I'm certainly not going back there! But I can't leave the manor either, not while Hamo is still missing. What am I to do?'

'You can stay here with me,' Edwin offered.

Janna moved over to investigate the small space between the fence of woven wattle and the woodpile. It was barely large enough to hide Edwin.

'I s'pose you could stay here,' Bertha said reluctantly. 'The animals are my responsibility. No-one else comes out here but me. And my father, when he needs more wood, but Edwin knows to stay hidden unless he hears my voice.'

'No, I thank you. I'll find somewhere else to hide.' Janna screwed up her face in concentration. Where could she go, and what could she do to help find Hamo? 'I wish I knew whether he was lost or taken!' she burst out.

'Taken? Who?' Both Edwin and Bertha turned to Janna in confusion.

'Hamo.' She pondered a moment, wondering if she could take them into her confidence. Yes, she decided. Three heads might be better than one at working out this puzzle. Besides, Bertha had lived here all her life, she might well know something from the past to help make sense of the present. 'I wish I knew whether Hamo's disappearance was connected in any way with what else has been happening here,' she said carefully, and began to tell them about the sprigs of rue that were left each time to mark the scene of the so-called 'accident'.

Talking about it helped to get the sequence of events clear in her mind, she found.

'I thought Hamo's disappearance was yet another "accident" when I found the posy of rue beside the door of the undercroft,' she said, 'but when Serlo accused me – us – of stealing the woollen cloth and goblets, I thought I must be mistaken, and that the rue was left to mark that instead. But now I'm not so sure.'

'Why? What have the accidents and Hamo going missing got to do with each other, then?' Bertha frowned at Janna.

'I wish I knew,' Janna said again. 'It's just that after I found the rue, I decided to search the barn myself to see if it meant anything. Serlo claims that the missing articles came from some wooden chests stored there, but I know they were all locked when I looked at them.' She frowned, worried that she already knew the answer to the question she was about to ask. 'Whoever took those things must have had a key to open the chests,' she said. 'So who would have a key?'

'The lord Hugh. Master Serlo. Mistress Tova, and maybe Gytha?' Bertha offered. Then she laughed, and shook her head. 'But that's silly. Why should any one of them want to cause harm to the manor – or to Hamo? Unless . . .' She stopped.

'Unless?' Janna prompted, dreading to have her suspicions confirmed by the carpenter's daughter.

'Well, Gytha's mother wants her to marry the reeve. Serlo has a good position and is held in great respect. He owns his cottage and the gore acres around it and, whatever happens to my lord Hugh once Hamo inherits this property, you can be sure that Master Serlo will keep his position here. But Gytha is determined that she'll wed my lord and no other.'

Janna nodded. This she already knew. She waited for Bertha to explain herself.

'I'm wondering if Gytha knows anything about Hamo's disappearance? It's terrible even to think it, but if something happens to Hamo then my lord Hugh will inherit all Dame Alice's fortune, including this manor. That would please Gytha greatly. Hamo is the greatest barrier to her becoming the lord Hugh's wife and the lady of his manor.'

'Gytha?' Janna hadn't considered the young beauty before. She wondered if there could be any truth in Bertha's words.

'Gytha must know that if my lord Hugh inherits nothing when Hamo comes of age, he will need to marry someone with a fortune. He certainly won't wed her,' Bertha continued, unconsciously echoing Janna's own thoughts on the matter. 'Maybe Gytha knows something about Hamo's disappearance? Maybe she's even the cause of it?'

'It's possible, I suppose,' Janna said dubiously. Did Gytha have the courage or the guile to carry out such a dreadful mission? It seemed unlikely. It seemed even more unlikely that she was involved in any of the incidents that had gone before. While she would have had the time and the opportunity to carry them out, she had no motive and nothing to gain from any of them. A sudden thought lodged like an arrow in Janna's heart. Could Hugh and Gytha be in this together, and working for their common cause?

'Watch Gytha, see where she goes, what she does,' she told Bertha. 'If she knows where Hamo is, sooner or later she'll lead you to him.'

Bertha nodded, looking self-important and proud. Janna was relieved that Bertha hadn't taken her guess to its logical conclusion. If Gytha had everything to lose when Hamo inherited the land from Dame Alice, so did Hugh. Whichever way she looked at the problem, it always came back to him. He, more than anyone, had good reason to kidnap Hamo, as well as the means and opportunity to carry it out. He would not have to use force. The boy would go with him willingly. She was about to say so, but found that Hugh's name stuck in her throat. She could not say it out loud, because she still didn't want to believe it. She would hide, and watch, and wait until she found proof of his culpability,

Janna decided. Then, and only then, would she call Hugh to account.

'I'd better go,' she said, and scrambled to her feet. Bertha stood up to accompany her. Edwin gave Janna an apologetic smile. 'I'm sorry you have to face this alone,' he said. 'But I'll come out of hiding just as soon as those travellers leave the manor, I promise you.'

'And then?' Janna queried. 'Will you come on to Winchestre with me?'

Edwin and Bertha exchanged glances. She spoke up for both of them. 'It is our wish to be wed, if the lord Hugh permits it,' she said. 'I have asked my father to take Edwin on as an apprentice and he has already agreed to it. Edwin's life lies here now, with me.'

Janna nodded in understanding. 'Good luck to you then,' she said, 'and I wish you both great happiness.' She turned to Bertha. 'Please keep close watch on Gytha and, if you have any further ideas about Hamo's disappearance, either of you, please tell me.' She gave Edwin a farewell salute, then followed Bertha out through the cottage, taking time to give her younger sister an awkward wave as she passed.

Needing to find shelter, Janna headed off towards the forest for the night, all the while keeping a lookout for telltale flickers of light from the searchers, and listening anxiously for sounds of the hunt. She'd sworn never to pass another night up a tree again, and so she looked around for somewhere else she might shelter – and found it in the sheep shed where she and Edwin had hidden once before. With relief, she hurried towards it, sure that she'd be safe there for the night, for it must already have been searched by others as well as by herself.

She debated gathering leaves and straw to make a softer bed, but decided against it. Even if she cleaned out the shed in the morning, she was bound to leave signs of occupation behind, signs that could be misinterpreted. With a sigh of resignation, she cleared a small patch of the hard flinty ground free of sheep's mundungus, and lay down. She was exhausted, but her thoughts churned endlessly, keeping her fretful and awake. Hamo. He must be feeling so frightened, and so alone.

And Hugh! Her suspicions seemed impossible when she recalled his kindness, his gentle touch as he comforted her after her mother's death. His kiss . . . Her body ached and burned with memories of Hugh.

At some time during the night she heard the sound of voices and leapt up, trying to judge whether she was safe, whether she had time to run. She opened the door a crack and peered out across the water meadows. The weary villeins were returning home, their torches burned as low as their spirits judging by the snatches of conversation that came her way through the still night air. Hamo was not found then. The hunt would start again at dawn. She dozed, awoke, and dozed again until a gradual lightening to the east told her that the sun would soon rise, and the searchers with it.

She scrambled to her feet and rolled her shoulders to ease their stiffness, then rubbed her arms to generate a little warmth. She was cold and hungry. She could almost smell the fresh bread baking in the kitchen, the rich scent of pig roasting on a spit, and was tempted to sneak back to the manor and ask Mistress Tova for something to break her fast. Instead, she slipped into the forest to find something to eat. Some mushrooms, hastily collected and eaten raw, helped ease the hollow emptiness in her stomach, while a few early raspberries added a touch of sweetness at the finish. The golden aura of the sun peeping above the horizon spoke of a fine day, a fact that added to her rising spirits, her confidence that Hamo was still alive and would be found.

Hugh – or Gytha? Janna shook her head, sure that the answer lay with the one who stood to gain the most from Hamo's death. She resolved to keep herself hidden until Hugh's return. After that she would follow him. If Hamo was alive, his first call must surely be to check on the boy, and when he did so, she would be there, following in his footsteps. She took comfort from the thought that if she was wrong, Bertha would be watching Gytha, ready to pounce if necessary. In the meantime, Janna sought shelter, needing to evade Serlo's watchful eye. She found an old beech tree close to the path through the forest, and climbed high into its dense, leafy crown.

Serlo was the first to come out of the manor, leading a group of villeins. Judging by their yawns and dragging steps, they had been woken early and given little time to break their fast. Janna stayed motionless in her hiding place as they crossed the river and came on into the forest, passing close beside her hiding place. She hardly dared even to blink in case someone caught a flicker of movement. She watched them disappear down the path, and wondered if they were also searching for her. If Serlo had bothered to send some bread and ale to the barn, or even taken the victuals to her himself, he would know she was gone. Everyone would have been warned to keep a lookout for her, and for Edwin.

The sun rose higher, warming the chill from the air and lightening the sky with its rosy rays. Janna's eyes felt heavy with sleep after her wakeful night. She lay along the length of a branch, and felt her eyes close in the drowsy summer heat. A swarm of gnats found her. She flapped an irritable hand at them but they continued to bite and tease her until she found herself thoroughly wide awake. She listened for sounds of the search but heard only the discordant clanging of the bell. Then there was silence.

To keep herself awake, she cast her mind back to what Eadgyth had told her about beeches. The tree had many healing properties but, of more importance to Janna right now, was something else Eadgyth had said. 'The beech is said to protect lost travellers. The old ones especially revered it because they believed the ancient gods wrote upon its bark and so the tree received their knowledge and wisdom. Even today, if you write a wish on a beech tree, it will be granted.' After a moment's reflection, Janna pulled out her knife and laboriously began to inscribe her father's name on the smooth grey bark. J O H N. 'Please let me find him,' she whispered, as she cut into the hard wood.

The long morning wore on, and Janna was almost asleep when the thudding of a horse's hooves jerked her upright. Hugh! She peered through the leaves to make sure, and recognised the green cloak coming towards her. He was riding the reddish brown steed he'd been on before, and he was moving fast. There was no time to lose if she wanted to keep him in sight. She slid down through the lofty branches, grabbing hasty handholds along the way, until she missed her footing and fell. She crashed down into thick leaf litter below the beech, landing almost in the path of the speeding horse. Startled by her sudden appearance, the horse reared and whinnied in fright. Its hooves lashed out and pounded the air. Hugh clung tight to the reins. As he fought to stay in the saddle, he tried to gentle the horse to stillness with his voice. 'Whoa there, easy up. Easy now.' He kept on talking until at last his mount stood calm. Then he looked at Janna, and frowned with displeasure.

'What on earth do you think you're doing?' he said curtly. 'You could have killed us both!'

'I . . . I'm sorry, sire.' Janna bent her knees in a hasty curtsy, tried to correct it to a bob, remembered that Hugh knew she wasn't a boy, got her feet tangled up, and fell over. Scarlet-faced, she scrambled up again, cursing her clumsiness and the ill-luck that had precipitated her descent. She had hoped to follow behind Hugh without being seen; she hadn't expected to confront him like this.

'Why were you hiding up a tree?' From the determined set of Hugh's jaw, Janna knew he would not leave without some explanation from her. She struggled to find something convincing to tell him, but nothing came into her mind. Eventually, she decided to stick to a version of the truth.

'I'm hiding from Master Serlo,' she explained.

Hugh was still gentling and patting the horse. As the bell tolled out once more, his frown deepened. 'There is no sign of Hamo, then?'

'No, sire.' Janna shook her head, almost convinced that Hugh's concern sounded genuine. 'The search has gone on all night, but he is not found.'

Hugh's lips tightened. There was a look of real distress in his eyes. 'I must find Serlo,' he told Janna. 'But before I do, tell me why you are hiding from him.'

'Master Serlo believes that I stole some things from the storage chests in the undercroft, but I swear to you, sire, that I did not.'

'If Master Serlo accuses you of theft, I am sure it is for a good reason. No!' Hugh held up a hand to stay Janna's outraged retort. 'I hold you in good faith, Johanna, and so I am sure he is mistaken in his belief. But what about Edwin? Your *brother*?' There was a wealth of sarcasm in the word.

Janna sighed. His question was fair, but she was unsure how to answer it. 'I have spoken to Edwin and I swear he knows nothing of it either.' Janna hesitated, but decided to continue with the truth, partly because Hugh already knew it. 'He has gone into hiding, sire, because he recognised the travellers who are staying at the manor. They come from his lord's own manor near Tantone, and Edwin is afraid they will return him there if he is found. He's trying to stay hidden for a year and a day so that his lord can no longer claim him.'

'That's what I suspected.' Hugh dismounted then, but kept tight hold of the horse's reins. 'And is there any good reason why I should not hand Edwin over to Master Siward so that his lord can make his own decision about him?'

'He . . . his lord is a violent man, sire. Edwin told me he was beaten regularly. In fact I have seen the scars of it on his back. The other villeins were also beaten. Even the lord's own family were victims of his rage.'

Hugh nodded thoughtfully. 'That accords with what Master Siward hinted at, but you haven't told me everything, Johanna. Or has Edwin not told you that when he ran away, he took his lord's favourite steed with him?'

'Yes, Edwin told me what he was accused of, but no, sire, he did not take the steed. He denied knowing anything about its theft, and I believe him. But he knew no-one else would, and so he ran away.' Janna hesitated. 'For certes, there was no sign of any horse when I met him in the forest, sire.'

'Humph.' Hugh was silent for a few moments. 'And what is Edwin to you, that you defend him so vigorously, Johanna?' There was a slight edge to his voice.

Janna smiled, rather flattered by Hugh's interest. Should she tell him he had nothing to fear, that Edwin was already in love with Bertha? A quick check with the reality of her situation wiped the smile from her face. She must never forget, for one moment, the reason behind her interest in Hugh. 'Edwin was hiding in the forest, just as I was, sire.' Better not mention her stolen purse, Janna thought. 'We decided it would be safer for both of us if we travelled together, and that's why we made up the story about being part-Welsh and everything.' Shamefaced, she looked at Hugh, willing him to believe her, to believe them both.

'You seem to tell lies so readily, Johanna, that I wonder how far I can trust you now?' Hugh's eyes rested on Janna with a steady gaze that cut right through her so that she felt as if her heart and soul were being peeled open. Whatever

Hugh found on his inspection seemed to satisfy some of his doubts, however.

'Very well,' he said curtly. 'I shall speak to Serlo. I shall make sure he knows you are innocent and must be left free. But for all your faith in Edwin, I will speak to him myself. I will find out the truth.' He hoisted himself back into the saddle. 'You will bring him to me tonight, Johanna, in secret if you wish. There is no need for the travellers to see him. But you must make him come or I shall believe the worst of him and then not only the travellers but the whole shire will be looking for him. He will be caught, he will be tried in my manorial court and, if necessary, I shall have him hanged.'

Janna gulped, knowing from Hugh's tone that he meant every word of his threat. 'There's something else you should know, sire,' she said, in a small voice.

'What?'

'Master Serlo locked me up in a barn, but I . . . I managed to escape.'

'And how did you do that?' In spite of Hugh's grave expression, Janna thought she detected the hint of a reluctant smile about his mouth.

'I cut through the thatch at the top of a wall. There's a bit of a hole there now.'

Hugh clicked his tongue in disapproval. 'I believe I've underestimated you in the past, Johanna,' he said then, 'but I won't make the same mistake twice. And I'll make sure that Serlo doesn't either.' He dug his heels into the horse's flank and it took off across the water meadows. Janna watched the horse and its rider cross the river and head for the manor house. She had no chance of keeping up with Hugh, but for all that, she must follow after him in case he led her to Hamo. The idea that he might have had a hand in his cousin's disappearance disgusted and repelled her. She so desperately wanted to trust him, yet she could not get past the thought that, with Hamo out of the way, Hugh would be Dame Alice's sole heir. He would be free to marry anyone then – including Gytha. Janna's mouth turned down in a sour grimace at the thought.

Her mood, as she followed him across the water meadows, was not improved by the memory of Hugh's last injunction. How was she going to persuade Edwin to come out of hiding and face him? He would think she had betrayed him, and in truth, Janna felt as though she had, although Hugh had given her no choice in the matter. With a heavy heart, she wondered what she could say that might make Edwin trust Hugh's word, and change his mind about staying hidden.

Trust Hugh's word! She tripped over the thought, and almost laughed at the bitter irony of it. It seemed disaster awaited them all, whichever way she looked.

She was almost at the manor house when she heard the distant sound of hoofbeats. She stopped to look behind her, and her heart turned over when she saw Godric. Surprisingly, for she had not known that he could ride, he was mounted and coming her way. As he rode closer, his face set so cold and hard against her, she knew that she was not forgiven. She looked beyond, to the party riding behind him. In front were Robert of Babestoche and, beside him, Dame Alice, his wife. The dame had a kerchief to her eyes; they were scrubbed red and raw from crying. At once Janna looked down to hide her face from them. She stepped quickly out of the party's way. Her heart went out to the mother of the missing child, knowing how frightened she must feel, and how bitter her grief would be if her only son had come to harm. Silently, desperately, she prayed that Hamo would be found alive. She also prayed that Godric would not blurt out her secret.

To her relief, and also to her shame, Godric ignored her. He rode past her, taking Dame Alice, Robert, their small entourage of servants and the laden sumpter horses on towards the manor. None of them spared a second glance at Janna, but she was shaking with fright and reaction as she stared after them. Robert of Babestoche here at the manor! She could hardly believe that the man who had wished her dead, who had incited the villagers against her and stopped at nothing to bring his wish to fruition, was now within reach. She groaned aloud as she recalled all those who could bear witness against her, if they had the mind to do so. Cecily would hold her tongue, she was sure of that, but would Godric? Or Hugh? Or Hamo, who was just a child and could know nothing of discretion?

She remembered then, and with a heavy sense of despair, that Hamo was not around to blurt out the truth. But she was still in danger and so she must hurry to those who might, albeit unwittingly, spell her doom with a careless word. She must warn them, for her sake, to be silent. She would start with Hugh, who didn't understand the danger in speaking her name aloud to his aunt. She would start with Hugh, in the hope that he would lead her to Hamo.

ELEVEN

THE GROOM WAS leading away the mounts ridden by Godric and his party, but there was no sign of them, or of Hugh, when Janna entered through the gate. She hurried up the stairs to the hall and, greatly daring, pushed the door open a crack and peeped through.

Alarm took her breath away. Hugh was in there already, along with his guests. Cecily was also in attendance, red-eyed and shamefaced. Only Gytha seemed to be enjoying herself as she plied them all with refreshments. Janna scowled at the young woman before turning to Cecily. How could she catch the tiring woman's eye, and ask her to pass on the warning to Hugh not to divulge her identity? Impatient and perturbed, she jiggled and bobbed about in an effort to attract Cecily's attention. At last Cecily looked her way. Her eyes widened in surprise. Janna beckoned to her, then stepped hastily back out of sight.

'Janna! What are you doing here?'

'I escaped. But never mind that now. You have to warn my lord Hugh not to tell Dame Alice or Robert that I've survived the fire.'

Cecily frowned. 'But what reason shall I give for such secrecy?' she asked nervously.

Janna was silenced. Cecily's secret couldn't be told, but without that truth nothing else made much sense. 'I've already told him that there are some who wish me harm,' she said at last. 'Could you just remind him of that, and ask him to keep my true identity a secret from everyone, including his own family?'

'Very well.' Cecily gave a reluctant nod. To Janna's relief, she set off at once and, without ado, bobbed a curtsy to the dame and then drew Hugh aside. At once Janna shut the door and escaped down the stairs and into the yard. Bertha ran over to her.

'You shouldn't be here, Janna,' she said breathlessly. 'Serlo's told everyone you're a thief on the run. Edwin too. People are out looking for both of you now, as well as Hamo.' In her agitation, she'd grasped hold of Janna's sleeve. She clutched onto Janna, her face tight with distress.

'Don't fret, mistress. And don't make a scene and attract attention our way.' Janna gently disengaged Bertha's fingers. 'I've spoken to my lord Hugh and he knows I am innocent, and Edwin too, but he still wants to see him tonight, in secret if necessary. If Edwin wants to stay here at the manor, you'll have to persuade him to come out of hiding. Do you understand?'

To Janna's relief, Bertha nodded. It was one hurdle out of the way. 'Have you been watching Gytha? What have you seen?'

Bertha drew a quivering breath. Janna knew her fear and distress was on Edwin's account, not her own. She waited for Bertha to compose herself.

'Gytha spent part of the morning out with a search party. She stayed with them all the time and only came back to the manor when she saw my lord Hugh return. She's upstairs with him now.' Bertha's eyes brightened with sudden amusement, her good humour almost restored as she continued, 'I was following Gytha as you told me, and I heard my lord tell her to make herself useful for once, and prepare some refreshments for his family. I must say he didn't sound very loving, or even very friendly.'

Janna stood still while she absorbed Bertha's information. 'You've done well,' she said slowly. 'Will you keep on watching?' She was fairly sure Bertha was wasting her time, but if she told her so, Janna knew the girl's suspicions might move on to a far more likely prospect. Besides, she might have misjudged Gytha, underestimated her pride and her ambition. The thought of Gytha's guilt was some consolation to Janna, even if she couldn't quite believe in it.

Bertha nodded, and walked back to keep watch on the stairs leading up to the hall. She flicked a hand in farewell, and Janna returned the gesture. She wondered what she should do while Hugh was engaged with his guests. Every instinct prompted her to join in the search, but she was sure there was no point to it, for if Hamo was going to be found, he would have been found already. Rather than rush around pointlessly, Janna decided instead to follow the leads she'd come up with, in the hope that Hamo's whereabouts might become clear to her. She could only pray that she would find him in time to save his life.

She could start by looking for Hamo's ball. As she began a careful search of the yard, she wondered if it was still there to be found. Even if Hamo had left his ball lying around, it was quite possible one of the young searchers she'd previously encountered in the barn had already made off with it. Hamo's ball was a prize worth having, being made of leather stuffed with dried beans, rather than the straw-filled pig's bladder that was the usual plaything of urchins. Without much hope, she poked and pried about bush and barn, and came at last to the reluctant conclusion that the urchins must indeed have found the ball first, for her careful search revealed no trace of it at all. Either it had been stolen, or Hamo had taken it away with him. It occurred to Janna then that there was still one place left for her to search. At the same time, perhaps she could also solve the mystery of the disappearing dog?

She hurried across to the kitchen garden, and peered behind the barrels where she'd first spotted Bones in hiding. She chided herself for being fanciful as her keen eyes scoured the area and found nothing. Disconsolate, she looked around the neat garden with its rows of herbs and vegetables, an abundance of food which brought juices seeping into her mouth when she remembered her scant breakfast.

She walked past a large bush of rue, and stopped to search for any signs of who might have been picking posies from it. Perhaps there was a footprint, or even something dropped which might help her identify the culprit. A pale glimmer deep within the foliage caught her eye, and she plunged her hand into the bush to investigate.

'Yes!' She seized Hamo's prized treasure with a shout of triumph. As she held the ball aloft, her spirits took a sudden nosedive for she understood now, without any doubt at all, that Hamo's disappearance was linked to what had gone before. It was a deliberate act by someone who wished him harm.

Hugh, she thought, with an ache of sadness that wrenched her heart. She must stick by him, tight as resin to a tree. Sooner or later, he would lead her to his cousin. She left the kitchen garden and positioned herself at the side of the barn where she could see but not be seen. There was nothing for it, now, but to watch and wait until Hugh emerged from the hall and went about his business once more.

Her feet were tired and her spirit weary from watching when Hugh finally clattered down the stairs from the hall. He was accompanied by Godric. They stood together, conferring, while Janna fumed impatiently. She desperately wanted to tell Godric what was on her mind, and enlist his help in tracking down Hamo, but she could not while Hugh was present. Of course it was quite possible, she conceded as she watched them part, that Godric would not speak to her. She could waste time with him instead of going after her prime suspect. Who, then, should she follow?

Caution won. She followed Hugh, even though she was sure Godric had seen her. He would think she was running after Hugh. It would turn him even further against her. She longed to speak to him, to try to explain, but she could not. Not when Hugh might be on his way to check up on Hamo even now. So she skulked about watching Hugh, ducking for cover behind walls and trees every time he looked around in case he spotted her.

He seemed in no hurry to join the search for Hamo, going first to the kitchen where he spent some time. When he came out, he was followed by Serlo. They spoke a few moments longer, and then Serlo strode off while Hugh went into the kitchen garden. Janna sidled after him, and watched him pull an apple from the tree. The apples were still not quite ripe and she suspected he was about to give himself a bellyache, but he made no attempt to eat it, walking instead towards the stable. Janna felt a sudden leap of hope. Could Hamo be hidden somewhere inside? She broke cover to creep after Hugh and took shelter in a stall while she waited for her eyes to become accustomed to the dim light.

'Johanna. Why are you following me about the manor?' Hugh's voice sounded weary and impatient. A hot blush flamed Janna's cheeks as she stumbled reluctantly from her hiding place.

'I . . . I . . .' She could think of no excuse that might explain her actions.

He stroked the horse's nose while he waited. The silence between them lengthened to snapping point. It was Hugh who gave in first. 'Was there something you wanted to say to me?'

Yes! But Janna was afraid to ask the questions that tumbled into her mind, for Hugh would know then that she suspected him of abducting Hamo.

'I . . . I wanted to change Arrow's dressing,' she muttered.

At once, Hugh lifted the horse's hoof so that she might inspect it, gentling the horse all the while. Watching him, Janna found it impossible to believe him responsible for deliberately injuring the animal, or for carrying out any of the other acts that had plagued the manor. He loved Arrow – just as Janna was sure he loved his cousin Hamo, as well as the manor that had been entrusted to his care. Janna knew Hugh to be kind, and she had thought that he was honourable. Gytha might not be quite so honourable, but Janna doubted she had either the resourcefulness or the will to snatch Hamo and bring about all the 'accidents' that had gone before, or even the wit to think of leaving posies of rue to mark what she was doing. But if not Hugh, or Gytha, then who?

Once again, something niggled at her memory. Was there something she'd overlooked, had someone said something that might shed new light on the people who lived and worked here?

Rue for repentance, rue for regret. But Eadgyth had said it could also be used to curse an enemy.

The significance of everything that had happened at the manor suddenly shifted and began to change, forming a different pattern altogether. And with the new pattern came an unexpected name. Perplexed, wishing she had time to sift her thoughts and make some sense of them, Janna bent to the task of removing the dressing. 'The wound is healing well, my lord,' she said, 'but you should not ride Arrow for a while yet.'

Hugh nodded. He produced the apple and held it out to Arrow. 'Don't forget I want to see Edwin tonight,' he said, over the sound of the horse's happy crunching. 'I've been speaking to Master Serlo, and I want some answers from you both. Too many accidents have been happening lately, seemingly without any explanation. There were no accidents until you and Edwin arrived at the manor.'

'We arrived at the manor before you did, sire. There were no accidents until you came home from Babestoche Manor.' Janna knew she was taking a risk, but perhaps it might provoke Hugh to deal honestly if he thought others suspected that his might be the hand behind all the incidents. And if he was innocent, as she was beginning to suspect he might be, then the more he could tell her, the closer they might come to understanding the reason for Hamo's disappearance. Feeling a little fearful, she kept her head bent while she replaced Arrow's dressing and waited for Hugh's reaction.

He went very still. 'What do you mean by that?' His tone rasped harshly.

Janna stood her ground, not allowing herself to be intimidated by him. 'I mean nothing by it, sire,' she said, in as respectful a tone as she could muster. 'You and Master Serlo seem to hold Edwin and me responsible for the troubles here. I'm only pointing out a fact in our defence.'

'Hmm.' Hugh inspected her closely. Janna flushed more deeply under his scrutiny, all too conscious of the rough smock and breeches that she wore. Automatically, her hand went to her hair, to smooth and tidy it. It was a shock to feel only stubble under her hands. Hugh lifted a sardonic eyebrow, understanding only too well her unconscious attempt to remind him that she had once been beautiful.

'Do you know anything about these accidents, Johanna, anything at all?' he asked in a more conciliatory tone.

Janna hesitated, then made up her mind. If she was going to defend herself and Edwin, and test him at the same time, she might as well do it properly, she thought. 'I know that a posy of rue has been left at the site of every mishap.'

'Rue?' She could have sworn his surprise was genuine, along with his question: 'What do you mean?'

'I mean that a posy of rue was left at the henhouse at the time the fox got in, and another was found beside the lamb that was slaughtered. I found a posy of rue near the byre after the animals escaped and destroyed the new wheat, and there was also a posy attached to the haystack next to the one that was fired. I found rue at the stable door on the day Arrow's shoe worked loose and the nail went into his hoof and . . . and I saw a posy of rue at the door of the undercroft, from where the woollen cloth and silver goblets were stolen.'

'And where are they now, these posies of rue?' Hugh sounded thoroughly bewildered.

'I . . . I was afraid that Edwin and I would be blamed for all that was going wrong, and so I destroyed them,' Janna confessed.

'You've told me lies in the past, Johanna. Why should I believe you now?'

And why should I believe you know nothing about what I'm telling you, Janna thought in turn. 'Because it's the truth, sire,' she said instead. 'I told lies in the past because I had to protect myself, but I have no need to tell lies about what's been happening here. Neither does Edwin. He *likes* it here, he wants to stay, he's told me so himself. Why should he try to destroy something when it is the means to his escape from his lord as well as his future livelihood?'

Hugh nodded thoughtfully. 'And Hamo?' he said carefully, going to the heart of the matter. 'Is his disappearance part of this same puzzle?'

Janna looked at him. Was he testing her, seeing how much she knew, or suspected, or did he really want to know? His face was gaunt, lined with worry and fatigue. She was almost sure his concern was genuine. 'A posy of rue was left outside the undercroft where he was playing with his ball,' she said carefully.

'You said goods have been stolen from the undercroft,' Hugh rejoined swiftly.

Janna nodded. 'And by someone who has a key to the chests, for they were all locked, sire.'

'And how do you know that?'

'I searched the undercroft when I found the posy of rue, just in case Hamo was hidden there.'

'Was he?' Hugh seized her arm. He sounded truly fearful as he begged, 'For God's sake, tell me if you know where he is, Johanna!'

'I do not know, sire. I wish I did.' Baffled, Janna shook her head while the last of her carefully constructed assumptions fell apart in the face of Hugh's anguish.

Hugh let go of her arm and began to curse under his breath. Then he turned on Janna. 'I must go out and search for the boy. You have given relief to my aunt in the past, Johanna. Will you see her again? Perhaps mix up some posset to ease her mind, for she is in great distress.'

'I can't!' Janna answered without thinking.

'Why not?' Now Hugh sounded cold and hard as he continued: 'I will pay you for your ministrations, if that is what is on your mind.'

'No! No, sire, it isn't that at all!'

'Then why will you not go to my aunt? Cecily begged me to keep your secret, she says you believe people wish you harm, but you cannot fear my aunt, surely?'

'But I do, sire. I fear everyone.' Janna stopped and took a

deep breath. She remembered what Hugh had said in the past about his aunt's marriage. Would he be sympathetic to her cause? 'I especially fear my lord Robert,' she said carefully.

Hugh frowned, but he didn't say anything. Janna knew she had come too far to back out now. She must go on, although she would not tell him everything she knew. She wouldn't betray Cecily. 'I asked you once before to keep my identity a secret,' she said. 'It was because I feared him. I believe it was he who incited the villagers to set fire to my cottage, even though they knew that I was inside. In fact, I suspect that was part of the plan, for the lord Robert wanted me either dead or gone from the manor. I want him to think he has succeeded in this. Indeed, my safety depends on it.'

'Why should Robert want your death? What do you know about him?'

It was a fair question, but one Janna was not prepared to answer, at least not without Cecily's permission. She stayed silent while Hugh waited for an answer. At last, when he saw she would say nothing more, he heaved a sigh and said softly, 'My aunt married unwisely when she chose Robert but, by calling in the priest to marry them at the church door, she now has the sanction of the church on her marriage and therefore cannot undo the union, no matter how much she might have come to regret it. That is why she summoned me for the birth of her baby, and that is why I stayed on at the manor for such a long time afterwards. It was because she suspected that Robert has turned his affection elsewhere. How am I doing so far, Johanna? Do you know what I'm talking about?'

His question caught Janna by surprise. She gave a reluctant nod.

'And I suspect you know a lot more than you're telling me?' Hugh waited for Janna's reply, but she stayed silent. Her own mother had died because Robert had tried to silence Cecily, but without proof Janna couldn't accuse Robert of anything. That hadn't stopped him trying to silence Janna with the willing aid of the villagers he'd incited. And she knew he'd try again if he realised his secret hadn't died with her.

'Perhaps you're not prepared to betray any confidences?' Hugh ventured.

Janna nodded again, relieved that he seemed to understand her position.

'Then tell me!' He grasped her once more by the arm, and thrust his face close to hers. 'Does any of this have anything to do with Hamo's disappearance now?'

'No. At least, I don't think so.' Janna looked up at Hugh, conscious of how closely they stood together. She could see the stubble of his beard, and smell the sweat on him after his hard ride through the forest. She closed her eyes, feeling suddenly faint with longing.

'Johanna.' His voice was gentle. 'I keep saying that I won't underestimate you, and then I go and do it all over again.' He gave a rueful laugh. 'But you still haven't told me why you've been following me about the manor, when you could have come straight to the stable if you really wanted to change Arrow's dressing.'

His question brought Janna back to the reality of her position. She blinked, and stepped away from him. Yet she could not break the tie she'd sensed between them. How far could she trust him with the truth?

'I'm looking for Hamo, sire. I wondered if you . . .' She found she could not go on.

'If I . . . know where he is? If I can lead you to him? Do you think I have him hidden somewhere?' There was a hard edge of anger behind the question.

Janna tilted her chin, assuming a bravery she did not feel. She found she was incapable of answering his question.

Hugh gave a short, hard laugh. 'I can assure you I don't know where Hamo is, and I'm every bit as concerned for his safety as you are. If you have any thoughts about where he might have strayed, I beg you to tell me so that we can look for him there.'

'I don't think he has strayed, sire. I believe he's been taken.' Janna felt a sudden doubt as she said the words. Had her longing for Hugh led her to misread the situation? For a brief moment, she didn't know whether or not to hope that she had. Then she reminded herself that everything pointed to abduction rather than happenstance.

'Taken? But why? And by whom?' Hugh looked stunned as the full import of Janna's words struck home.

Could her suspicions be correct? A name was on the tip of Janna's tongue, but she found she could not utter it. Not yet, not without further thought. Not without proof. 'I don't know, sire,' she said instead.

'But you thought I was responsible?' Hugh nodded before Janna could answer the question. 'Yes, I can see why you might think it in my interests to have Hamo out of the way.' He took hold of Janna's shoulders and grasped her tight. 'You must believe me, I know nothing of any of this,' he said earnestly. His jaw set into a determined line. 'But by God, you can be sure I'll get to the bottom of it. No-one will be safe from my questions, no-one.' He let her go and took a step back. 'Not even Edwin,' he added. 'Go and fetch him now. I will question him along with everyone else.' And before Janna could protest, he strode out of the stable.

TWELVE

JANNA LOOKED DOWN at the ball she was still clutching in her hand. All her fine theories about Hugh's guilt had been blown away, and she was more than glad of it, for there was someone else now to take his place. She'd seen and heard several things that could suggest a possible motive for what had been happening, but before she could do anything to find Hamo, she would first have to prove that what she was thinking could be true. Edwin would have to wait. She had far more important things to do right now than go looking for him.

Taking care to keep her face hidden lest Robert or Dame Alice should see her, she went in search of Cecily. She didn't have to look far. The tiring woman was moping about the kitchen garden once more. Bones was with her, still tied to the old piece of rope. Even as Janna watched, the dog lifted a leg and sent a liberal spray over a patch of parsley. Janna pulled a face, hoping that the cook was as punctilious as her own mother had been when it came to washing herbs before using them.

'Cecily,' she called, in case the tiring woman hurried away now that her charge had done his duty. She tucked Hamo's ball behind her back as she approached. Bones barked and wagged his tail, and she bent to give him a pat, pleased that he stood four-square on his paws, seemingly without discomfort.

Cecily gave her a woebegone smile. 'I'm glad Serlo saw sense and let you go free, Janna.'

Janna grinned in return. 'Actually, I escaped. But it's all right, my lord Hugh knows about the missing goods. He knows I am not to blame, and he has spoken to Serlo about it.' Surprised, the tiring woman opened her mouth to question Janna further. 'Will you tell me again about the last time you saw Hamo?' Janna hurried on, unwilling to waste time on explanations.

Cecily's eyes filled with tears. 'I left him over there.' She flung out her hand towards the staircase which led upwards to the hall.

'And he was playing with his ball?' Janna confirmed.

Cecily nodded.

'This one?' Janna pulled it out from behind her back and showed it to the tiring woman.

Cecily gasped. 'Where did you get that?' She took it from Janna and peered at it as if it might reveal the secret of Hamo's whereabouts.

'I found it here in the kitchen garden, hidden within a bush of rue. And I found the dog here, too. I think he'd been beaten. He was frightened.'

'But . . . who? Why?'

'I'm working on it.' Janna took Cecily's hand. 'Try not to worry,' she said gently. 'I think I'm close to finding an answer. If I'm right, none of the blame for Hamo's disappearance will fall on you.'

'Do you know where he is? Is he still alive?' Cecily's face shone with new hope.

'I hope so.' It was as far as Janna was prepared to go right now. She released Cecily's hand, frowning as she noticed a patch of tiny blisters on her own hand. They were itchy and sore. Janna scratched them absent-mindedly. 'You said you were called away to speak to the cook about Hamo's meals. Who called you away?' She waited for an answer, willing Cecily to speak the name in her mind.

'Master Serlo,' Cecily answered readily. 'I asked his advice about Hamo. I wanted to know what Hamo might do about the manor farm to keep him occupied, for he is such a bright and merry boy, I knew he would not be content to stay by my side all the time. I thought Master Serlo might arrange for him to learn to ride, perhaps, or become more proficient with his swordplay, for I know he loves to pretend to fight just like his cousin Hugh. Serlo suggested I speak to the cook about providing good fresh food for Hamo, for he is growing apace and is always hungry.'

Serlo! No-one had been more assiduous in the search for Hamo than the reeve. No-one was more proud of the manor farm. In Hugh's absence he had taken charge of it as if it was his own. He had nothing to gain from setting a fox amongst the hens, or killing a lamb, setting fire to a haystack, destroying the new wheat or laming Hugh's horse – or even snatching a child. He had nothing to gain but the destruction of Hugh's reputation. Janna's next thought sent her heart plummeting down to her boots. Serlo might have started out with the intention of discrediting Hugh in the eyes of his aunt, perhaps hoping that it would further his own interests.

But snatching Hamo meant a larger purpose altogether, a purpose Janna couldn't bear to think about.

If there was anything in Serlo's past to shed light on his actions now, the cook would surely know, Janna thought. She was a know-all and a gossip, and she must be made to talk. Conscious that time was passing and that the more pressing need was to find Hamo rather than working out how to force Serlo to show his hand, Janna turned to Cecily.

'I'm going to make up a posset for Dame Alice, for I believe the lady is in sore distress,' she told Cecily. 'Will you come to the kitchen and fetch it by and by? I beg you, if you value my life please don't tell ma dame, or Robert, where it comes from.'

Cecily nodded. 'I have kept your secret, as I vowed I would,' she assured Janna.

'But please tell my lord Hugh that I have made up the posset, as he asked.'

Cecily's eyes widened as she came to understand the full implications of all Janna had told her. The lord of the manor had reached an understanding with a lowly peasant who dressed as a boy and worked as a farmhand. A smile twitched Janna's mouth as she read the girl's bafflement.

'I must go up to ma dame.' Cecily thrust the end of the rope into Janna's hand. 'Please take the dog. It upsets Dame Alice to have it near by, while my lord Robert gives it a kick every time it comes close to his boot.'

Janna gave a small huff of sour amusement. She could quite well believe it of Robert. The man was a bully, afraid of no-one save his wife. And the thought of anything that might jeopardise his comfortable life, Janna amended.

As Cecily climbed the stairs and vanished into the hall, Janna tugged on the rope to lead Bones to the herbs she wanted to pick for Dame Alice's posset. Wild lettuce and valerian would help to calm and soothe her, banish nightmares and help her to sleep, while motherwort, sweet marjoram or any of several other herbs would build her strength and lift her spirits. She glanced at the dog as she picked the roots, leaves and flowers she needed. He'd been washed, his coat was clean and shining. In fact, the dog was starting to look almost handsome. 'Where were you when Hamo was taken?' she asked, sure in her own mind that Bones had been used as bait to trap Hamo, and that the dog had then been dumped, along with Hamo's ball, once the child was safely out of sight. Or dead.

She hurriedly pushed the thought away. She could not afford to give in to despair, not while there was the slightest chance that Hamo might still be alive. 'Did you see Hamo?' she asked Bones. 'Do you know where he is now?'

The dog looked at her with bright, intelligent eyes, and whined softly. Janna gave him a pat and straightened, clutching her handful of plants. She hurried off to the kitchen, with Bones trotting willingly beside her. He'd obviously decided that the kitchen was his favourite place, and he strained on his lead to get there, setting up a frantic sniffing and barking once inside.

'Get that mongrel out of here,' Mistress Tova said savagely, as she swiped a piece of bacon away from the dog's quivering nose.

Janna set down the fragrant herbs she carried. She surreptitiously slid her hand over a piece of bacon fat before dragging Bones outside. While he was busy gulping down the titbit, she tied him to a post, leaving him in view of the door so that she could watch out for him. Then she went back inside, determined to put the cook's gossip to good use for once.

The cook glanced sideways at Janna. 'Master Serlo was in here looking for you – and your brother. You're in a lot of trouble, both of you. He says there are some goods missing from the undercroft.'

'My lord Hugh knows that we are both innocent of this crime,' Janna said quickly.

Mistress Tova gave a suspicious sniff, as if to smell out the truth. 'Doesn't do to get on the wrong side of Serlo,' she muttered darkly.

It was the opening Janna was waiting for.

'Tell me about Master Serlo, mistress,' she said. She hooked a pot of water over the fire to boil, and began to prepare and chop the herbs she'd picked. 'How is it that he lives in such a substantial home and is allowed to keep all those fields for his own?'

'This manor once belonged to Serlo's family.' Unable to resist a good gossip, the cook came over and settled her bony backside onto a stool. 'The land was confiscated by William the Bastard after the great battle at Hastings,' she confided. 'The king gave this estate as well as several others to Dame Alice's grandfather, who had fought with him and so was rewarded for his service. Serlo's family lost their land and their livelihood, and were reduced to the status of villeins on a manor they had owned for centuries before that.'

Janna was silent as she absorbed the cook's information. This was the link that completed the puzzle. It was also a familiar story. Many Saxon thegns had been dispossessed of their lands after the Norman invasion. William had even taken an inventory of everything he'd conquered, right down to the last hide and plough, cow and pig, mill and fishery, and had kept a record in what everyone now called 'the Domesday Book' for it seemed like a final reckoning of their lives. But the commissioners had many arguments to settle first, so it was said, for the thegns did not give up their land and possessions lightly, while the Norman barons were always greedy to claim more than their entitlement. It had caused great hardship, anger and misery at the time. It seemed that the memory of past greatness and great wrongs did not die easily.

'Ma dame inherited the property through her own family, but Serlo still takes great pride in the estate,' Mistress Tova continued, confirming the direction in which Janna's thoughts now lay. 'It was to reward him for his good offices that my lord Hugh granted him the right to live in a cottage that had once belonged to his family and gave him the gore acres as his own, on the understanding that the work was done in Serlo's own time and that it would not take anything away from his attention to the rest of the manor.'

She hesitated, torn between loyalty to her daughter and confiding her innermost fears. 'In truth, John,' she said then, 'I have urged Gytha to encourage Serlo's attention, for I know he is keen – more than keen – to wed her. In faith, the reeve is besotted with her, he is sick with love, but Gytha will have none of him for she means to marry my lord and no other.'

Janna nodded. She'd seen how Serlo looked at Gytha, and how disdainfully the young girl treated him in turn. Serlo must know that he had a rival for her affections, and who he was. How he must hate being subservient to Hugh, especially as all this had once belonged to his own family! 'And does the lord Hugh encourage her in this expectation?' It took all Janna's courage to remain calm as she waited for the cook to reply.

Mistress Tova sighed. 'He does not,' she admitted sadly. Then she brightened slightly. 'But my lord is lonely, and my daughter is beautiful. While he breathes, there is hope for her.' She thought for a moment. 'And if Gytha's ambition comes to nothing after all, Serlo will still have her and she must have him. She will see that he has much to offer and that she could do a lot worse than take him for a husband.'

Indeed, Serlo had much to offer, Janna thought. No wonder he worked so hard about the manor, if Gytha was his intended prize. If he could take Hugh down at the same time, that would make his prize even sweeter. She recalled her first meeting with Serlo. 'See how well my flock is doing,' Serlo had boasted to the forester while she and Edwin were in hiding. His words had led Janna to believe that they were taking refuge on Serlo's own property, yet the fields he'd shown the forester were not his own but were part of the manor he oversaw for Hugh.

Janna nodded thoughtfully. Serlo's slip of the tongue should have alerted her to his real purpose right from the start. Having already reclaimed a substantial property for himself, the reeve meant to have it all. By discrediting Hugh, he hoped to drive him off the manor farm and out of Dame

Alice's good graces, leaving himself in charge. But he must have known that, even if his plan succeeded, his power could only last until Hamo came of age.

Janna's hand stilled on the knife she was using to cut the herbs. With a cold feeling of dread, she finally acknowledged the unthinkable. Hamo's visit to the manor was unexpected, as was his ducking in the river, but Serlo had wasted no time using those events to his own advantage. Hamo's death could be made to seem the result of yet another accident. With Hamo dead, and Hugh out of the way, the path would be clear for Serlo to petition Dame Alice for the right to reclaim what had once belonged to his family. She would surely be agreeable, for by that time the manor would hold only the worst of memories for her.

Janna felt sick. Her hands began to tremble so badly she set down the knife lest she cut herself. Serlo. He had been left in charge of searching the manor grounds and forest in Hugh's absence. How easy for him to lead the search away from Hamo. How easy for him to ensure that Hamo – or Hamo's body – would never be found. Was Hamo alive, or dead? A hot tide of rage swept over Janna. She clenched her hands. If Hamo was dead, perhaps buried in the forest somewhere, they might search for ever and never find him. I can't allow that to happen, Janna vowed. Alive or dead, he *must* be found.

A sudden thought lifted Janna's spirits slightly, and gave her a thread of hope on which to cling. Dame Alice would never relinquish the manor to Serlo while there was the possibility that Hamo might one day be found. Only his dead body would be enough to convince her either to sell or

241

give the manor farm to Serlo – and so far, there was no dead body. Did that mean Hamo was still alive? Could Serlo be waiting for the hunt to be called off before causing the 'accident' that would bring about the boy's death? If that was the truth of it, then Serlo must be keeping Hamo captive somewhere – but where?

In his own cottage? It seemed the most likely place, but it was also the most dangerous. Serlo was the villeins' reeve, the first person they would call on if they had a grudge or a grievance to air. And for the same reason he was also the first person Hugh would call on. Anyone entering Serlo's cottage in search of him would find Hamo. It was surely too big a risk. But if not the cottage, then where? The fields round about? Janna considered the possibility, but only for a moment. There was no shelter out there to hide a child, not for any length of time. If Hamo was anywhere in the fields, he would certainly have been found by now.

The forest? If Serlo had managed to take Hamo there without being seen, it would make the best hiding place of all, Janna concluded. He could choose a spot, somewhere wild and undisturbed, knowing that the grave would never be found. He would be safe then to carry on his mission to reclaim his stolen land, with or without Hamo's body.

Janna sighed. This was all thought and supposition; she had no proof to accuse Serlo of anything, nor would she unless Hamo could be found to bear witness against him.

A sudden pang of doubt shook Janna as she remembered how Serlo had hidden them from the forester. He had given them shelter for he had recognised that they, too, were of Saxon stock, and his instinct had been to protect them from the terrible justice of the forest law instituted by Norman kings. Even though they'd been expected to work hard in repayment for Serlo's kindness, she and Edwin had been grateful, so grateful. And now here she was, ready to suspect him of the worst deeds imaginable: kidnap and murder.

'Gytha was always proud. Of course she has many talents as well as being beautiful.' Mistress Tova was still talking.

'Has Gytha spent any time with the young lord, with Hamo?' Janna interrupted, her certainty in Serlo's guilt suddenly shaken. No matter how unlikely it might seem that Gytha was guilty, she couldn't afford a false accusation against someone as powerful as the reeve.

'No, she dislikes the child. Oh!' Mistress Tova put her hand to her mouth, too late to take back the words she obviously wished she'd never said. 'I didn't mean it quite like that,' she said nervously. 'Gytha's very good with children, but she resents the fact that the young lord will inherit this manor when he is of age. Even so, she's very upset by his disappearance. She spends every free moment out searching for Hamo. Poor little lad. He must have run off in a great hurry, for Mistress Cecily left him alone only while she talked to me, and she raised the alarm just as soon as she realised he had run away again.'

Janna hastily finished chopping up the herbs and threw them into the boiling water. A growing sense of urgency possessed her. The cook had given her much to think about and she was anxious to get moving.

'This is a posset for Dame Alice, to help her rest,' she said. 'Let it boil for as long as it would take to milk a goat or a sheep, then take it off the fire and let it cool. I pray you, keep the mixture for Mistress Cecily, who will be along presently to fetch it for ma dame.' Not giving the cook any time to argue, she rushed out of the door, pausing only to untie Bones. Delighted, the dog yipped and ran around in circles, almost tripping Janna as she set off across the yard.

'Behave yourself!' She nudged Bones out of the way with a not-too-gentle foot, and hurried on. She had to find Hamo – and for that, she had to find Serlo.

Her hand was smarting quite badly now. Janna looked down at the rash, remembering how she'd plunged her hand into the bush of rue to retrieve Hamo's ball. She should have taken more care, wrapped something around her hand to protect it, she thought, recalling that rue was harmless enough except when the sun shone on it and brought oil to the surface of its leaves, the oil that had caused her skin to blister.

The elusive memory flickered once more, and in a sudden Janna had it, the last proof she needed of Serlo's guilt. He, too, had once had a rash on his hand, the same rash that came from picking rue. She remembered that she'd offered to make him up an ointment for it, hoping to deflect his accusations about the straying cows – and the fox in the hencoop and the slaughter of the lamb. If only she'd thought of this before, so much harm could have been avoided!

She understood now, the posies of rue and what they meant. Rue to curse Dame Alice, and to mark his revenge against her for taking his land. She would repent that theft and suffer the consequences.

She remembered how quick Serlo had been to correct her when she'd hinted that Hamo might have been taken, how he'd called Hamo 'silly' for wandering away and getting lost again. Janna closed her eyes and groaned aloud at her own stupidity as she realised something else. Serlo had seen her with the posy of rue. No wonder he'd been so quick to act against her. He would have had a key to the chests in the undercroft and could easily have taken the missing goods. Perhaps his aim was to throw Janna off his trail if he suspected that she knew what he was doing, but it was much more likely that he meant to use the stolen goods as an excuse to banish her and Edwin from the manor. He had certainly used them to discredit her. He'd made quite sure that, if she voiced her suspicions, she would not be believed.

More convinced than ever, now, of Serlo's guilt, and with a corresponding lightness of heart that Hugh was innocent of every charge, Janna thought of someone else who might help in her quest to find Hamo. Someone she could trust. Someone skilled at tracking signs, and who knew the forest better than anyone else, better even than the forester. Godric. If Hamo was hidden or buried somewhere in the forest, Godric would be able to follow the passage of whoever had taken the child.

Hamo must be alive, Janna thought. He *must* be! Her imagination tortured her with images of the boy's bright face, his open, trusting nature. She wondered if he could hear the bell tolling to bring him home. He would not understand what was happening to him, why he was being held captive. He would be so frightened. Janna's hands clenched in impotent rage. She would have battered the truth out of Serlo with her bare fists if she'd thought it would help her cause. But punishment could come later, once Hugh found out the full extent of his reeve's treachery. In the meantime, their best hope of finding Hamo rested with Godric.

Taking care to keep out of Serlo's way, for he was everywhere about the manor supervising the search parties, Janna walked quickly to the gate with Bones yapping at her heels. She was about to pass through when Bertha pounced on her once more, and drew her into the shelter of a barn.

'You must be careful, Janna,' she said in a low voice. 'I heard the lord Hugh tell Serlo that you're innocent of all crimes and he's not to lock you up again, but the hunt is still on for Edwin. Serlo means to have you followed in the hope you'll betray Edwin's hiding place. You won't do that, will you?'

'Of course not.' There were no doubts now in Janna's mind about Serlo's guilt, but it seemed likely that Edwin was to be made the scapegoat for all that had happened. She couldn't allow that.

'You don't have to watch Gytha any more,' she told Bertha. 'I know she's innocent, and I also know who's guilty of these crimes, although I have no way of proving it unless I can find Hamo.' She glanced quickly over her shoulder to make sure they were still unobserved. 'Go to Edwin when you can, when it's safe, and tell him he's not to show himself on any account until we find Hamo.'

'Is Hamo still alive then?' Bertha's eyes shone with hope.

'Pray God that he is, otherwise we are all doomed,' Janna said grimly. She walked to the door of the barn and peered out. Serlo was nowhere in sight. 'Have you seen Godric anywhere?' she called over her shoulder.

'I saw a stranger go through the gate a little while ago,'

Bertha answered. 'Was that Godric? He walked down to the ford. I think he plans to search in the forest.'

'Good. Thank you, Bertha.' Pulling Bones behind her, Janna left the barn and hurried off in search of the villein. At the same time, she kept a sharp lookout for Serlo. To her relief, there was no sign of him or of Hugh but, as she forded the river, she caught sight of Godric. He was about to vanish into the thick green barrier that marked the edge of the forest.

'Ho! Godric, wait for me!' she shouted, and put on a burst of speed to catch up to him.

He hesitated. Janna knew that he'd heard her cry out. It was too far for her to see his face, but she could imagine him scowling as he made up his mind whether or not to obey her command.

He stayed where he was, and she was grateful for it. 'Godric!' she panted, as soon as she was within earshot. Although he'd waited, he'd turned his back on her and seemed absorbed in studying the myriad hues of green in the foliage ahead.

'What do you want?' He turned and scowled at her.

Janna bent over, holding tight to her aching side. 'You have to help me,' she gasped.

Godric's face closed against her. He took a step away. 'I have more important things to do with my time, Janna,' he said distantly. 'I'm looking for Hamo.'

'So am I,' Janna said impatiently. She straightened. 'I think I know what's happened to him. Listen to me.' And she poured out her story, trusting him with all the truth including her suspicions about Hugh, leaving nothing out in her desperation to convince him to help her. 'I know how good you are at following signs,' she finished breathlessly. 'If Hamo's hidden somewhere in the forest, I know you'll be able to find him, Godric.'

His expression remained dubious. 'People have been searching through the forest for days, trampling tracks everywhere. How will I know whether I'm on Serlo's trail or someone else's?'

'Oh.' Janna's hopes deflated instantly. 'I hadn't thought of that.' She took some comfort from the fact that at least Godric had listened to her, and that he was taking her suggestions seriously. But his objection was sound. 'Then we'll have to follow Serlo after all,' she declared, adding honestly: 'You'll have to follow him, Godric. He's watching out for me, he thinks I'm going to lead him to Edwin – which I'm not. Bertha's gone to warn Edwin. She loves him, and she'll make sure he stays hidden until it's safe for him to come out.'

Godric nodded. It seemed to Janna that he was looking more friendly as he said, 'I doubt Serlo will make any move towards Hamo in the daylight. If he's making a show of searching for him, he'll continue while people are around to watch. I suspect we'll have to wait until it's dark, Janna.'

'So you do believe me? You'll help me?' Janna looked up at Godric with shining eyes. He caught his breath, and quickly turned away. 'I'll help you,' he said gruffly. 'But I suggest we also keep on looking for Hamo.' He hesitated. 'It would be easier for Serlo to keep him hidden if he was already dead, you know that, don't you?'

'I refuse to even think it.' Bones had started to bark and Janna cuffed him gently with her foot. 'Sshh!'

'We don't want to attract Serlo's attention.' Godric turned on Bones. 'Can't you shut him up?'

But Janna was no longer listening. 'No-one's searched Serlo's cottage, of course. It's over there.' She pointed a finger to show Godric where she meant. 'I don't think he's got Hamo hidden there, but we should probably search it if we can.'

She became aware that Godric wasn't looking, and waved a hand in front of his eyes to get his attention. Suddenly, and taking Janna completely by surprise, he pulled her into his arms and kissed her hard.

'Umph . . . ssfflk.' It was too hard to protest with Godric's lips pressed against her own, but Janna did her best.

'Serlo's coming our way,' Godric muttered, before kissing her vigorously once more.

'But he thinks I'm a boy!' Janna protested, when she could speak once more.

'No, he doesn't.' Godric kept his arms around Janna, and his mouth close to her ear as he whispered, 'He saw you in the river and I believe he's been asking questions about you ever since. I also heard him ask Cecily why she thought you were a girl.'

Too alarmed by Godric's observations to think straight, Janna melted into his embrace. They stood locked together in a long and lingering kiss. To Janna's surprise, she found she was rather enjoying herself.

'That's enough,' she muttered at last, and pulled away. At once Godric let her go, but his eyes were bright and his face was flushed as he looked at her. Janna found it hard to meet his gaze. 'We've done enough kissing to convince the reeve,' she mumbled.

Godric shook his head. 'He's still coming towards us,' he whispered. 'But he might think twice about having you followed if he believes your affection lies with me and not with Edwin.' He bent to kiss her again.

'You! John – or whatever your real name is. I want a word with you!'

Reluctantly, Janna freed herself from Godric's embrace and braced herself to face Serlo. He came striding up to them with a thunderous expression. In spite of her resolve, Janna found herself shrinking against Godric, badly needing his strength and support. Beside them, Bones continued to bark.

'If it were left to me, you'd be gone from this manor by now, and with a beating to send you on your way, you and your so-called brother!' Serlo stood over Janna, glowering at her. Godric placed an arm around her shoulders and scowled right back at the reeve.

'You may have the ear of my lord Hugh, but I know how many lies you've told,' Serlo blustered, ignoring Godric. 'Unless you tell me where your brother is hiding, I'll make sure my lord Hugh finds out the truth about you, about who and what you really are.'

Several comments came to Janna's mind, not least the fact that while Hugh already knew the truth about her, he certainly didn't know the truth about his reeve. But she held her tongue, knowing that she must not, under any circumstances, put Serlo on his guard.

'Where is your brother?' Serlo thrust his face close to hers, and Janna took an involuntary step backwards.

'She doesn't know where he is.' Godric pulled Janna into the crook of his arm and held her tight.

'This is no time for courting,' Serlo growled. 'You get back to wherever you came from, and leave the girl to me.'

'I'm staying right here to help look for the young lord.' Godric kept his arm around Janna.

Serlo glared at them both. 'Very well, then. I believe the boy may have tried to find his way home to his own manor but strayed off the track and got lost in the forest,' he snapped. 'You two can go and look for him.'

It was too good an opportunity to miss, and Janna moved off with alacrity, tugging the furiously barking Bones behind her. The reeve's next words stopped her dead. 'And get rid of the dog. If Hamo calls out, I want to be able to hear him.' Noticing Janna's surprise, the reeve continued, 'I'm coming with you. And so are they.' He raised a hand and beckoned several villeins forward. Urk and his mother were among the group.

Janna had a sudden feeling she and Godric were being enticed into a trap, but there was little they could do about it now. She dragged Bones over to Urk. 'Will you look after Hamo's dog for me please, Gabriel?' she asked, including Mistress Wulfrun in her friendly smile.

'Ooh, yes!' The boy fell to his knees and began to pat Bones with great enthusiasm. The dog wagged its tail at him, but kept on barking.

'I'm sorry, mistress. I don't know what's got into him,' Janna apologised to Urk's mother. 'Do you think Gabriel could play with him for a bit, and keep him quiet?'

'Gabriel has a way with animals, 'tis true,' his fond mother agreed. She nodded. 'Go on, then. We'll keep an eye on the dog for you.'

'Thank you.' Janna wasn't sure who would take priority where Mistress Wulfrun was concerned, Urk or the dog, but she knew she could trust the woman to do her best. Keeping close to Godric, Janna followed the villeins and Serlo into the forest.

'I really am sorry about your mother, sorry that I wasn't there to physic her,' she apologised, thinking Godric must listen to her now after what had just passed between them. The memory brought a blush to her cheek, and she quickly looked away.

'I'm sorry too,' he said soberly. 'It's true what I told you before. No matter what some of the villagers might have said to you – and I know Mistress Hilde was one of them – they regret it now, and repent the action they took against you. Especially Mistress Hilde. There is no-one to make up the cream that your mother once provided, and her skin is red raw with scratching.'

Janna felt a moment of fierce satisfaction. 'You know she killed my cat, don't you? It was a warning to me, she said, not to lie with her husband. As if I *would*!'

'She lives to regret her deed. She says now that your cat walks with her wherever she goes. She is in mortal fear that it will smother her new baby. But no-one else can see the cat. No-one believes her. Her fancies have turned her mind too far from the truth.'

'You are so right!' Janna said quickly. ''Tis Hilde's guilt that torments her now, guilt for crucifying my cat!'

Godric's face darkened in remembered anger. 'I don't know how you could have held me responsible for that, Janna, not even for a moment. You should know I would never do anything to harm you. Why, I . . .' He clamped his lips together, and marched on.

'I know that now.' Janna hurried after him. 'I'm sorry, Godric, truly. I haven't been kind, or fair, to you at all, and I deeply regret it.' She felt a weight ease off her heart. She'd treated Godric so badly; it had been a burden on her conscience. She'd thought she'd never see him again so it was a great relief to her, now, to have the chance to apologise. 'Forgive me?' She gave him a tentative smile. When he flashed a reluctant grin in return, her spirits soared. Then she remembered the task that lay before them, and her joy evaporated immediately. At once she looked towards Serlo. He was watching them. In fact, he seemed far more interested in keeping them in sight than in pretending to search for the missing boy.

Fear threaded through Janna and tightened into a knot of anxiety in her stomach. Serlo had already shown himself to be quick and resourceful, and utterly without mercy. Soon enough he would make a move against them. What was in his mind? One small thought brought Janna some consolation. While Serlo was watching them, he was unable to act against Hamo. She only hoped that, when the time came, she and Godric would be able to outwit the reeve and find Hamo in time to save the boy's life.

ThIRTEEN

THE BELL CONTINUED to toll at intervals through the weary day, the sound growing fainter as they moved further away from the manor, until finally it ceased altogether. Knowing they were wasting time, Janna grew impatient, but they couldn't start their own search under Serlo's watchful eye. The sun burned fiercely, its heat penetrating even the dim forest, parching her mouth and throat. She wished she'd thought to bring something to drink, and something to eat too.

At Serlo's signal, the villeins came together late in the afternoon to eat their dinner. Janna realised their steps had taken them close to the path again as she watched the villeins settle deep in the shade on either side of it, and unstopper leather bottles of ale to slake their thirst. She swallowed hard, trying to bring some moisture into her mouth. They must be moving back towards the manor, she realised, as she heard the faint tolling of the bell sound mournfully through the silent forest.

'You can follow this track after you've eaten your dinner,' Serlo told the villeins. He turned to Janna and Godric. 'You will continue the search with me.'

'What's he playing at?' Janna whispered as Godric came over to her.

He shrugged, and produced his own leather bottle, which he offered to Janna. She took it gratefully, and swallowed several mouthfuls of ale. It was warm from the heat of the day, and tasted somewhat of leather, but it ran down her parched throat like liquid gold.

'Thank you.' She handed the bottle back, and accepted a piece of bread and cheese from Godric. 'You're saving my life here.'

'Again.' His smile took the sting from the word. With a weary sigh, Janna sat down, her back propped against a tree. Godric collapsed beside her, and they sipped and chewed together in companionable silence for a time.

Looking around, Janna read the despair on everyone's faces. They had given up hope of finding Hamo, and were only going through the motions of searching for him now. In fact, they'd given up altogether, she realised, as Serlo directed them off down the path towards home.

'Come!' He beckoned them up to follow him. Janna knew that the trap was baited and ready for them. She knew also that she was the one Serlo wanted, not Godric. His life would not be in danger if he went with the reeve.

'Get after him,' Janna hissed, thinking to seek safety with the departing villeins. 'I'll go to his cottage and look for Hamo.'

'It's you he's interested in, not me, so he won't go anywhere unless you're there too.' Godric grasped her arm and hauled her along with him after the reeve. 'If Hamo is hidden somewhere in the forest, you can protect him while I take care of Serlo. We can search the cottage later.'

Janna recognised the wisdom of Godric's reasoning and stopped resisting him. In single file, they tramped after Serlo, moving from light to deep shadow, and never in a straight line. 'Did he do it? Did he do it?' a song thrush called, answering its own question: 'Come out! Come out!' There was a rustle and flutter of wings as it flew off. Serlo stood quietly for a moment to make sure they were still following him, then began to push his way through the forest once more.

'I wonder where he thinks he's going?' Godric sounded puzzled as he padded after the reeve. Janna shook her head. She wondered if either of them knew, for she herself was lost, had been lost for most of the day.

'He's already been this way once before,' Godric stopped and looked at Janna. 'He's taking us around in circles.'

'He obviously doesn't realise you know the forest better than he does!'

Godric shrugged, and set off after Serlo once more, keeping a careful lookout for any sign of Hamo. Janna marvelled how silently he walked. 'Aargh!' She gave a muffled scream as a sticky spider web suddenly wrapped around her face. Frantically, she clawed it off, sure that she could feel the tickle of spider legs threading through her hair, down her neck, against her skin inside her smock. She beat at herself with both hands, hoping to squash the insect dead. Distracted by the spider, not looking where she was going, her foot sank into a hole, giving her ankle a painful wrench. She stifled a cry, but tears came into her eyes with the pain of it. She limped towards Godric, who was waiting for her. Serlo had vanished.

'It's as I thought,' Godric said, as she came up to him. 'Serlo's been leading us around in circles, and now he thinks we're lost. He's done it on purpose.'

'What about Hamo? Where is he?'

'Nowhere Serlo's leading us, that's for sure.'

'Serlo must have him hidden in his cottage after all.'

Godric lifted his shoulders and spread his hands in a helpless gesture.

'We must find Hamo. We *must*!' Janna was frantic. 'Let's go back and look, Godric. Quickly, while Serlo is still in the forest.' A horrible thought stopped her. 'Do you know where we are? Can you find your way out of here?'

To her relief, Godric nodded. 'Let's play Serlo at his own game first and buy us some time. Follow me, Janna, close as you can, and walk quietly.'

To Janna's immense surprise Godric cut away at an angle from where they'd come, and silently began to make his way through a dense grove of trees. At once, she went after him. She could only hope he knew what he was doing.

Without warning, he jumped onto a fallen branch. The sudden crack sent her heart leaping in fear. She frowned, puzzled by his antics. 'What . . .?' He pressed his finger against her lips. They waited a few moments.

Nothing happened. Janna listened intently, but she couldn't hear anything, nor was there any sign of the reeve. Godric picked up the fallen branch and hit it against a tree. The dull thud echoed through the forest. 'Janna! Come see what I've found,' he called. 'I doubt Serlo will be able to explain this away!' Again, he cautioned her to silence.

Above their heads, birds began to twitter and sing, serenading the closing of the day. But Janna knew Godric wasn't listening for birds. She strained her ears to hear if his ruse had worked, and became aware of a furtive rustling. Animal or human? Evidently Godric knew the difference for he grabbed her hand and swept her away and around a patch of holly, then pushed through a thicket of hazel, snapping twigs and swishing branches as he passed. He was making more noise than a charging boar. Putting his finger to his lips once more, he stopped and looked behind, waiting.

This time Janna could hear the faint swish of Serlo's boots on dry leaves. Satisfied that he'd taken the bait, Godric drew Janna off in a different direction, cutting silently through a long stand of tall beeches and oaks then scooting across a patch of open grassland. He gave another raucous call. 'Janna! Where are you?'

Janna was right beside him, but she'd worked out now what he was up to, and she grinned up at him. She couldn't see the reeve, but she could hear him. He was still coming their way. Godric set off again, this time moving deep into a grove of yew, an impenetrable maze of knitted branches and leaves. 'Call my name,' he whispered, and Janna did as she was bid. The note of desperation in her voice wasn't all fake. She was frightened, as much for Hamo's sake as their own, by this deadly game of hide and seek in the forest. Serlo knew, now, that they were on to him, and that they would betray him if they could. He couldn't afford to let them leave the forest alive.

'Call again,' Godric prompted, and Janna did. She listened, heart thumping hard in her breast. There was a smothered cough, and then the faint sound of Serlo's panting breath as he came after them.

Godric nodded his head, satisfied. 'Come,' he whispered. 'Quiet as you can.' He took her hand and led the way, slipping silently through the dense growth. Once out of the copse, he kept on moving in a straight line through trees and weedy clearings, picking up speed all the way. To Janna's amazement, they suddenly emerged from the forest almost directly in line with Serlo's cottage.

'Hurry!' Godric urged, and began to race down towards the water meadows. But Janna had noticed the shed where once she and Edwin had sheltered. If it came to defending themselves against the reeve, a weapon would be handy. She hastened inside to retrieve the sword, feeling a great relief to find it still in its hiding place. Ignoring the dull ache of her wrenched ankle, she sped after Godric, following him down through the water meadows and across the river.

The door of the reeve's cottage was locked and barred against them. 'The devil take him,' Janna cursed, even as she acknowledged that this spoke of Serlo's having something to hide. 'Hamo!' she called, and beat on the door with her fist. 'Are you in there?'

Silence. Godric was peering through a shuttered window, trying to see inside the cottage. 'Hamo!' he bellowed, not caring now who might see or hear them. 'Hamo!' They both stopped and listened. Nothing moved. There was no sound in answer to their calls. Janna knew a bleak despair. If Hamo was in there, he had been silenced – perhaps permanently.

Godric pulled out his hunting knife. Large and very sharp, it was the knife he used for protection when walking through the forest. Not caring about the noise he was making or the damage to Serlo's property, he hacked into the wooden shutters, tearing and splintering them. Wordlessly, Janna handed him the sword, and he wasted no time in using it to slice through the shutter, making a large enough space for Janna to crawl through. At once she put her foot into Godric's cupped hands and launched herself through and into the cottage.

'Hamo!' she yelled, as she hit the ground. She rolled over and sprang to her feet. In spite of the heat, a fire smouldered in the hearth, and Janna waited a moment for her eyes to adjust to the dim light. There was no sign of anyone. With dragging steps, she went to the door and unbolted it. Sadly, she shook her head in answer to Godric's unspoken question. She stepped aside to let him enter.

Together they opened the remaining shutters to let in the light, then began a systematic search through the cottage. Janna's eyes narrowed. Two wooden trenchers lay on a table, as if waiting for food to be placed on them for the evening meal. Two trenchers? Janna felt a sudden surge of hope. 'Hamo?' she yelled. 'It's Janna, and Godric. There's nothing to be afraid of, we're here to help you escape.' She listened intently, felt her heart double thump as she heard a noise, but then realised it was the faint yapping of a barking dog.

'I'm sure Hamo's about somewhere,' she told Godric, 'and I'm sure he's alive!' She pointed at the second trencher. 'Look! Where do you think Serlo's got him hidden?'

Godric shrugged, looking baffled. Once more they searched through several unlocked chests and around the meagre pieces of furniture within the cottage, including the coverings and frame of a rather fine wooden bed which stood hidden behind soft drapes in a small alcove off the main room. With increasing desperation, they searched even those places far too small to hide a little boy, just in case there was some clue to Hamo's presence, anything at all.

The sound of barking grew louder. A dog was coming this way. Bones? Suddenly there was a furious scratching at the door, accompanied by a series of short, sharp yips. Desperate to stop the noise before it attracted any more attention, Janna hurried to open it.

Bones shot in. Janna could swear that the dog was surprised to see her. He wagged his tail but kept on moving, sniffing at the ground until he suddenly stopped and sat, almost as if he was keeping guard. The beaten earth of the floor was covered with rushes. By the look of them, they'd been down for some time and needed changing. Janna frowned and looked more closely. The rushes near Bones seemed unevenly distributed, as if they'd been recently disturbed. Bones was still barking, but not so ferociously now. He looked up at Janna with bright eyes. Janna thought he was trying to tell her something. 'You were here before, weren't you, Bones?' she said softly. 'Where is Hamo? Do you know?'

The dog whined, and scratched at the rushes, scattering them. Janna looked at Godric. 'There's something buried down there.' She felt sick as an image of Hamo's small body interred in the earth came into her mind. 'Careful!' She flung out a hand as Godric's knife flashed out and he knelt to dig. 'You don't know what's down there,' she breathed.

Janna knelt beside him and they began to dig into the soft earth with their bare hands. The earth shifted easily, testament to the fact that it was the gateway to something below. With a feeling of dread, Janna plunged her hands deeper into the soil. She frowned as her fingers jabbed against something hard. Cautiously, she began to throw handfuls of earth to one side, fearing what might be revealed. A small wooden panel came into view. Janna frowned at it. 'Why would anyone want to bury this?' She lifted it, and the answer was instantly revealed in the dark hole beneath.

'It's a trapdoor.' Godric crawled forward and peered down the hole. 'Hamo?' he called softly.

Janna listened intently. She thought she could hear something, but even as she strained to identify the sound, it ceased. She must have imagined it, she thought reluctantly. 'I guess this must be a storeroom?' She craned over to peer down into the darkness.

'I'll go and have a look,' Godric offered.

'No.' Janna was grateful that he'd put himself forward, but she took hold of him to push him aside. 'I'll go,' she said steadily. She looked about the room for something to light her way. Her eyes widened as she noticed a fat beeswax candle rather than the rush light she would have expected to find. A fine bed. A beeswax candle. Serlo must be saving them to impress Gytha – if only he could lure her to his cottage as he must have lured Hamo. The thought stiffened her resolution to find the missing child. 'Will you light that candle so I can see what's down here?' she asked Godric.

He shook his head. 'Let me go. You don't know what you might find.'

An image of Hamo's dead body came into Janna's mind. No! She wouldn't, she couldn't think the worst. 'If Hamo's down there, and alive, he might think you're Serlo,' she said, her voice wobbling slightly with the effort to be brave. 'He'll be much less frightened if he sees me.'

Acknowledging the truth of her words, Godric gave a reluctant nod. As he stood up to light the candle from the fire in the hearth, Bones jumped down the hole in front of Janna. He started barking once more, short furious yips that echoed the urgency they all shared. Wasting no more time, Janna grabbed the candle from Godric, picked up the sword and dropped down after the dog, ducking her head under the low ceiling.

A thin shaft of light shone down through the trapdoor. The rest of the cellar was in darkness. The air was stale and smelt of damp earth. Janna held the candle out so that its light was shed more widely. A quick glance confirmed the cellar's purpose. It was crammed with barrels and chests and newly combed fleeces, the latter piled high and ready for market. Truly this was a treasure trove, and not all gained by the honest toil of Serlo's hands either, Janna was willing to stake her life on it. How long had he been planning to take over the manor, deceiving Hugh and amassing wealth at his expense so that, when the time was right, he would be in a position to make a worthy offer to the dame for her property?

Banishing Serlo's dishonesty from her thoughts, for there would be time enough for Hugh to take revenge on his trusted reeve, Janna looked about for Bones. She could hear him barking still, but the dog seemed to have disappeared.

'Janna,' Godric's anxious voice called out. 'Are you all right?'

'Yes, but there's no sign of Hamo. Come down and help me look.'

Janna dripped a little hot wax onto one of the barrels, and secured the candle to it. With the small light to see by, she and Godric began a thorough search of the cellar. Almost the first things she found were the silver goblets and the length of woollen cloth supposedly stolen from the undercroft. 'Look!' She snatched them up with a cry of triumph, pleased that she would be able to prove her innocence beyond question now.

Everything else was sealed tight. From their weight, Janna knew that the chests and barrels were not empty. She also knew that if Hamo was concealed in one of them, he must surely be dead for there would be no air inside to sustain him. Despairing, she thumped hard on their sides, calling Hamo's name. She didn't think he'd be able to hear her above the cacophony of barking, but even that might comfort Hamo, if he was alive to hear it. Where was the boy? And where was Bones? She listened for the direction of the dog's frantic barking, then followed the sound towards a row of barrels shoved against the earthen wall at the far side of the cellar. The barks came from behind them. Janna realised that there was a narrow gap between the barrels and the wall. She hoisted herself half up onto one of them in order to peer over and down into the gap between. And drew in a painful breath, and then another. The dog was wedged there, standing guard over a small, still body.

'Hamo!' Janna's cry echoed through the low chamber as she shoved at the heavy barrel barring her way, leaning all her weight against it so that she could get to him. Godric rushed to help her and, as soon as there was enough space, Janna darted in and crouched down beside the child. He lay unmoving, but his eyes, wide and staring, gleamed in the faint light from the candle. Janna put her hand on his forehead, dreading to feel the chillness of death against her fingers. But his skin felt warm, although he did not move, or say anything in answer to her frantic question, 'Are you all right?' Then she saw why. Hamo's feet and hands were tightly bound, and so was his mouth.

A great fury shook Janna. 'He's alive!' she shouted, as she crouched down beside the child and, with shaking hands, unfastened the gag that covered his mouth.

Hamo moistened his lips with his tongue. 'Are you Janna?' he whispered, and Janna nodded, swallowing over a huge lump that had somehow got stuck in her throat. Godric shoved her aside. He whipped out his knife and slashed through Hamo's bonds.

'Hamo!' Janna reached out to take him in her arms. Instinctively the child shrank away, moving as far from Janna as he could go. He cowered against a barrel. Bones pushed past Janna and began to lick Hamo's face. Hamo pushed him away.

Janna knew rage and a grief beyond anything she'd ever experienced. Serlo had done this. He'd destroyed Hamo's open, trusting nature. He had stolen his innocence.

'It's all right, Hamo.' Janna kept her hand outstretched, but made no further effort to touch him. 'You're safe now. Master Serlo can't harm you any more.'

'We have to get out of here,' Godric said urgently.

'Just wait a few moments.' Janna inched closer to Hamo, willing him to take her hand.

'I'll go for help.' Godric rose from his knees and reached up to the opening in the roof of the cellar. 'I'll tell the lord

Hugh that Hamo is safe. I'll tell his mother too. And I'll suggest the lord brings men at arms with him when he comes.'

'No, don't go.' Janna tugged on his tunic to stop him. 'If Serlo comes back, we'll need you to defend us. But we can't leave just yet. Hamo's in shock. He's going to be too stiff to walk after being tied up for so long. Just give him a little time to recover.'

Godric nodded. He squatted down beside Janna, and gave Hamo an awkward pat on the shoulder. The boy gulped, and pressed himself harder against the barrel. Godric cast a helpless glance at Janna.

'Bones found you,' she said, with determined cheerfulness. 'Do you know, he kept on barking and barking at Serlo. He knew what the reeve had done. And he came straight here as soon as he managed to escape. He showed us where to dig to find this cellar. He's a smart dog, is Bones.'

'Bones was here before.' Hamo's voice was so quiet they strained to hear it. 'Serlo told me he had Bones. That's why I came away with him, even though Mistress Cecily told me not to go anywhere without her. But Bones was missing and I wanted to find him.' His voice hardened as he said angrily, 'Serlo kicked Bones, I saw him. He *hurt* Bones.'

'I know. I know.' Janna felt somewhat reassured by the fire that had come into Hamo's voice when he spoke of his beloved pet. His silence and apathy had frightened her. She felt even more reassured as Hamo suddenly flung his arms around Bones. Miraculously, the dog had finally stopped barking.

'Look at all this!' Godric gave a silent whistle as he gestured at the riches that surrounded them. 'I'll wager my life that the lord of the manor doesn't know about this secret storeroom!'

Janna nodded in agreement. 'Serlo will be hanged for his deeds. The lord Hugh will never forget or forgive what he has done.' Her words brought home to her the danger of their position, and she stirred uneasily. Serlo wouldn't go willingly to face his punishment. In fact, he'd stop at nothing to prevent his secret being found out.

'We should go.' Godric voiced her misgivings. 'The sooner we get Hamo safely to the manor house, the better.'

And the safer we'll be too, Janna thought. 'Do you think you can walk?' she asked Hamo.

He nodded, and climbed stiffly to his feet. 'Ow!' His face crumpled and he began to hop around as he felt the prick and sting of blood flowing freely through his cramped limbs once more.

'Up you go!' Godric swung him up and hoisted him through the hole in the floor. 'Now you.' He turned to Janna just as a muffled scream rent the air. She snatched up the candle to see better, while her heart pounded in fright.

'I have the boy and this time I'll show no mercy.' Serlo's face appeared briefly as he bent down to smile at them. 'As for my cellar – no-one knows about it so no-one's going to find you here. Its contents will keep . . . but you won't.' His chuckle was cut off by the sound of the solid oak panel thudding into place, sealing them into the earth.

'No! *No!*' Janna screamed the words in defiance, while beside her Bones began to howl. She pushed against the panel, but Serlo held it down. Godric sprang to her aid and, together, they strained to shift it. Scraping sounds above told them that Serlo was shifting something over the trap-door to hold them fast. They were trapped, sealed tight into an earthen tomb. No-one knew they were down here, no-one would come looking for them. Soon enough their air would run out. The candle would flicker and die, and so would they. And so would Hamo. Janna looked at Godric in despair. 'What are we going to do now?' Her voice was almost inaudible against the noise being made by Bones.

But Godric had already seized up the sword. Arm raised above his head, he began to saw away at the wooden panel. Janna leaned over, and slid his knife from its sheath. She began to attack the other side of the panel. Silently, desperately, they sawed through the wood, neither of them voicing their fear that their air would run out before they could cut a hole big enough to escape through.

'Help!' she shouted, just in case there was anyone around to hear her. She put her full voice into the cry. 'Help! Somebody, please help us!'

Time seemed to slow to a crawl. Terrifying images ran through Janna's mind as she realised that Serlo would have to carry out his threat now that events had forced his hand. It was a miracle the child had survived as long as he had but from now on his life could only be measured in minutes, unless he was already dead. She had promised Hamo that he was safe, that Serlo could never harm him again, and she had failed him. The knowledge was shattering; she felt almost paralysed with grief and fear. 'Hurry!' she begged, although she knew Godric was as frantic as she was to escape.

The air in the small cellar was being used up; she could smell that it was gradually becoming foul with their breath. She could hear Godric panting, or perhaps it was her own gasps for air that she could hear. She put her hand over her nose and mouth to see if it would help to filter the foulness, but instantly felt as if she was suffocating. She quickly snatched her hand away and took in several deep breaths. It was not enough to satisfy her need. She looked about for Bones. He'd collapsed on the ground nearby. Janna could see the rapid rise and fall of his tiny stomach as he fought for breath. Beside her, Godric sawed on with grim determination.

The candle flickered, and died. They were lost in the darkness. Somehow, their fate seemed even more horrible now they could no longer see each other. Janna stopped cutting for a moment, and reached out to touch Godric. She needed to connect with someone. She needed to feel she was not alone. He took her hand, and kissed it, his lips warm and moist on her skin. Neither of them said anything as he released her and began sawing at the wooden slab once more. They worked in silence for a time, until there was a crack and part of it fell away.

'We're through!' Godric shouted. Janna sensed movement beside her as he reached up to feel the opening. Why was no light shining through? Her question was answered by Godric's next words.

'There's something else, something solid blocking the way,' he said dully. 'Serlo must have pulled a heavy chest over the trapdoor to make sure we can't escape.'

Janna closed her eyes, swept by a wave of fierce anger that this was to be their fate. 'Help!' she screamed again. 'We're trapped in Serlo's cottage. Somebody, please help! For the love of God, please save us!'

FOURTEEN

'Bones! Bones, where are you?' The voice sounded muffled, far away. Janna wondered if she was imagining things. She put a hand on Godric's arm. 'Sshh.' She listened intently, sure she'd heard a voice.

'Bones? Where are you?'

'Here!' Janna shouted frantically. 'We're here under the ground of Serlo's cottage! Bones is here too!'

There was a long silence. Janna suspected she must have been hallucinating after all. Perhaps it was a lack of air that made her conjure up what wasn't really there.

'Did you hear anything, Godric?' she asked at last, reluctant to give up this tiny fragment of hope.

'Something. I don't know. Yes, maybe.' He raised his voice. 'Help!' he shouted. 'We're trapped in a cellar underneath Serlo's cottage. There's a trapdoor with a chest or something on top of it.' He stopped and they listened intently. Silence. Then Janna heard a faint creaking above her head. Her heart leapt high with elation. 'We're down here!' she shouted. 'Hurry! Please, please hurry!'

There was a sudden waft of air, tinged faintly with smoke from the fire in the hearth. Janna sucked it gratefully into her lungs. A faint beam of light from the fire slanted down through the darkness of the cellar, the light becoming brighter as their saviour dragged a wooden chest out of the way. Janna bent to pick up Bones, then looked upwards to see who was there. Peering down at them with a worried expression, but as welcome as the angel Gabriel himself, was Urk. 'Gabriel, well done!' she greeted him. 'You've got here just in time! Here, take Bones.' She thrust the dog at Urk and turned to Godric.

He cupped his hands together and Janna put her foot in the cradle. Without wasting any more time, he heaved her upwards while, from above, Urk grasped her arms and hauled her through. Then it was Godric's turn. Snatching up the sword, he pushed it through the trapdoor then pulled himself up after it. 'Thank you,' he said. 'Thank you for saving our lives.'

Urk smiled his big smile at them both, and turned aside to pick up Bones. The dog had recovered somewhat, and licked Urk's hand.

Godric took only a moment to catch his breath before seizing hold of Urk and Janna and hustling them out of the cottage and into the darkening night. 'Go and fetch the lord Hugh,' he told Urk urgently. 'Tell him he must come at once. Tell him Serlo has taken Hamo. Tell him to bring men at arms to hunt Serlo down.'

Urk looked bewildered. He clutched Bones tighter to his chest. 'Bones ran away,' he said slowly. 'I had to find him. I didn't want Serlo to see me so I had to wait till he went away from his cottage. Serlo has Hamo.'

'Yes, yes I know,' Godric said impatiently. 'What did I just tell you, Gabriel?'

'Go and fetch the lord Hugh,' the boy repeated obediently. 'Tell him Serlo has taken Hamo. Tell him to come at once. He must bring men at arms to hunt Serlo down.'

'Good boy.' Godric patted his shoulder. 'Hurry, it's almost dark. There's no time to lose.'

Still the boy hesitated. 'Go!' Godric gave him a shove.

'You can take Bones with you. Look after him,' said Janna, understanding at last what was delaying their messenger. 'And thank you for finding us, Gabriel. You're a real hero!'

Urk's face split into a smile. He set off at speed, straight as an arrow towards the manor house. Janna could only hope that he would remember their message, and that Hugh would believe it.

Although impatient to be on the move, Janna forced herself to stand quietly. She peered across the fields, scanning the landscape carefully in the lambent light of the evening sky. They had no way of knowing where Serlo had taken Hamo, for there was no sign of him now. If he hadn't risked dumping the boy in the forest before, he certainly wouldn't risk going there now, not while bands of villeins might still be roaming about the water meadows in search of Hamo. Not the forest then. Where else might he go?

'I can't see them anywhere,' Godric muttered, sounding discouraged. 'You realise, don't you, Janna, that Serlo can't afford to leave the boy alive. We may already be too late.'

'No!' Janna said fiercely. 'I'm not giving up, not yet. It's not quite dark. People will be out searching for Hamo. Serlo will take him somewhere that's already been searched, where he knows they won't be seen.'

'This copse?' Godric flung out a hand to indicate the grove that stood guard over Serlo's cottage.

Janna thought for a moment. 'We'd better check. He may have taken Hamo there just to shut him up.' Her voice caught in her throat. She swallowed hard. 'But I don't think Serlo would leave him there. It's too close to his cottage. The villeins might well come in here to collect dead wood, while the pigs will soon be foraging for acorns and beechmast. Serlo would know that a grave must be found sooner or later.'

Her eyes widened as an idea flashed into her mind. 'What about the river?' She turned to Godric, her eyes full of hope. 'It's already been searched thoroughly, but no-one will question another drowning, not when Hamo so nearly drowned that first time. Come on! But we'll search the copse first, just in case.'

Sword in hand and ready for use if necessary, she set off through the trees. Godric hurried after her, sheathing his knife and uncoiling his slingshot as he ran. 'Please, God, don't let us get there too late.' Janna repeated the prayer under her breath as they inspected the small copse. In spite of their fears, there was no sign of a small body or the reeve among the bracken and weeds that grew rank beneath the trees.

'He's not here.' Janna wiped her sweating face on the sleeve of her smock. Godric nodded in agreement and, together, they left the shelter of the grove and ran down towards the river. It spread before them like a long silver snake in the dim evening light. Finally Janna stopped for a moment, and bent over, clutching hold of her aching sides.

'He'll be hiding somewhere among the trees,' she gasped, 'but where?'

At the sound of her voice, Godric glanced behind him, then turned and hurried back to her. He bent down and quickly selected a handful of flints. Janna straightened and looked towards the river, narrowing her eyes to see more clearly, watching for any movement that might betray the reeve's whereabouts. Finally she shrugged. 'We can't waste any more time,' she said. 'Let's split up. You go downriver,' she stuck a finger towards the mill, 'and I'll go upstream. Quiet as you can. Serlo mustn't hear us.'

'No.' Godric stood his ground. 'You can't face Serlo alone. We must stay together.'

Janna stuck out her jaw, looking stubborn. 'I mean it,' Godric warned. 'I'm following you, whichever way you choose to go.'

Janna clicked her tongue. 'Look,' she said impatiently. 'The closest cover of trees is over there. Maybe that's where he's taken Hamo. He can't risk the boy being seen, not while there are people about.' Without hesitation, she began to run once more, with Godric keeping a steady pace beside her.

As they came closer, Janna slowed and tried to quieten her panting breaths. Godric crept forward; she followed close behind him. It was dark in the thicket of young alders that crowded beside the river bank but, even so, they had no trouble spying Serlo. Janna felt an unutterable relief as she saw the small boy beside him, his hand held tight in the reeve's larger hand, being dragged along against his will. Alive! Hamo was still alive. He was quite silent, and Janna's fists clenched as she imagined what Serlo must have done to keep him quiet. Truly he would pay dearly for his treatment of the boy.

Godric crept stealthily forward, slingshot at the ready. He was gaining on Serlo, who was encumbered by the struggling Hamo. Janna knew how accurate a shot Godric was, but even so her heart beat hard with fear. What if he should miss, and bring Hamo down instead? She stopped, hardly daring even to breathe, frightened that she might make some noise and alert Serlo to their presence.

'Be careful,' she prayed, knowing that Serlo wouldn't hesitate to use Hamo as a shield against any attack. She couldn't bear it if, in the end, it was Godric who brought the boy to harm.

Godric had stopped now, and was busy fitting a flint into his weapon. Janna wondered which part of Serlo he would aim at, and prayed that the flint would find its mark.

Godric took another step forward. A twig cracked and snapped. Serlo whirled and saw them. At once, he pulled Hamo in front of him. Janna saw that he held a knife at the ready. No wonder Hamo had been so silent, she thought, feeling despair as she understood that they were powerless now to save him. She reached out a hand to Godric, to stop him from doing anything stupid that might jeopardise Hamo's safety. But she was too late. His arm swung around. As Serlo whipped the knife up to the boy's throat, Godric loosed the flint. For several long moments time seemed to stand still. Then, with a grunting sigh, Serlo fell to the ground, taking Hamo with him.

Numb with shock, Janna stayed frozen, listening to the fearful silence. Finally she forced her legs to move. She ran

forward, dreading what she might find: that Serlo had had
time to slit the boy's throat; that even now Hamo might be
dying or dead. She became aware that Godric was beside her
as she fell to her knees beside the reeve. There was blood
everywhere. Neither Hamo nor Serlo was moving. She
reached out to Hamo with a trembling hand.

'Ohhh.' It was a long drawn-out sigh of relief as she saw
that the blood spattered over Hamo's tunic had come from
the reeve. The flint had hit Serlo's forehead. It was bleeding
profusely, and so was a long cut in his arm where his knife
had sliced through his sleeve as he'd fallen.

Ignoring Serlo, Godric snatched Hamo from the reeve's
limp hands and carried him to safety, while Janna bent over
Serlo to inspect his wounds and determine if he was dead or
merely stunned. She wanted the reeve alive to face Hugh, to
know public humiliation and disgrace before the hangman
put an end to his pathetic, miserable life. As she leaned
closer, his hand shot out and grabbed her. She cried out, but
it was too late. Serlo had her firmly in his grasp. She lunged
for his fallen knife, but he was too fast for her. He snatched
it up and staggered to his feet, holding her in front of him as
a shield against any further harm.

'Drop the sword.' She felt the prick of his knife against her
throat. Frightened into silence, she obeyed his command.

Godric put Hamo down. He rose to his feet, knife in hand,
and faced the reeve. Janna stared at him in despair. He could
do nothing to save her without risking her life at the same
time.

The reeve pulled Janna closer. He pressed himself against
her; his arms became a tight band around her, trapping her

tight. She couldn't move; there was nothing she could do to free herself. Fighting panic, she waited numbly to see what would happen next.

'Give me my life, or I'll take hers.' Serlo's voice rumbled behind her. Godric nodded acceptance. He dropped his slingshot and slowly sheathed his knife.

'No!' Janna's mind suddenly cleared. She remembered how she'd been trapped like this once before. She knew there was a way out after all. Before Serlo could move, she raised her foot and stamped down with all her strength onto his instep. He stumbled, loosening his hold as he struggled to keep his balance. Janna wrenched herself free and ran towards Godric. With a wide gesture, he swept her out of his way while, with his other hand, he pulled his knife out of its sheath. There was a glint of silver in the dim light, then Janna heard a thud.

Serlo lay on his back on the ground, with Godric's knife embedded up to its hilt in his chest.

'Your life, Serlo, instead of hers.' Godric walked to the reeve, gave the knife a twist and pulled it out. Serlo's fingers plucked feebly at the air, then fell nervelessly to his side. He gave a faint sigh and his body went limp.

Knowing that he was no longer a danger, Janna rushed over to Hamo. He was curled up in a ball. His eyes were wide with terror; his whole body was shaking. Not giving him any chance to retreat this time, she scooped him into her arms and held him close. For one long, heart-stopping moment, he stayed rigid. Then, with a strangled yelp, he burrowed into her and began to cry.

'You're safe now,' she comforted him. 'You really are safe

now. Serlo's dead. He'll never harm you again.' She glanced sideways as a faint drumming came to her ears. Horses! She caught a glimpse of torches.

'We're here!' Godric shouted. 'We're down by the river!'

The drumming sounded louder. 'Is the boy safe?' Janna recognised Hugh's voice, and felt an overwhelming relief. She bent over Hamo, fighting tears. 'Your cousin Hugh is here,' she told him. 'He'll take you back to the manor, Hamo. Your mother and father are there. They'll be so glad to see you. So glad.' A sudden thought brought fear to Janna's heart. 'Don't tell them my name,' she said urgently. 'Please just call me "John".'

'John,' Hamo echoed. There was a moment's silence, and then came the question. 'Where's Bones?'

Janna didn't know whether to laugh or cry. She hugged Hamo tighter. 'Bones is safe too,' she said. 'Urk has him, he's looking after him for you. Urk saved Bones and he also saved us. He let us out of the cellar so we could chase after you and Serlo. You're safe now, Hamo, I promise you. Everything's going to be all right. Everything.'

The nightmare was over. The knowledge filled Janna's mind and heart, and left her overflowing with joy.

FIFTEEN

THE MOMENT OF peace and thanksgiving was quickly over as Hugh leapt off his destrier and hurried over to check for himself that Hamo was alive and safe. Not wasting any more time, he pulled Hamo up onto Arrow and galloped back to the manor house with him. A joyful pealing of bells told of their safe return. Meanwhile Hugh's men at arms fashioned a litter and carried Serlo's body home, stashing it safely in a barn to await burial. He had escaped justice on earth, he'd cheated the gallows, but he would have to account for his actions in the highest court of all. Janna hoped that he would be condemned to hellfire for ever.

Hugh had summoned Janna and Godric into the solar and now they sat in comfort, with a hot bowl of pottage and a meat pie to bring new warmth and life to their tired bodies, and a jug of ale to wash it down. Hugh had expressed his thanks, as well as the gratitude of Dame Alice, and had then set to questioning them about the night's events and what had gone before. Between them, Janna and Godric had given him a full account of all that had led up to this moment. But Hugh had still more questions for them.

'What made you suspect Serlo in the first place?' He looked to Janna to answer his question.

Janna paused mid-chew. 'Lots of little things,' she said indistinctly, then hastily swallowed her mouthful. 'When we first came here, when he saved Edwin and me from the forester, he talked about "my sheep".'

'Saved you from the forester?' Hugh quirked an eyebrow.

'It's a long story,' Janna said, continuing hurriedly, 'I thought, from Master Serlo's words, that the manor belonged to him.' She gazed up at Hugh, blushing slightly and hating herself for it. 'I didn't know it belonged to you. I wouldn't have stopped here if I'd known that.'

Hugh's eyebrow rose higher.

'I also saw the way Serlo looked at Mistress Gytha, and the way she looked at you.'

'Me?' Hugh spluttered. 'But Gytha is just a child!'

'She's old enough to wed – and she has a certain amount of ambition in your direction,' Janna commented dryly.

Hugh shook his head in wonder. 'I had no idea her thoughts lay with me. Although I must confess I had . . . er . . . noticed lately that she was . . . er . . .'

He could hardly have failed to notice what Gytha had been so determined to display! Janna hid a sly smile.

'. . . but I thought, when the time came, that Gytha might make a match of it with Serlo,' Hugh stammered on.

Janna interrupted his musing. 'And Serlo was desperate to have her. But he understood her ambition only too well. He knew he had to improve his station if he was to have a chance with her, and it was to be done at your expense.'

'Hence the spate of so-called "accidents"?' Hugh ventured.

Janna nodded. 'But it went further than that. He was stockpiling goods to sell at St Edith's fair at Wiltune, or perhaps even at Winchestre. Mistress Tova told me he takes several cartloads to the fair every year, your produce as well as his own. You'll see the quantity of chests, barrels and fleeces which he has stored in his cellar. There's far more than he could have come by through honest toil.'

'I certainly knew nothing about them,' Hugh said grimly, 'but I should have questioned Serlo earlier. Although we've had fair seasons for some time now, the manor farm has not been as productive as I'd expected. I had no idea Serlo was robbing me blind.' He shook his head and growled in anger.

No wonder you were so keen to visit your aunt and make yourself agreeable, Janna thought. She wondered if the dame had asked questions of Hugh, if she'd been having second thoughts about leaving him in charge of what should be a profitable manor.

'It's a hard lesson to learn, but I will be less trusting and I'll take more of the reeve's duties on my shoulder in the future,' Hugh continued.

'The woollen cloth and silver goblets Serlo accused me of stealing are also down in the cellar,' Janna added, anxious to clear both her and Edwin's name. 'My guess is that Serlo planned to sell them as well.'

'I see now how his mind worked.' said Hugh. 'With Hamo gone and me discredited, my aunt would have been anxious to cast off this manor with all its unhappy memories.'

Janna nodded in agreement. 'Serlo couldn't have known that Hamo would visit you, but once Hamo vanished the first time he saw how a second disappearance might work in his favour. I think he snatched Hamo with the intention of drowning him, but he was unable to carry out the deed because Mistress Cecily was so quick to raise the alarm. With so many villeins out searching, he knew he'd be noticed. So instead, he decided to keep Hamo alive for a little while longer. My guess is that he planned to take him away in one of the carts with all his goods for sale, and drown him somewhere along the journey, past where anyone might have searched the river for him before. Once Hamo's body was found, he could then approach ma dame with his offer.'

Hugh's lips tightened. He muttered a savage oath against his once-trusted reeve.

'I'm sorry Serlo is dead and that you cannot bring him to an accounting for his deeds,' Godric ventured. 'I would not have thrown my knife at him by choice, but I knew that if I let him get away with Janna, he would have killed her rather than let her go free to speak the truth about him. I have never killed a man before but if I had to, I would make that choice again.'

'You made the right decision. I am glad that you were there,' Hugh reassured him. 'I only wish it had never come to this. If I'd read the signs right from the start, all this might have been avoided.' He looked at Janna. 'Why did Serlo leave rue at the scenes of his crimes? What was he thinking?'

'I didn't understand, until the cook told me how Serlo's family had once owned this manor. It seems they were forced into servitude after the Conquest. The rue was both his curse and his message to your family to repent that theft.' Janna didn't add that she felt a sneaking sympathy with the reeve's grievance, although she could never condone what he had done.

Hugh nodded thoughtfully. 'You have all my gratitude for finding Hamo and opening my eyes to Serlo's true nature.'

'Don't forget Gabriel . . . Urk,' Janna said quickly. 'But for him, we would have died in that cellar. If he hadn't come in search of Bones, and then faithfully conveyed Godric's message to you . . .' She shuddered, marvelling at how narrowly they had all escaped death.

'Urk will be rewarded, as will his family. But for my part, I am indebted to you for rescuing Hamo not once but twice, and bringing him home alive.' His warm smile encompassed both Janna and Godric. 'Please be assured that you have a home here for as long as you like, and for ever if you wish it.'

Janna's mouth went dry. She couldn't find the words to answer him. But Godric spoke up.

'I thank you, my lord, and I would indeed like to stay here.' He shot a quick glance at Janna, then said hurriedly, 'But I am tied to Dame Alice's manor. I cannot leave without her permission.'

'You can leave my aunt to me,' Hugh said confidently. 'I have lost my most trusted reeve. Although the villagers will elect a new one, I'd like to have an honest man by my side, if you'll agree to it, Godric?' A mischievous smile tugged at the corners of his mouth. 'I venture to suggest that you would be far more to young Gytha's taste than Master Serlo ever was.'

Speechless, Godric and Janna exchanged glances.

Godric found his voice first. 'I have my own cot and land at Babestoche, sire,' he said. 'If I came to you – '

'You would not lose by it.' Hugh cut him off. 'Master Serlo's cottage and lands lie vacant now. They are yours, as my reward to you for saving Hamo's life.'

'That . . . that is very generous of you, my lord.' As Godric absorbed the full extent of Hugh's generosity, his face blazed alight with hope and high expectation. He turned to Janna, but before he could say anything, Hugh addressed her directly.

'And Edwin?' he queried. 'What has become of him? Has he had a hand in any of this business with Serlo?'

'No, sire! He planned to stay in hiding until your visitors left the manor and it was safe for him to come out. But if you wish to speak to him, you'll find him sheltering with Bertha, the carpenter's daughter.'

Hugh tilted his head to study Janna. 'And will he want to stay here with you, do you think?'

'Not with me, my lord. He wants to stay here with Bertha.'

'And so he shall.' Hugh's mouth curved into a wide grin. 'What about you, Johanna? How can I reward you for your deeds this day?'

Janna gazed up at him, at a loss for words. A reward? It was something she hadn't looked for, didn't want. Unless Hugh could help her find her father? Could she ask him to do that?

'I must confess, I would like you to stay on at the manor, but in a lady's attire if you please,' Hugh continued. 'I cannot get used to you in the guise of a man.' His gaze narrowed slightly as he looked more closely at Janna's smock and breeches. 'Where did you find those clothes you wear?' he asked.

Janna was thrown by the unexpected question. She blushed deep as she wrestled with her conscience. 'I . . . I stole them, sire,' she confessed.

'From the barn that burned down so suddenly on my aunt's demesne?'

Janna pondered what to say. It had been an act of defiance to set fire to the barn, to pay back Robert of Babestoche something in kind for his evil deeds. But she'd also wanted to hide the evidence she'd used to deduce his true nature, as well as the evidence of her theft. She could explain all that to Hugh, but would he understand? Worse, would he tell his aunt? If she was charged in a manorial court for her misdeed, the penalty would be heavy indeed.

She was saved from having to answer as the door from Hugh's bedchamber was suddenly flung open. Dame Alice bustled into the solar, closely followed by her husband.

At the sight of Robert, Janna quickly turned aside. She bowed her head as she hastily rose to make her obeisance.

'Please, sit down and finish your supper.' In spite of her red eyes and obvious exhaustion, Dame Alice's face shone radiant with relief. She took a handful of silver coins from her purse and set them down on the table in front of Janna and Godric. 'This is your reward for bringing my son home safely,' she said, her voice trembling with emotion. 'But no silver, or words, or anything I can do, can ever convey to you my most heartfelt gratitude.' She took Janna's and Godric's hands and held them tight. 'Thank you,' she said huskily.

'It was a pleasure to serve you, ma dame.' Godric spoke for both of them. Janna was desperately racking her brains for an excuse to flee the room. Had Hamo spoken her name? Did they already know who she was, or had Hamo remembered to keep her secret?

'I know you, of course, Godric, but I don't know your companion. John, is it?' Unexpectedly, the dame reached out and took Janna's chin, raising her face towards the soft candlelight that bathed the solar. Janna had no choice but to look at her, and also at Robert, who was standing behind his wife.

The dame sucked in her breath in a sudden hiss. 'Could it be . . . are you really Johanna?' she asked, in a tone of wonder.

'His name's John,' Hugh said harshly, suddenly awake to the danger Janna faced. 'And if you've finished your supper, John, you can go now.'

'Not so hasty, Hugh!' the dame protested. But Hugh's words came too late to save Janna. As she'd looked at the dame, so had she seen realisation dawning on Robert's face: a flash of involuntary fear, followed by an expression of fierce resolve that told Janna he would not be intimidated by her knowledge, and that he would kill her rather than risk his affair with Cecily and his role in her own mother's death being found out. She was in mortal danger once more.

'Come, John. Come with me.' Hugh grasped Janna's arm and marched her out of the solar and into the hall. Godric snatched up the silver coins and followed them.

'I'm so sorry,' Hugh apologised, once they were safely out of hearing. 'I didn't tell them you were here. I thought they would stay in my bedchamber with Hamo.'

'The lord Robert knows who I am. He recognised me,' Janna whispered. She was shaking with fright. She had never before encountered such anger, such vicious hatred. Now that Robert knew she was alive, he would have to act to silence her. She was filled with dread at the very thought of it.

Hugh looked thoughtful. Then he said, 'They'll be going home soon, and probably taking Hamo with them. There'll be no danger to you then, Johanna. In the meantime, I am sure I – and Godric – can keep you safe.'

Beside Janna, Godric stiffened. 'I can look after Janna perfectly well on my own, sire,' he muttered.

'But I don't want to be looked after by anyone!' Janna retorted angrily. 'How can I live any sort of life if I'm constantly watching over my shoulder just in case the lord Robert returns here to visit?'

'You would be safe with me if we were wed,' Godric said eagerly. 'I have a cottage and land of my own here now. I have more than enough to support a wife.'

Hugh's glance swivelled quickly from Godric to Janna. He seemed suddenly unsure of himself.

Janna took a moment to consider. She'd hurt Godric's feelings once before on this matter; she must not do so again. Marrying him would not answer her problem, but how could she explain that to him? How could she explain to both of them the idea that had been forming in her mind ever since Hugh had told her of the abbess's knowledge of her mother, the idea that now seemed absolutely perfect? It would keep her safe from Robert's wrath. It was the answer to everything.

'Even if we were wed, Godric, that would not keep me from harm,' she said steadily. 'I still know my lord Robert's secrets.' She stole a quick glance at Hugh. He did not know what Janna knew: that Robert had murdered her mother and also the reason why. Nor must he find out, for it was Cecily's secret. But Godric knew everything and he was the one Janna was anxious to convince. 'While I live, I am a threat to him, and he knows it. I had thought, by pretending my death and changing my identity, to keep myself safe. My strategy has come to naught. All that's left for me now is to find a place of refuge, of safety, where my lord Robert will not be able to touch me.'

She tilted her chin and faced them both. 'I have decided to seek shelter at the abbey at Wiltune.'

'You're going to take the veil?' Hugh exclaimed, thunder-struck. Godric said nothing, but Janna saw his face crumple. He looked absolutely shattered.

'No! No, but I will stay there for a time.' Long enough to talk to the abbess. Janna raised her hand to touch the purse at her waist, felt the outline of the precious parchment, the letter from her father. She had another reason for going to the abbey. She smiled at the thought of it. If she could, if she was allowed, she would stay long enough to learn to read and write. If she could only read her father's letter, it would help her find him, help her solve the secrets of the past. Her heart felt lighter; new courage flowed through her veins as, at last, she saw the way ahead. 'I thank you for your offer, my lord, and for yours too, Godric.' Impulsively, she caught hold of his hand and held it to her cheek. 'You are very dear to me, but my mind is made up,' she said firmly.

'Then, with your leave, sire, I will escort Janna to Wiltune.' Godric still looked stunned as he turned to Hugh.

'Tonight,' Janna added. Not for anything would she spend another night here, not now that Robert knew who she was.

'Tonight,' Hugh confirmed, but he looked every bit as unhappy as Godric about Janna's sudden decision. 'But are you quite sure . . .?'

'Yes, my lord,' Janna interrupted. 'I am quite, quite sure.'

The iron gates of the abbey clanged shut behind Janna. Godric looked at her, and felt a great desolation in his heart. 'Goodbye, Janna,' he said quietly. 'God go with you.'

'Goodbye, Godric.' Janna stretched her hand through the gate, and drew him closer. She puckered up her lips and blew him a kiss, then gave a rueful smile as she heard the tut-tutting disapproval of the nun waiting behind her to take her to the abbess. She would miss Godric; she would miss them all, she realised. After living alone with her mother for so long, she'd found a place within the small community of Hugh's manor. It had given her new confidence to know that she was liked and valued there, and that she could make a life for herself even without her mother's guidance. It was hard, now, to walk away from everyone she had come to know. It was especially hard to walk away from Godric, and from Hugh.

She'd escaped from Robert, but not from her own heart, she realised. Perhaps time out from the real world might give her a chance to get her emotions in order, as well as giving her the opportunity to learn the skills she needed for the journey she must make if ever she was to find her father.

Perhaps time out might give her the chance to forget about both Godric *and* Hugh? Janna knew that she would do well to succeed in that, for while she was locked in here, Gytha would have the run of the manor and be free to choose whoever might have her. Looking closely into her own aching heart, Janna knew that in Gytha's shoes, she would find it hard to make a choice between Godric and Hugh. Better perhaps to be in her own shoes here at the abbey, with no choices left to her at all.

'Come,' said the nun. She beckoned Janna forward and Janna followed, turning her back on Godric, and on the outside world. In an effort to scrape up some courage, she set her shoulders square and tilted her chin. One thought gave her comfort. She was Johanna, daughter of John. Wherever she went, and whatever she did, she would make her father proud of her. Finding him was her goal now. For the time being, romance would just have to wait.

GLOSSARY

aelfshot: a belief that illness or a sudden pain (like rheumatism, arthritis or a 'stitch') was caused by elves who shot humans or livestock with darts

ague: fever and chills

alewife: ale was a common drink in the middle ages. Housewives brewed their own for domestic use, while alewives brewed the ale served in alehouses and taverns. A bush tied to a pole was the recognised symbol of an alehouse, at a time when most of the population could not read.

apothecary: someone who prepares and sells medicines, and perhaps spices and rare goods too

besom: a bundle of twigs attached to a handle and used as a broom

breeches: trousers held up by a cord running through the hem at the waist

boon work: at busy times in the farming year (such as haymaking and harvest) villeins were required to work extra days in the lord's fields. In return, they were given food and ale.

canonical hours: the medieval day was governed by sunrise and sunset and divided into seven canonical hours. Times

291

of prayer were marked by bells rung in abbeys and monasteries beginning with matins followed by lauds at sunrise; then prime, terce, sext, nones and vespers at sunset; followed by compline before going to bed.

'caught red-handed': literally with blood on your hands, evidence that you had been poaching in the king's forest

cot: small cottage

cottar: a medieval villein (serf) who occupied a cottage and a small piece of land on his lord's demesne, in return for his labour

demesne: manors/land owned by a feudal lord for his own use

Domesday Book: commissioned by William I after he conquered England in 1066, the book is a meticulous reckoning (for taxation purposes) of who owned what in England, from manors, mills and land holdings down to slaves, pigs and ploughs

farthing: one quarter of a penny

feudal system: a political, social and economic system based on the relationship of lord to vassal, in which land was held on condition of homage and service. Following the Norman conquest, William I distributed land once owned by Saxon 'ealdormen' (chief men) to his own barons, who in turn distributed land and manors to subtenants in return for fees, knight service and, in the case of the villeins, work in the fields.

forest law: from William the Conqueror's time, royal forests were the preserve of kings and the 'vert' (living wood) and the 'venison' (the creatures of the forest) were protected and managed. The laws caused great hardship to the peasants, who needed timber for building and kindling, while hunger tempted many to go poaching – but they faced punishment, and sometimes even death, if caught with blood on their hands.

gore acres: the odd corners of fields too awkward to plough

gorget: a cape with a hood, worn by the lower classes

hayward: manorial official in charge of haymaking and harvest, and the repair and upkeep of hedges and ditches

heriot: a death duty to the lord of the manor, usually the best beast, and sometimes also some household goods, such as metal utensils or uncut cloth. This constituted 'payment' for the loss of a worker.

hue and cry: with no practising police force other than a town sergeant to enforce the law, anyone discovering a crime was expected to 'raise a hue and cry' – shouting aloud to alert the community to the fact that a crime had been committed, after which all those within earshot must commence the pursuit of the criminal.

kirtle: long dress worn over a short tunic

leechcraft: a system of healing practised during the time of the Anglo-Saxons, which included the use of herbs, plants, medicines, magical incantations and spells, charms and precious stones.

medale: a drinking festivity after the lord's meadows have been mown.

mortuary: death duty paid by a villein to the parish priest – usually the second-best beast

nostrums: medicines

ploughshare: along with the coulter, the iron cutting parts of a plough. The coulter is a blade or wheel that makes the

preliminary cut through the soil; the share is the cutting
blade of the plough.

posset: a hot drink with curative properties

pottage: a vegetable soup or stew

reeve: the reeve (steward) was usually appointed by the
villagers, and was responsible for the management of the
manor. Shire reeves (sheriffs) were appointed by the king
to administer law and justice in the shires (counties).

rush light: a peeled rush dipped in hot animal fat, which
made a primitive candle

scrip: a small bag

skep: a beehive fashioned from woven straw and covered
with a cloth to keep out rain

strip fields: a system of farming was practised in medieval
time, whereby two fields were ploughed and sewn for
harvest in summer and winter, while a third field lay
fallow

sumpter horse: a packhorse used to transport goods

tiring woman: a female attendant on a lady of high birth and
importance

villein: peasant or serf tied to a manor and to an overlord,
and given land in return for labour and a fee – either
money or produce

water meadows: the farm land on either side of a river that
floods regularly

week work: two or three days' compulsory labour in the lord's
fields

wortwyf: a herb wife, a wise woman and healer

AUTHOR'S NOTE

*T*HE *JANNA MYSTERIES* is set in the 1140s, at a turbulent time in England's history. After Henry I's son, William, drowned in the White Ship disaster, Henry was left with only one legitimate heir, his daughter Matilda (sometimes known as Maude). Matilda had an unhappy childhood. At the age of eight, she was betrothed to a much older man, Heinrich, Emperor of Germany, and she was sent to live in that country until, aged twelve, she was considered old enough to marry him. Evidently she was beloved by the Germans, who begged her to stay on after the Emperor died, but at the age of twenty-four, and childless, Matilda was summoned back to England by her father. For political reasons, and despite Matilda's vehement protests, Henry insisted that she marry Count Geoffrey of Anjou, a boy some ten years her junior. They married in 1128, and the first of their three sons, Henry (later to become Henry II of England), was born in 1133.

Henry I announced Matilda his heir and twice demanded that his barons, including her cousin, Stephen of Blois, all swear an oath of allegiance to her. This they did, but when Henry died, Matilda went to Rouen (Normandy) for his burial while Stephen went straight to London to gather support, and then on to Winchester, where he claimed the Treasury and was crowned King of England.

Not one to be denied her rights, Matilda gathered her own supporters, including her illegitimate half-brother, Robert of Gloucester, and in 1139 she landed at Arundel Castle in England, prepared to fight for the crown. She left her children with Geoffrey, who thereafter stayed in Anjou and in Normandy, pursuing his own interests. Civil war between Stephen and Matilda raged in England for nineteen years, creating such hardship and misery that the *Peterborough Chronicle* reported: 'Never before had there been greater wretchedness in the country . . . They said openly that Christ and His saints slept.'

I became interested in this period of English history while researching *Shalott: The Final Journey*, when Callie meets Matilda at Arundel Castle as part of her quest. As this new series began to fall into place, I realised that this time of shifting allegiances, of fierce battles and daring escapes, of great danger and cruelty, formed a perfect setting with many plot possibilities. Janna's travels will bring her into the company of nobles, peasants and pilgrims, jongleurs and nuns, spies and assassins, and even the Empress Matilda herself.

With England in the grip of civil war, secrets abound, loyalties change and passions run high, and Janna will encounter the darkest side of human nature: the jealousy, greed, ambition, deceit and fear which so often lead to betrayal and murder. As well as solving the mystery of her past, Janna's mission is to find out the truth and bring the guilty to judgment, but she will need great courage and insight to escape danger and solve the crimes she encounters along her journey.

For those interested in learning more about the civil war between Stephen and Matilda, Sharon Penman's *When Christ and His Saints Slept* is an excellent fictional account of that history. On a lighter note, I have also read, and much enjoyed, the *Brother Cadfael Chronicles* by Ellis Peters, which are set during this period. While Janna's loyalty lies in a different direction to Ellis Peters' characters, her skill with herbs was inspired by these wonderful stories of the herbalist at Shrewsbury Abbey.

I have set *The Janna Mysteries* in Wiltshire, England. Janna's quest for truth and justice will take her from the forest of Gravelinges (now known as Grovely Wood) to royal Winchestre, seat of power where the Treasury was housed. I've kept to the place names listed in the *Domesday Book* compiled by William the Conqueror in 1086, but the contemporary names of some of the sites are: Berford – Barford St Martin; Babestoche Manor – Baverstock; Bredecumbe – Burcombe; Wiltune – Wilton; Sarisberie – Sarum (later relocated and named Salisbury); and Winchestre – Winchester.

The royal forest of Gravelinges was the only forest in Wiltshire mentioned in the *Domesday Book*. While it has diminished in size since medieval time, I have experienced at first hand how very easy it is to get utterly lost once you stray off the path!

Wilton was the ancient capital of Wessex. The abbey was established in Saxon times and became one of the most prosperous in England, ranked with the houses of Shaftesbury, Barking and Winchester as a nunnery of the first importance. Following the dissolution of the monasteries during the reign of Henry VIII, ownership of the abbey's lands passed to William Herbert, 1st Earl of Pembroke. Some 450 years later, the 18th Earl of Pembroke now owns this vast estate. A magnificent stately home, Wilton House, stands in place of the abbey and is open to visitors.

While writing medieval England from Australia is a difficult and hazardous enterprise, I have been fortunate in the support and encouragement I've received along the way. So many people have helped make this series possible, and in particular I'd like to thank the following: Nick and Wendy Combes of Burcombe Manor, for taking me into their family, giving me a home away from home and teaching me about life on a farm, both now and in medieval time. Mike Boniface, warden of Grovely, who guided me through the forest by day and ensured that I also saw it (and the badgers!) at night. Pat Sweetman from the USA, who warned me about rue, and who kindly shares her knowledge of herbal medicine with me. Gillian Polack, mentor and friend, whose knowledge of medieval life has helped shape the series and continues to give it veracity. Linsay Knight and the team at Random House for their faith and support, and Zoe Walton, for her care and skilful editing. My thanks to you all.